R. D. TARVER

FOURTH MANSIONS PRESS
CHARLOTTESVILLE, VIRGINIA

CONTENTS

HELL PATROL

Copyright © 2020 R. D. Tarver

"Hell Patrol"
Words and Music by Glenn Tipton, Rob Halford and K. K. Downing
Copyright ©1990 EMI April Music Inc., Crewglen Ltd., Ebonytree Ltd. and Greargate Ltd. All Rights on behalf of EMI April Music Inc., Crewglen Ltd. and Ebonytree Ltd. Administered by Sony/ATV Music Publishing LLC, 424 Church Street, Suite 1200, Nashville, TN 37219
International Copyright Secured All Rights Reserved
Reprinted by Permission of Hal Leonard LLC
"Hell Patrol"
Written by Kenneth Downing, Rob Halford, Glenn Raymond Tipton
Published by Round Hill Songs II
All rights administered by Round Hill Music LP

Fourth Mansions Press, LLC
Charlottesville, Virginia
fourthmansions.com

ISBN: 978-0-578-82580-9

Cover art & design ©2020 Anthony Roberts
Interior layout & design by Anthony Roberts
blackmindseye.org

For the metal gods…

HELL PATROL

PART I

PROLOGUE

"Hell," Henry's father began. "Hell was a warning."

Henry braced against the ominous string of words propelled by his father's gruff and booming voice.

Even in his few short years, he had come to realize that there were times when being a professor's son definitely had its drawbacks. More specifically for Henry, those times were in the early morning hours when his father would try out his new material on the captive familial audience before his lectures at the University.

"More than just an antiquated Bronze Age treatise on morality, some scholars also believe the concept of Hell served as an allegory among Neolithic pastoralists," his father said, adjusting his notes. "A dire portent heralding an encroaching evil that threatened their way of life—the walls of civilization, and the rule of law that lay at their foundation."

Held hostage by the morning's lesson plan, Henry did his best to sit still and feign interest as his father continued to fill the small study with stuffy-sounding words.

His younger sibling, Vincent, was far less reserved. Like their father, Vincent was quick to summon a foul temper which could manifest at any moment. Such a disruption had the potential to prolong the mock lecture and disrupt the day's itinerary. Henry had a tight schedule to keep. *The Herculoids* were on in an hour.

The professor shuffled his notes atop the sleek cherrywood dining table. "As nomadic hunter-gatherers shifted towards agrarianism, their world began to grow smaller, ushering in increasingly dynamic social landscapes in place of natural ones. Along with civilization came humanity's descent into sin."

Henry cringed as his brother's tiny voice filled his ears.

"Why would the nomads want to live behind the walls when they could roam free?" Vincent asked.

"Shh. Save the questions for the end," Henry said, cupping his hand over his little brother's mouth.

The professor let out a hearty laugh.

"An excellent question, dear boy—are the walls of civilization inevitable? Are they necessary for humanity to thrive? And what is the long-term cost of circumscribing our species from the natural world?" He pulled at his thick salt-and-pepper beard, pausing occasionally to brush the dandruff from the lapels of his tweed blazer as the questions lingered unanswered.

Vincent wriggled in the heavy wooden chair. "I hate the walls," he said, undoing his wool cardigan and tossing it on the floor.

"Ah yes, resistance," replied Henry's father. "In an attempt to resist the negation of freedoms imposed by this new cultural development, the disenfranchised often expressed their displeasure by clinging onto tradition and reverting back to the old ways."

His father trotted over to a nearby bookcase. In one deft motion he pressed down on a concealed lever and sidestepped the bookcase as it swung away from the wall, revealing a hidden panel. Inside the secret space was a shelf covered in old, dusty books, an acrylic display case filled with ancient artifacts, and an array of strange-looking electronic equipment mounted to the interior. Above the display case, a large sepia-colored world map spanned the breadth of the panel. The map was marked with strange sigils and handwritten annotations that Henry could not decipher.

His father selected one of the tattered, leather-bound volumes from the shelf and closed the panel.

He wiped off the cover of the book, sending up a plume of dust made visible by the solitary beam of sunlight that pierced through the stained glass window of the otherwise darkened study.

"The ancients utilized fables, parables, and folklore as the means of escape to overcome the challenges of straddling the dichotomous spheres of *physis* and *nomos*."

"Are you going to read us a story?" asked Vincent, eagerly eying the book. "I want to hear the one about the Devil and the violin."

"You've heard that story a million times," chided Henry. "There's more to life than music, you dork."

Vincent made a face at his brother.

His father ruffled Vincent's hair. "As you like *Tartini's Dream*, my son, you will certainly enjoy this story—and rest assured, there is music involved." He paced around the table holding the book as he spoke. "But before we begin, I want you both to consider the following: what if there was a more literal interpretation of these ancient descriptions of Hell? Is it possible that we have mistaken allegory for anecdote?"

Vincent let out a high-pitched squeal that forced Henry to cover his ears. He watched in fear as his father tried to retain his composure at the outburst.

"Very well, lecture over," his father said, switching on a nearby reading lamp. "Time for a story."

Henry let out an internal sigh.

His father opened the weighty tome and took his seat at the table. "Within an oasis surrounded by barren desert, the delicate flower of civilization had begun to blossom and, along with it, the preservation of humanity's cumulative knowledge of the primeval." His father paused, repeating the line under his breath as he scribbled down a final note before continuing. "These cultural transmissions of knowledge—ancient tales and whispers in the dark—were cemented into the walls of the cities of Uruk and Mari that were erected out of the swamps and marshland of the Fertile Crescent."

Vincent scrambled out of the chair and fell to the ground. He kicked off his shoes and dug his heels into the plush Persian rug that surrounded the cluttered dining table. "This story better have music in it," Vincent said as he crossed his arms. "And it better not be boring."

"Be quiet, it's starting," Henry said. He sat next to his brother on the rug and held him still as their father began to read from the ancient book.

✠ ✠ ✠

According to one such tale, on a particularly still night on the eve of the vernal equinox, Mendak the shepherd and his two eldest sons, Kabu and Ninshe, were slowly navigating their flock over the unforgiving terrain of the upper Tigris highlands—an inhospitable landscape marked by craggy ravines and treacherous cliffs.

Their destination was the small agricultural settlement of Tethe, an outlier community soon to be incorporated into the ancient city of Assur, where they would trade the wool and milk provided by their flock for grain.

A heavy spring rain had forced the shepherd and his two sons to shelter the flock for the night before continuing their journey.

The youngest of the two brothers, Ninshe, had become distracted from his chores, tossing stones through one of the narrow fissures from within the cliffside hollow that overlooked the waters of the Tigris river below.

Hearing his father's call, the boy ran back to the shelter entrance where Mendak was preparing a fire. Ninshe approached cautiously, seeing the beads of sweat that had formed on his father's furrowed brow.

"Have you finished the fence like I asked?"

"Yes, father," Ninshe replied. He pointed to the makeshift barrier of date palm branches and mardi reeds, constructed to protect the flock from jackals and hyenas that roamed the countryside.

"Then come and play us a song while your brother makes our supper," Mendak said. "Your mother would be ashamed at how seldom you use her gift."

"Yes, father." Ninshe produced a thin reed pipe from his pack—a recent gift from his mother who had encouraged him to take up the instrument to help his father calm the flock. His fingers fumbled over the small holes as he tried to replicate the tune his mother had taught him.

A loud crash interrupted the performance as all eyes turned towards the mouth of the shelter.

One of the ewes had managed to topple over a section of the protective barrier that held the sheep at bay. Ninshe watched in horror as she bounded over the fallen branches and ran out into the darkness beyond the fire.

Mendak called to his sons to drive the ewe back into the shelter as he tended to the rest of the flock. Ninshe and Kabu chased after the sheep, who had followed a game trail into a ravine carved out by the waters of the mighty Tigris river.

The brothers followed the bleating of the runaway sheep as it ran inside a narrow opening in the cliff face along the edge of the river.

"You go in first and scare her out," commanded Kabu. "I'll wait out here and watch the trail in case she comes out another way."

"Father says I'm not to follow your words anymore now that I am of age," said Ninshe.

"Father is not here, and I am the eldest."

"Father says there is no power over man other than the gods."

"Father also says to obey your elders. I am the eldest. I know best. Now get in there before I tell him that it was you who neglected your duties—this is all your fault." Kabu punctuated the sentiment with a hard shove that nearly knocked Ninshe off his feet.

Ninshe submitted and entered the mouth of the small cave. The sound of the sheep's hooves clattering against the limestone outcrop echoed off the cavern walls. His flint too wet to spark a flame to light his lamp, Ninshe proceeded into the darkness by feeling his way along the wall of stone.

"Come girl, come on out. This is no place for either of us if the rains keep coming," said Ninshe. The rising water from the nearby river was seeping into his sandals as he called out to the animal.

He pulled out the small reed pipe from his pack and began to play a soothing melody to calm the frantic sheep. The cavern picked up the song and washed it about like the waters of the swelling river. The notes lingered in the air long enough for

Ninshe to play against his own pipe, forming an interplay of dissonant notes that grated against the air. A fierce thunderclap answered back, splitting through the night sky.

Unsure if it was a trick of sound caused by the approaching storm, or the lingering echo of his pipe, Ninshe thought he heard the unmistakable sound of a distant horn blowing from beneath the ground in the deep darkness of the cave.

Without warning, the ewe suddenly shot past the boy and out into the coming storm. Ninshe turned to catch the sheep, and in the process slipped and fell, dropping his pipe. As he crawled in the darkness to find the instrument, another deep, bellowing blast shook the cavern.

The sound was deafening, causing Ninshe to cup his ears as he ran towards the lightning flashes that filtered in through the cavern entrance. Leaving behind his mother's gift, he fled from the source of the terrible noise as he began to feel the presence of another within the cave.

☩ ☩ ☩

Outside, Kabu was tying a length of rope around the neck of the runaway ewe who had wandered casually over to him on the trail. He looked to the entrance of the cave for any sign of his brother. Thunder filled the air as the storm grew in intensity.

He called out to his brother. "Ninshe, quit fooling around! We need to get back to the shelter."

The crackling of tree limbs resounded throughout the ravine.

Kabu turned to examine the sound and watched awestruck as every tree in the palm grove began to bend towards the ground. At first, he had assumed the force of the storm was responsible for the strange occurrence. Then he noticed that the unseen force that propelled the trees seemed to emanate from the center of the grove pushing outward, forcing the trees to bend out in all directions against the wind.

A second thunderclap threatened to break the night sky in two.

A strange bellow, sounding off like a deep horn blast, echoed in the wake of the thunder. Kabu stood frozen as a large, shadowy giant emerged from the cavern, dragging his brother's lifeless body in tow.

Lightning reflected off the ornate golden crown that adorned the demon's monstrous countenance, revealing a great, solitary horn that erupted from the creature's snarling snout.

The beast tore the horn from its flesh and held it to its lips, creating an earth-shattering clarion call. The sounding of the horn caused the very earth to open up beneath its clawed feet. The great demon dragged Ninshe's body down into the parting ground, which sealed behind it as it descended into the depths of Hell.

Unable to believe his eyes, Kabu ran to the site where the demon had taken his brother beneath the ground only to find the fractured pieces of his brother's reed pipe atop the undisturbed soil.

⚔ ⚔ ⚔

Henry's father closed the book and leaned back in his chair. "Now that we have provided some context, what insights might this ancient tale reveal about its authors?"

"They were scared," offered Vincent. "Scared of the demon."

"Demons aren't real, stupid," Henry replied. "It's just a made-up story to scare children into doing their chores."

The comment elicited an elbow from his younger brother.

"What do you think, Vincent? Is Henry right?"

Vincent thought for a moment as he considered his father's inquiry.

"The demon was afraid too."

"Interesting observation. And what do you think the demon was afraid of?"

"The boy's song."

CHAPTER ONE

HELL HOLE OF DEATH

1

Jesse Lynn watched the sky for any sign of weather as he lay on the roof of the family station wagon —"Jaws," as his mother called it. A solid steel behemoth, the great white '78 Pontiac LeMans sat parked beneath one of the numerous pecan trees that surrounded the double-wide trailer he currently called home.

Home.

The word was beginning to lose all meaning.

Any metro-area yokel with a working TV set knew it was only a matter of time for one of these tornado magnets to bite the big one. He closed his eyes and tried to commune with the wind.

A placid blue sky stared back through the branches that diffused the glare of the late-afternoon sun. With no cataclysmic storm likely to manifest any time soon, Jesse would be forced to contend with the new lodgings for the foreseeable future.

A condoling wind rustled through the trees, shaking loose their bounty, whose tough shells resounded off the trailer's metal roof like the spring hailstones common to this part of the Southern Plains.

Thanks, but you need to step it up if we're ever gonna get out of this dump.

The trailer was a recent acquisition that his stepdad, Randy, had bought off of one of his old army buddies. It reeked of cigarette smoke and stale beer; Jesse even thought he had seen some bullet holes in the walls of one of the back bedrooms.

"It's just for a few weeks while we get the old ranch house fixed up," his mother had promised. "Until then, we're just going to have to make it work."

Jesse contemplated the transition into his new environment as he toyed with the frayed hem of his favorite T-shirt—a hand-me-down from his older brother, Rick. There were holes in both of the armpits, and the inverted pentagram that held the faded Slayer logo was barely visible, but it was still his favorite.

The sound of the truck rattling down the dirt road drew nearer; it plodded along like a rusty old comet, dragging a long tail of dust up the gravel drive.

Bessie. That was the name Randy had given his old '77 Chevy Bonanza. How did people arrive at the names of their inanimate objects? And why was the pool of names so shallow? He watched the truck pull up the drive, saddled with what remained of his earthly possessions.

Randy's tall, wiry frame emerged from the dissipating dust cloud. He nodded to Jesse as he rolled up the sleeves of his shirt, revealing a tattoo of an eagle carrying a sword in its talons. The ink had long faded from its original black to a dark-greenish color set within the canvas of tan, leathery skin.

The lenses of Randy's transition glasses had grown dark. The optical effect created the impression that his stepdad was always pissed off about something.

"Little help, Boss?" asked Randy.

Bessie's tailgate was broken, requiring Jesse to stand on the rear tire to reach over the side of the pickup bed to retrieve the cargo.

He made a quick scan of the bed's contents. Wedged between the wheel well and a pile of boxes rested his prized possession: a Fender Squire bass with a rosewood fretboard and black nitro finish that his parents had bought him on his thirteenth birthday.

Jesse had taken the modest manufacturing afforded to the base model and added several upgrades—namely a replacement of the stock pickups, machine heads, and the addition of a locking bridge. Even though it was his first project guitar, he was still satisfied all these years later with the work he had done.

He slipped the gig-bag strap over his shoulder and pulled out two boxes: one labeled KITCHEN, the other embellished with a hand-drawn skull and crossbones and the words RICK THE PRICK in bold black marker.

He brought the boxes into the trailer and deposited the first on the kitchen counter where his mother was battling what remained of the previous tenants—an embedded squadron of red wasps. She had managed to corner one of the bogeys behind the blinds of the kitchen window with a broom.

"Thanks, hon." The words came between labored breaths as she pivoted back and forth on the balls of her feet. "Did you put your brother's bed together like I asked?"

Jesse shrugged. "Can't. The frame got busted up in the move, so I gave him mine."

"And where are you going to sleep?"

"I'll just put my mattress on the floor. No big deal."

She swatted at the blinds just as a pair of yellow-tipped antennae emerged from between the slats. "He can't just sleep in a regular bed. He needs the adjustable frame to elevate his legs." The insect folded its legs neatly up under its abdomen and fell twirling to the ground like a downed fighter jet.

Appearing satisfied with her conquest, she opened the window and called out to Randy. "What happened to Rick's bed? Jesse said the frame got busted."

"I said it's not a big deal."

His mother's mouth gaped open. "That bed cost almost two thousand dollars *after* insurance. They're not going to shell out for another one."

Jesse relented. He knew when it came to his brother's health, or money, that it wasn't the hill he wanted to die on.

She swept up the wasp carcass into the dustbin and slammed the contents into the trash can. "I'm sorry to be the bad guy, but it actually *is* kind of a big deal."

"He's not a baby. He'll be fine."

His mother continued to yell at Randy through the open window as Jesse set off to deliver the remaining parcel.

He expected to find his brother fast asleep, as was generally his habit at two p.m. on a Saturday. Instead, Rick was at his desk in the customary meditative trance that accompanied one of his sacred listening sessions. Jesse observed the ritual elements: headphones resting atop his gleaming white dome, oversized wire-rim glasses laid down on the desk, and the smell of recently lit incense that announced the sanctity of the rite in progress.

Sensing the presence of another, Rick raised his hand, palm out, towards the source of the intrusion.

Jesse set the box down on the desk and pulled on the left ear of his brother's hi-fi headphones. "You're welcome, dickhead. Also, mom found out about the bed." He let go of the padded headphone speaker, allowing it to thump against Rick's skull in a manner that satisfied Jesse more than it should have. The headphone cable danced back and forth a few times before it came to rest next to the turntable that spun hypnotically at his brother's side.

Jesse received a blow to the arm before Rick motioned for him to quiet. He produced a second pair of headphones and handed them to Jesse, who accepted the gift with reverence. Jesse jettisoned the gig-bag, stuffing the bass in the corner of the cramped, shared space before slapping the headphones over his ears and slumping to the floor.

Rick leaned forward over the arms of his wheelchair to reset the needle, knocking over a stack of photos pulled from a nearby shoebox. The topmost photo was an image of Rick and his late girlfriend, Julie, sitting on a motorcycle.

Jesse had coveted the bike, a '77 400cc Honda Rebel, given to Rick by their biological father. The smell of the leather seat and the grip of the handlebars came rushing back, along with the many hours he spent sitting on the bike, pretending to ride it. Rick had even taken him out on it a few times before the accident. "Sissies sit on the sissy bar," he would always instruct.

"Abandon all hope, ye who enter here," Rick said, carefully dropping the stylus on the record.

An eruption of unbridled electricity broke from the crackling vinyl. Jesse was immediately pulled in by the sound. A barrage of heavy kick drums settled into a bombastic cadence, an ominous prelude forecasting the inevitable sonic assault that would follow.

A pair of screeching guitars ripped through the pulsing rhythm, neighing like bucking broncos as they were broken into submission by the soaring vocal swarm that rose above it all.

Jesse recognized Rob Halford's unparalleled range and vocal command as the track raged forth. He motioned for his brother to hand him the LP cover that stood propped up on the turntable lid to confirm his intuition.

He held the album cover, transfixed.

A winged chrome warrior, fist raised high, clutched the throttle of a demonic serpent cycle whose wheels, composed of gleaming metallic saw blades, hovered over an apocalyptic cityscape poised to sink into the fiery depths of Hell.

Jesse closed his eyes, entering into the divine soundscape conjured by the living metal gods themselves—Judas Priest.

As the second track ripped along, Jesse felt the tingle of goosebumps pushing up the hair on his arms. No sooner had he begun to lose himself in the music than he began to feel a sharp turbulence as he was pulled from his celestial orbit, crashing back into the mundane realm where he opened his eyes to find his mother standing before him, arms crossed.

"Is the truck empty?" she asked.

Jesse pulled the headphones from his ears and tossed them on the desk, aiming for the stack of photos. The disruption ejected Rick from his trance. An expression of shock gave way to understanding as Rick followed Jesse's cue by placing a picture frame over the stack of loose photos. The frame held a recent polaroid of the Lynn brothers seated around their mother during her fortieth birthday celebration.

"I'm going, I'm going," sighed Jesse. "Rick was just showing me the new record."

"Randy has been running back and forth on the interstate all day long. The least you could do is make an effort to pitch in." She caught her breath as she examined the state of disarray that permeated the cramped bedroom.

Jesse put his hands up in an attempt to diffuse the coming onslaught. "Okay, don't freak out. I said I'd do it."

"This place is a pigsty, Jesse. You start a new school on Monday. Get it done." She looked to the cluttered desk and picked up the framed polaroid that lay on top. "Oh, geez, I hate this picture."

"Because it reminds you how close to death you are?" asked Rick.

She swatted Rick's shoulder with the frame. "You're not off the hook either, mister. You're supposed to be finishing with these boxes, not warping your brother's mind." She handed the frame to Rick. "I want them all unpacked before supper."

"Yes, ma'am."

She stopped on her way out the door. "Boys, I know this is rough, but we have a chance at a new start here, and I need to know you are all on board." She gestured to the mess as she continued. "The longer we spend moving into this hole in the wall, the longer it will take to finish up your grandparents' house."

"We're on board," said Jesse.

Rick nodded in affirmation.

"Okay then," she sighed. "Because if not, I'm going to send you both to stay with your Aunt Nancy so we can get some actual work done around here."

"Oh no," said Rick. "Please don't force us to live in a retirement castle on Grand Lake with our cool aunt, tossing back cocktails with all the hot divorcee trim."

Her smile faded. "She lets you guys drink?"

"Only when we take the boat out," the brothers answered in unison.

His mother threw her arms up in the air and left the room.

Once she was out of earshot, Rick turned to Jesse. "Nice save, fuckwad." He fished out the picture of Julie and the motorcycle from the stack of spilled photos and put it inside the desk drawer. "So help me—if you so much as put a scratch on my headphones."

Jesse gestured to the LP cover. "So it finally came?"

Rick nodded. "Despite the best attempts of the Reno dipshit brothers." He retrieved the LP cover and inspected it for any damage. "Six months, one week, and two days late, but she finally arrived."

"Sweet. Can you make me a tape?"

"One step ahead of you, little bro." Rick reached into the cassette deck mounted below the turntable and pulled out a newly minted cassette tape. He placed it in its case and handed it over to Jesse, who received the offering as if it were a holy relic. "This is going to change everything you've ever thought about Priest."

2

Jesse and Randy had finished unpacking the truck by the time the sun had begun to recede beneath the trees. The two had worked in silence until the chore was done.

As they carried in the last of the moving boxes, Randy turned to Jesse before entering the trailer. "Try to go easy on your mother for a while. All right, Boss?"

Jesse looked to the ground, unable to meet Randy's eyes. "Yes, sir."

They passed from beneath the greying sky and into the warm light of the small kitchenette where his mother was cutting up vegetables next to a skillet filled with sizzling ground beef. Jesse's stomach grumbled as he inhaled the welcome preparations for mealtime.

With his mother's back turned, Jesse grabbed the soft-pack of GPCs on the kitchen table, shaking it to jostle a few cigarettes loose towards the torn-out corner of the pack.

"I'm gonna go take a walk up by the house. Be back in a while."

His mother called over her shoulder, "Dinner will be ready in an hour. Don't be late."

"Yes, ma'am."

"And promise me you'll stay clear of the Old Townsite," she started. "You remember what happened to little Jimmie Shankly? He fell down that mineshaft and —"

"And broke both his little legs, and no one could find him, so he starved to death, cold and alone—yeah, I know."

"Such an awful story." She shivered, presumably imagining Jesse in place of the dead boy at the bottom of the mine. "By the time I was your age nearly every one of your uncles had gotten stitches, or worse, from playing around in that death trap."

"Don't worry, I'll be fine." Jesse kissed his mother on the cheek and grabbed his jean jacket off the coat rack before striding back out into the evening air. "This place is practically Mayberry. What's the worst that could happen?"

3

As he walked the property, Jesse was reminded of the time spent at his grandparents' ranch when he was younger. It was a strange sensation to retrace the steps of your previous self across a landscape also marked by the passage of time. The longing for stability—for home—felt that much more elusive as he plodded along the bittersweet trail of memories.

The tawny, rolling hills lapped up the static horizon, a scene worthy of a picture frame that his mother might have hung from one of the woodgrain wall panels inside the trailer.

A lone grain silo stood some distance from the house, dilapidated and worn. He recalled the lazy afternoons spent inside the silo shuffling through owl pellets with his cousins, and the ossuary of small rodent bones that had amassed there over the years.

The ancient space possessed an eerie energy, rife with the potential to spur a child's imagination towards the sinister. Jesse could remember *knowing* that some ancient evil had taken up residence within the ailing structure, though the passage of time had dulled the potency of the spell.

He lit a cigarette and headed towards the old ranch house.

As the house came into view, he saw a flash of light streak across the windows from inside. *Probably just some meth-heads looking for something they can pawn. Welcome to Macomb Springs. New start, my ass.*

As he approached the front door, he could hear laughter and the sound of breaking glass coming from inside the house. Music wafted out from one of the shattered front windows. Jesse recognized Ozzy's vocals bellowing out the chorus of "Bark at the Moon," *the title track of his third solo album, released on Epic Records in November of 1983.*

The data arose spontaneously, flowing naturally into his stream of consciousness. Ever since Jesse was a child he had exhibited uncanny musical recall. He could hear a song once—any song— and tell you the name of the song and the band that played it. And if he liked the song, he could even tell you what album it was from, the label that released it, and the year it came out.

The side door next to the garage on the east end of the house had been left ajar. Jesse finished his cigarette, listening to the commotion coming from inside the house. As he drew nearer, he heard a voice from inside.

"Hey, shut up for a second. I think I heard something."

The music stopped.

A long-haired teen wearing a backwards ball cap stepped out from the shadows of the interior of the empty house. In his hands he brandished an empty beer bottle, and on his face, a pubescent attempt at a mustache.

"Hey, man, this is our squat." The words squeaked out from behind a row of large, rodent-like teeth that showed beneath his upper lip.

A second voice called from the darkness. "Yeah, this one's taken. Go find your own, perv."

Jesse stepped on the butt of his cigarette, and let his eyes adjust to the dark interior of the house. He felt for the familiar shape of his pocket knife inside the watch pocket of his jeans and took a step forward.

Before he could cross the threshold, a teenage girl dressed in all black with matching black makeup stepped out from the shadows. The girl waved a bundle of smoldering herbs in the air and positioned herself between Jesse and the other two vagrants. She scanned Jesse for several moments before she finally spoke.

"It's cool. He's projecting a benevolent aura."

Appearing satisfied with the assessment, the others stood down.

She took a step closer to Jesse. The whites of her eyes cut through the murk of violet ashes that streamed in through the undressed windows—a well-suited ambience forged in the dying embers of daylight.

"I'm Mal. This is Alex." The crash of a glass bottle breaking against the stone fireplace followed her introduction. She nodded towards the sound as she continued. "And that abomination of nature calls itself Rust."

"That's 'cause I'm all metal, and you know it," Rust called out from the shadows.

"So who are you supposed to be?" she asked. The words were tinged with an electricity almost made visible as they charged the air in the darkened doorway.

"Jesse."

"What the fuck do you want, Jesse?" asked Rust.

"This is my grandparents' house."

"Oh shit," Mal said. "We didn't know anyone still lived here."

"They're dead."

"Gnarly," said Alex. The utterance drew a stern look from Mal. "I mean, sorry dude." Alex fetched his boombox from the mantel above the fireplace.

"Oh hey, do you think I can bum one of those?" Mal pointed to Jesse's flattened cigarette butt. "These moochers took my last one."

Jesse nodded and reached into his jacket to pull out one of the loose cigarettes. Before he could offer it to her, Rust swooped in and swiped it out of his hand.

"Thanks pal," Rust said. He pulled out a silver Zippo etched with a skull and crossbones and lit the cigarette.

Even in the low light, beneath the long strands of greasy curls, Jesse could see that his eyes were full of storms.

Jesse handed another smoke to Mal, who leaned in for him to light it. "Such a dick, dude," she whispered. "I promise not all of us around here are such assholes." The small flame revealed the stark contrast of her fair pallor against the dark makeup. "We just stopped by to drink a couple beers. Totally thought this place was still abandoned."

"My parents are supposedly fixing it up." Even in the shadows, he found it difficult to maintain eye contact with her and hold a conversation at the same time. "They were supposed to be done before school started, but I guess that's not going to happen with the move and all."

"Ugh, I've been trying not to think about that shithole."

"You guys go to Macomb Springs High?"

"Like we have a choice," Alex said. "It's like the only school around for a hundred miles, unless you wanna learn how to shoe a horse."

"So where do you live?" Mal gestured towards the empty interior. "I mean, while your family fixes this place up."

"They're holding me and my brother hostage in this shitty trailer down the way. We have to share a room. It fucking blows." *Do I sound like an idiot? What the fuck am I even talking about?* The metallic *clink* of Rust's Zippo brought Jesse back to the moment.

"Come on, let's bail," said Rust. "This place sucks anyway." He brushed shoulders with Jesse as he exited the house with Alex close on his heels.

"Welcome to the neighborhood, dude," laughed Alex. "Cool shirt." He pressed play on the boombox's cassette player and ran to catch up with Rust.

Mal lingered behind, allowing some distance between herself and the others. "We're going down to the Hell Hole. You wanna come?"

"Hell Hole?"

"Yeah, it's this lame smoke-hole near the old coal mine." She pulled at an errant strand of raven-black hair that had become stuck in her lipstick. "We get suspended if we're caught smoking near school grounds. It's like all there is to do around here."

"Sure." Jesse cringed as the word left his mouth. His mind's eye spun up the image of his mother having to lower Hamburger Helper down to his broken body at the bottom of a derelict mineshaft.

He followed Mal through the field of golden buffalo grass towards the edge of the woods.

Not far into the dense forest, they came upon an old gravel service road and the remnants of a concrete retaining wall that held back the natural rock outcrop that surrounded the mine entrance. The surviving segments of a rusted railing assisted in the steep-graded descent towards the bottom.

Alex and Rust were already inside the Hell Hole—an artificial vestibule constructed around what remained of the sealed mine entrance. Jesse remembered the spot well, as it was a constant source of ire for his mother every time the family visited his grandparents.

As one of the last observable vestiges of the original Macomb Springs townsite, located much to the southwest of the present sprawl, the mine had been a refuge for ostracized teenagers for generations. The hand-carved stone arch that surrounded the entrance had been bricked up and gated off ever since Jesse was a child. The ravages of time—along with a healthy dose of vandalism—had left the seal beneath the arch as little more than a visual deterrent.

As Jesse followed Mal into the Hell Hole, the air became cool and damp, and smelled of mold. A pile of half-melted candles lined the graffiti-covered brick seal. Segments of an ancient rail cart track were visible beneath the crumbling concrete slab before disappearing behind the gate, snaking deeper into the mine. The gate was so rusted it looked like it would crumble if touched; it was all that stood between them and the inner workings of the mine. Jesse was relieved to find the barrier intact.

Alex switched sides on the cassette tape. The gentle ringing of acoustic guitars reverberated into the cavernous hollow as the opening of "Beyond the Realms of Death," *a B-side power ballad by Judas Priest, from the album* Stained Class, *released on Columbia Records in 1978*, began to play.

"Is that an Rx-5150?" asked Jesse.

Alex nodded. "Yeah man, and it's totally metal—says so right there."

Jesse got the reference before Alex pointed out the stylized METAL insignia located at the bottom center of the cassette deck door. He didn't have the heart to tell Alex that *metal* in this case was just a reference to tape quality. Jesse had coveted the Panasonic line of boomboxes for some time, but could never come up with the cash to buy one.

"Hey Mal, why don't you come sit by me and we can do one of your séances?" asked Rust. He let out a loud belch to accompany the request, eliciting an audible chuckle from Alex.

Mal recoiled, pulling Jesse away to avoid the gaseous assault. "Barf. You smell like bologna." She took a seat on the ground opposite the others and motioned for Jesse to sit next to her. "And you know séances don't work unless you know the names of the spirits you want to contact, right?"

"What about those guys who blew their heads off?" asked Alex. He tapped on the boombox as he continued. "I heard they were listening to this record when it happened."

"Don't even mention those losers," said Rust.

"That's not how it works," said Mal. "You have to conduct the séance in the same place where they died."

Alex beamed excitedly at Jesse. "Speaking of séances—before we moved here from the city, my sister went to high school at Putnam City North with—"

"Sean Sellers, yeah, yeah," Mal interrupted. "We've heard it a million times."

"And one night after the murders, she went with her friends to his parents' house up in Summit Place—back when it was still abandoned." Alex stretched his tongue over his large front teeth to moisten his lips as he continued. "They tried to summon the spirits of his dead parents, but instead, the board spelled out the name *Ezurate,* just before it caught on fire and burned up."

"Ezurate?" asked Jesse.

"That was the name of the demon that possessed Sellers. The one that made him kill everybody."

"He totally stole that from Anton LaVey," added Mal.

"Sounds like somebody's been watchin' the *700 Club* again with his Jesus-freak parents," said Rust.

Alex ignored the jab and furrowed his brow as though deep in thought. "Damn. What the hell were those guys' names? It's driving me nuts."

Jesse saw the opening and went for it. "James Vance and Raymond Belknap were listening to the album *Stained Class* before entering into their suicide pact during the winter of '85." Jesse regurgitated the line from one of the articles he had read in Rick's archives. "Only Belknap was actually successful though."

Rust spat out his beer. "Holy shit! Look at this Poindexter go."

Jesse sat on the ground next to Mal and crossed his legs underneath him. "My brother is totally into Judas Priest. I mean, me too—but he's like obsessed. He has a box of newspaper clippings from the trial and everything." Jesse suddenly felt as if he were dominating the conversation. "It's practically all he's talked about until he finally got a copy of the new record after it was delayed in court."

Alex squealed at the mention of the much-heralded release. "Dude, that record is like impossible to get a hold of. You *have* to get him to make me a tape of it."

"Actually," Jesse reached into his pocket and produced the cassette Rick had given him, "he already made me one." As he gently handed the tape to Alex, a sudden silence fell over the group as though some profound ceremonial ritual had taken place. The handwritten label read PAINKILLER, flanked by two inverted pentagrams sketched on either side—one of Rick's illustrations. "It's going to change everything you've ever thought about Priest."

Alex reached into his jean jacket and offered Jesse a warm bottle of Budweiser.

"What the fuck, Alex? I thought you said you didn't have any more," complained Rust.

"It's awesome. We were just listening to a couple tracks," Jesse said, taking a swig of beer before passing the bottle to Rust.

"That's cool. So you guys are like, close?" asked Mal.

"Yeah, I kinda take care of him even though he's older." Jesse shrugged. "He was in a bad motorcycle accident."

"Sounds like a regular Evel Knievel."

"Don't listen to him," Mal said. "Rust is just trying to impress you by being a dick."

Alex swapped out the cassettes and turned the volume up on the boombox. The title track resonated off the surrounding stone, creating a natural reverb effect.

Jesse chimed in after the first track ended. "This next song is my favorite. I mean, I haven't heard the whole album yet, but I think it's my favorite."

"What's it called?" asked Alex.

"'Hell Patrol.'"

Rust and Alex exchanged a look that could have been fueled by either terror or unbridled excitement. As if guided by some telepathic communication, they both jumped to their feet and shouted in unison over the music, "Hell Patrol!"

"Great. You just gave them their band name. Now we'll never hear the end of it."

Jesse felt his heart skip a beat as he watched the two bang their heads until the track was finished.

"You guys have a band?"

"Hardly—they don't even have all the instruments."

In an effort to push through the awkward lull of silence, Jesse seized his opportunity. "That's cool. I used to have a band—sort of. We had to move before we got any gigs or anything."

"No shit? What do you play?" Alex asked.

"Bass."

The seed had been planted.

Jesse offered the information coyly, knowing that his preferred instrument was generally in short supply among would-be rockers. "I haven't taken any lessons or anything. Pretty much all self-taught."

"You wanna be in the band?" Alex blurted out. "We need a bass player." The offer was followed by a swift punch on the shoulder from Rust.

"Sure. I mean, if that's cool."

"Come on, Rust," Alex pleaded, rubbing his shoulder.

Rust downed the remainder of the bottle of beer, appearing suddenly disinterested in the conversation. "I guess you can try out. If you don't suck maybe you can stick around until we find someone better."

"You haven't even heard him yet," Mal said. "But I've heard you guys, and you aren't exactly in a position to refuse talent."

"What do you want from me, woman? I said he could try out." *I'm in the band.*

The thought resonated through Jesse's mind along with a flood of images portending the future that lay in store. Despite the immensity of the social victory—and on the first encounter with the inhabitants of his new world, no less—Jesse's mundane responsibilities wormed their way to the forefront of his mind.

"Shit. Does anyone know what time it is?" he asked.

Mal pulled back the row of cascading bracelets that lined her forearm to reveal a black Swatch with a spider on the watch face. "Almost 7:30 p.m."

"I gotta run."

"I'll walk with you." She pointed to the distance beyond the ranch house. "I live just over there."

"Thanks for the tape," Alex said.

"We meet here at the Hell Hole before practice on Sundays, two p.m., sharp," said Rust.

"Cool."

4

Mal led the way back towards the ranch house. Despite the heavy, military-issue combat boots, she traversed the thick underbrush gracefully.

"You still back there?" She turned to face Jesse while holding back her raven-colored hair. "You walk like a ghost."

"Sorry," Jesse shrugged.

"You don't have to apologize." She pushed on his arm gently. "Unless you really are a ghost."

"I'm pretty sure I'm real."

The exchange was interrupted as Mal became distracted by something in the distance. She grabbed Jesse's hand, pulling him down behind a thicket of stubby mesquite trees just off the Old Townsite service road.

Jesse followed her eyes as they peered out from behind the tree line. There in the distance, barely visible in the fading twilight, he could make out the silhouette of a bearded, bespectacled man atop the road-cut outcrop that loomed above the mine entrance. The man tended to an array of strange-looking scientific equipment installed atop the rocky outcrop. He was wearing headphones and scribbling readings from the equipment into a notepad every few seconds.

"Do you think he saw us?" asked Jesse.

"Relax, he's not wearing a uniform. He's not going to arrest us or anything."

"Maybe he's a meteorologist or something?"

"Doubt it. We haven't had a tornado in this part of the state in like twenty years. The town was built on an old Chickasaw burial ground."

"All right—then maybe he's some kind of sex pervert that spies on teens at the local make-out point?"

Mal turned to Jesse and gave a wry smile. "But we're not making out."

"No—I know," Jesse stumbled. "But that's probably what he wants to see—because he's a sex pervert."

The man turned towards their hiding spot and adjusted his headphones over his ears just as the words left Jesse's mouth. He seemed to be looking right at them through the undergrowth at the edge of the tree line.

"Nice try." Mal took Jesse's hand. "You could at least offer to buy me dinner first."

They ran through the woods, laughing at the strange, bearded fellow who followed them quizzically with his eyes. They kept running until they came upon a rusty barbed wire fence that separated the forest from the adjacent pasture.

After crossing back through the sea of buffalo grass, they stopped to catch their breath once they were in sight of Mal's street—a collection of small, sad homes that lined a winding gravel road that ran alongside the endless expanse of pasture.

"So," Jesse spoke up, "you never told me what you play."

Mal rolled her eyes. "Please—I'm an artist."

"Oh yeah? Like drawing and painting and stuff? My brother can draw pretty good. I'm terrible at it."

"You ever heard of Mick Rock or Annie Leibovitz?"

"They were in Heart, right?"

She laughed. "Hardly. Their instruments *actually* made musicians famous." She planted her feet and leveled her shoulders at Jesse. "I'm a photographic artist."

"Cool. So you'll be at practice, too?"

"Don't hold your breath. Those guys suck."

5

The next day, Jesse arrived at the Hell Hole with his bass slung over his shoulder and a 20-watt combo amp under his arm. He had paced around the concrete enclosure for a good while before finally noticing the rolled-up piece of notebook paper crammed in between the gate's wrought iron bars.

He tugged at the piece of paper, pulling it free from the rusty iron gate. In doing so he caused one of the loose bricks to separate from its mortar and fall behind the crumbling seal. He was held captivated by the whisper of darkness now visible beyond the gate.

Like the grain silo on his familial land, the mine was also a relic of his childhood, but one that still retained the attribution of otherworldly powers ascribed by his youthful imagination; however, unlike the silo, the passage of time had somehow increased the sense of foreboding that he felt upon gazing into the dark abyss. The Gothic stone archway that rose above the gate did little to allay the baleful portent.

He unrolled the loose piece of notebook paper and tried to decipher the crude instructions. A lone x appeared at the end of a perforated line drawn to indicate his path. He held the paper and oriented the dark circle in the center marked: YOU ARE HERE. Suddenly feeling the fool, he lugged his gear back up the concrete incline and into the woods towards his destination.

Jesse stopped to disentangle a patch of thorns that had snagged on one of the many holes in his ripped-up jeans when he heard a disembodied voice call out from the woods.

"You find yourself, a lowly sell-sword, on an overgrown road heading east. Ahead, you spy a gathering of kobolds who have erected their camp along your path. What do you do?"

"Very funny, guys."

"The kobolds detect your presence and begin a ranged attack."

A hefty dirt clod exploded against the trunk of a large oak tree, inches from Jesse's head. He wiped the dirt from his eyes and called out to the forest. "Are we gonna do band practice, or play D&D?"

Another clod struck true, thudding against his chest. Jesse jumped behind the tree to avoid the next volley. Deciding to avoid further target practice for his attackers, Jesse called out again to the woods.

"Fine. I cast Magic Missile on the kobolds." He proceeded to make the necessary calculations and specified his attack. "I'm a level twelve magic user, so that gives me nine missiles—I direct them all on the leader." He picked up a handful of acorns and hurled them towards the unseen assailants.

"The kobolds make a successful saving throw versus spell damage. You are unsuccessful in your attack."

Another volley of dirt clods flew through the trees on all sides; one of the projectiles knocked over the combo amp.

"All right, fuck this." Jesse picked up his gear and began to leave. "I'm out of here."

Silence followed the proclamation.

Finally, the voice called out once more from the trees. "*The kobolds wish to formalize a truce so that band practice may begin.*"

A towering, broad-shouldered colossus emerged from the forest beside Rust and Alex. Jesse was more disarmed by the unwavering ear-to-ear smile that he wore than the youth's unusual stature, or his roughspun tunic. A mop of dense auburn hair flowed in his wake as he moved towards Jesse.

"Congratulations sell-sword! You have passed the rite of initiation," spoke the large teen.

"Good job, dude," Alex's squeaky voice crackled through the still fall air. "You're in." He brushed off the dirt from Jesse's jean jacket as he chuckled to himself from behind his oversized front teeth.

"Glad I could provide the entertainment."

Alex cocked his thumb towards the large youth. "That's Mazes, he plays drums. You guys are the rhythm section."

"No hard feelings?" Mazes asked as he clasped Jesse's forearm. "Before you joined our party of seasoned adventurers, I had to make sure you were up to snuff. I must say, I am pleasantly surprised. Very quick on your feet, young mage."

Jesse hurried to keep pace with Mazes's long strides as the giant swooped up his gear under one of his massive arms.

Alex saddled up next to Jesse and pulled him aside as the others continued ahead. "Sorry about the theatrics, man. Mazes is cool." He followed the gargantuan youth with his eyes as he crested the hill, and lowered his voice. "He's just a little off."

"No shit. What's with the name?"

"A couple years ago he was involved in this really intense D&D campaign." Alex snickered. He glanced around and lowered his voice even more. "I heard he stayed up for almost a week straight, strung out on white cross, while the game went on, nonstop. He ended up going full on *Mazes and Monsters*, like in that shitty Tom Hanks movie. He had some kind of seizure and attacked the neighbor's dog."

"Holy shit."

"Yeah. His parents put him in a mental institution for a couple months," Alex shrugged. "At first we just thought it was all an act so he could get homeschooled. But he's been pretty much stuck inside his character ever since he came out of the funny farm."

Jesse felt slightly unnerved as Mazes picked up a felled sapling and held it aloft as though it were a sword. He plodded ahead in front of the others, parrying and thrusting his way through the woods, presumably fending off hordes of imaginary foes that threatened to impede his party's progress towards band practice.

"Luckily, he was playing a chaotic good paladin."

Mazes struck the sapling against a dead limb overhead, causing it to come crashing down in the middle of their path. A strange-looking organic nodule the size of a football had become dislodged from the branch, and rolled towards Rust's feet.

"Bees!" Rust screamed as he bounded farther ahead up the trail.

Alex stepped on the outer shell of the ovular pod and crushed it open beneath his shoe. The act of destruction revealed multiple disc-shaped layers that made up the internal support structure of the hive. Each layer was composed of a lattice of symmetrical honeycombs—hundreds of them. With the exception of the amber-colored goo stuck to the bottom of Alex's shoe, the beehive appeared empty.

"It's okay, there's nobody home," Alex said.

Jesse kicked at a cross section of honeycomb that was filled with a white gelatinous substance. The sight of the inner workings of the hive had a certain creep factor that was hard to explain. Each cell of the honeycomb matrix was perfectly identical. It was like seeing something that shouldn't exist—order derived from chaos.

"Royal jelly," said Mazes. He hung his head and sighed. "Pity this bounty will go to waste."

"All right dorks, can we get on with this?" asked Rust. He called down to the others as he leaned against a tree, running a switchblade comb through the shock of greasy curls that sprouted above the shaved sides of his head.

"So where do you guys practice?"

"Alex's place," answered Rust. "His parents are 24/7 Jesus freaks, so we pretty much have the run of the place."

Alex's lips parted into a toothy smile. "They're doing Bible Jeopardy after Sunday service today, so they won't be back until late."

They walked for a time towards the east, passing through the undeveloped farmland that stretched between the high school and the eastside residential district. As they ventured past Mal's street, Jesse caught himself feeling desperate for any sign of her.

Finally, the group arrived at a modern residential development still under construction. A showy brick step wall announced the gated community where Alex lived. Jesse felt out of place amidst the cookie-cutter suburban landscape with its manicured lawns and overpriced yuppie-mobiles. A few sidelong glances from the neighborhood denizens confirmed the feeling was mutual.

Mazes and Jesse walked side by side through the row of open, intersecting backyards. At one point, Jesse gestured towards Rust, who strode confidently in front of the group, immune to the upper-crust surroundings. "Let me guess, he's the singer?"

"Astute observation, young mage." Mazes smirked. "He is indeed the minstrel of the party."

They followed Alex through the side door of one of the houses—a large, two-story number with a grey brick exterior, nestled beneath a wood-shingled roof. Jesse tried to shrug off the sense of alienation as they set up their gear in the garage and began tuning up.

"I hereby call to order the first gathering of Hell Patrol!" shouted Mazes.

"Christ." Rust shook his head. "Where's the off button on this guy?"

Mazes took a seat behind a well-worn trap set where he followed the announcement with an ear-splitting cymbal crash. Jesse noted the running split in the cymbal and wondered at the cost required to maintain the giant's hardware.

"All right, newbie," said Rust. "Let's see what you got."

"You know any covers?" asked Alex.

"My old band used to do a lot of AC/DC songs."

"Come on man, we're not amateurs. Do you know any *real* covers?" asked Rust.

Jesse cycled through the catalog of bass tabs he had memorized from *Guitar Player* magazine.

"Okay, I got one." He turned on the combo amp and plucked his E string a couple of times to dial in his volume. Before he could talk himself out of it, Jesse launched into his best attempt at the intro of "N.I.B." by Black Sabbath, *from the seminal album* Black Sabbath, *released in 1970 on Vertigo Records*. He channeled his inner Geezer as he pummeled the strings with his fingers.

Wearing a mask of excited recognition, Alex rushed to throw his guitar over his shoulder, nearly dropping it in the process.

Mazes followed suit with an overbearing hi-hat count, but landed true on the beat just as the first verse kicked in. Jesse had never heard anyone play the drums that loud before. It was like watching Bonham on steroids.

The groove was stilted, out of tune, and clumsy, but contagious all the same.

Rust grabbed the mic with both hands in true Ozzy fashion and belted out the opening verse. His vocals were powerful, with just the right amount of gravel—somewhere on throat-bleed scale between Paul Di'Anno and Udo. While he was a far cry from Rob Halford or King Diamond, he could also hit the head voice high notes when he had to, and with a tasteful amount of vibrato, too.

Alex was the most technically proficient of the band, but not in an over polished, masturbatory Steve Vai or Yngwie Malmsteen kind of way. He channeled the blues-tinged darkness of the pentatonic prison, but in a way that made it his own. A disciple of the Left-Hand Path in the tradition of Jimi and Iommi, the southpaw strumming was an added visual bonus to his playing.

Jesse was no showboating Sheehan, but he could hold his own, and he knew his instrument's role as the glue that bound the rhythm to the riff.

Two hours and a modicum of improvement later, the brotherhood of Hell Patrol was forged in homage to the progenitors of heavy metal. After a few minutes into the logistical planning of their spring tour of the West Coast, a brilliant flash of light filled the garage.

The group turned to see Mal behind her camera.

"I'm not here, just be candid," she instructed. "Try to act like this isn't your first promo shoot, and I'll do the rest." She fanned the air in front of her face as she continued. "Also, someone should really let in some fresh air. It smells like balls and feet in here."

CHAPTER TWO

IN THE LAIR OF THE ICE QUEEN

1

A heaping pile of scrambled eggs was deposited next to the stack of toast on Jesse's plate. He wolfed down his breakfast, half-listening to his mother prattle on.

"And don't forget to introduce yourself to your teachers. New kids always start out at a disadvantage."

"This is high school. No one does that."

"Don't be shy, you're a very smart kid—stand up and be recognized."

Jesse obeyed her suggestion in the literal sense and stood from his chair with an open-mouthed, enthusiastic grin. He nodded his head up and down vigorously, causing the mouthful of half-chewed eggs and toast to fall back to his plate.

His mother erupted in a loud, ornamental yelp, and chased Jesse from the table with a kitchen rag. "And please change that shirt. No one wants to be friends with Satan."

He looked down at his prized Slayer shirt and brushed it off for good measure. "Give it a rest, will ya?"

He knew by the clamoring of dishes she had whisked into the sink that he had inadvertently drawn a line in the sand.

"Jesse, this is the *buckle* of the Bible belt. Remember that boy up in the city a few years back who killed his parents after he shot up that convenience store?"

"How could I forget? It's like all anyone talks about around here."

The door to the back bedroom creaked open.

"That's bullshit, Mom," Rick called out.

She ignored the intrusion. "People don't trust kids anymore, so don't give them a reason not to like you. You can be a very likable young man when you want to be."

"Sean Sellers is an asshole and deserves what he gets," Rick continued, undeterred. "He's just a cog in the political machine intent on blaming the ills of society on something they can't understand."

Sensing one of Rick's tirades coming on, Jesse began to gather his things for school as he felt the temperature change in the room.

"You're just regurgitating the scripted propaganda perpetuated by the religious right. The Moral Majority and the PMRC are on a witch hunt to try to silence anyone who would make it harder for them to maintain their control over an increasingly secular society."

His mother shook her head, bracing herself over the sink. "Thank you for the history lesson, Rick."

"Death to false metal," Rick replied. The door slammed shut followed by a blast of loud music.

"Well that's just great! Now you got your brother all excited. You know it's not good for him to get worked up."

"Mom, he's fine. You have to stop babying him. He's a grown man."

She wiped her face before escorting Jesse out the door. "You're going to be late. Randy is waiting in the truck." She handed him a crisp five dollar bill. "This is for lunch. Don't spend it all on cigarettes."

"Yes, ma'am."

He heard the screen door swing open after him. "Have a good first day of school, hon. You're gonna do great!"

2

Jesse floated through his first four class periods daydreaming about the events of the past weekend. With the exception of art class, which was dedicated to developing a series of Hell Patrol logos in various stylings (e.g., Death, Thrash, NWOBHM, etc.), the day was a dull blur. Though he lacked the artistic talents of his brother, Jesse figured his sketches might be enough for Rick to work with, given the proper motivation.

If there was one thing Rick knew, it was music. Before the accident forced him into exile from the industry, Rick the Prick had even roadied for Metallica, for fuck's sake. He was on his way to building a name for himself as a promoter before fate stepped in and traded out his motorcycle for a wheelchair.

His older brother had long ago instilled in him the importance of the almighty logo—the symbolic vessel that transported the essence of the band into the mind of a potential fan. Rick had a two-pronged theory about logos.

First, the logo required admission past the eye of the beholder. If the visual appeal was satisfactory, it didn't matter what string of syllables were cobbled together that served to utter the name aloud. Those would eventually become meaningless through time.

As testimony to Rick's wise council, Jesse reasoned that no one is really thinking about a hearing-impaired feline when they hear the name Def Leppard. It was just a pattern of sounds that conjured an association to the band's music.

There was a science to it.

Secondly, a good name could be ruined by a shitty logo, while conversely, a good logo could carry a shitty name. Fortunately for Jesse's new band, the latter was not an issue.

The end of fourth period concluded with the arrival of lunch hour. Jesse waded through the sundry offerings of the cafeteria, eventually settling on an overcooked chili dog that smelled like fish sticks and an order of greasy curly fries. A strawberry fountain drink topped off the nutrient-poor assemblage of heat-lamp stink.

As he slid his tray through the checkout line, his eyes were drawn to the bright sunlight that streamed in from the atrium. There he saw her, her raven black hair almost blue in the direct sunlight.

"Hey, you gonna pay for that?" The inquiry came from a bleary-eyed cashier. Jesse reached into his wallet and laid the five-dollar bill that his mother had given him on the counter, and left without his change.

He pushed through the glass double doors and entered the atrium where he was waved over to one of the aluminum picnic benches.

"Yo, Jess, saved you a seat." Alex motioned to an empty spot next to Mal.

Before Jesse could sit down, a dark shadow filled his vision. The force of the collision nearly knocked him off his feet, causing the chili dog to fall to the ground and spilling the strawberry soda across the tray.

"Watch where you're going, freak," said one of the letterman jacket-clad varsity football players who filled the center row of benches. He scowled at Jesse from beneath a fire-engine red flattop while two of his teammates began running mock play patterns with Jesse's fallen chili dog.

Jesse took the seat next to Mal, trying his best to stave off the wave of rage that was boiling up from beneath his reddened cheeks.

Mal stole a handful of the soggy fries from his tray and dunked them into a concoction of ketchup and mayonnaise that seemed to be her only staple.

"How did you know I love soda fries?" She spoke with a mouthful of food, making sure to reveal the contents of her open mouth in the process.

"Seriously, don't mention it," Jesse said, forcing a smile.

"So you must be Jesse?" The inquiry came from a curly-haired girl wearing a green army jacket and cat-eye glasses seated across from Mal. "Don't mind those assholes."

Jesse nodded.

"This is Kara." Mal took a drink as she choked down the fries. "She's like the only human I can tolerate in life."

Nearby, one of the football players was tripped up by his team-mates' horseplay and fell, jettisoning the contents of his backpack on the ground. A spiral notebook slid under the table near Jesse's feet and was quickly snatched up by Rust.

"Oh shit," Rust whispered as he thumbed through the notebook. "Anybody want Kenny Summers's algebra homework?"

"Unless those are workout notes, or phone numbers of slutty cheerleaders, it probably isn't worth copying," said Kara.

"I got a better idea." Rust dipped his finger into a ketchup container and sketched an inverted pentagram on the first blank sheet inside the notebook. Once the sigil was completed, he dropped the notebook to the ground and slid it with his foot back towards Kenny's fallen backpack.

Unaware of the subterfuge, Kenny bent over to pick up the notebook along with the rest of the contents of his backpack. The other varsity players took turns trying to execute a wedgie from his exposed underwear.

Alex and Rust exchanged a sly grin.

"He is going to freak," Mal whisper-screamed.

"Totally." Kara looked around. She lowered her voice to Jesse. "His dad taught my Sunday school class when I was a kid."

"Watch and learn, losers," Rust muttered under his breath as he stood from the table. He knelt beside Kenny and began helping him gather his stuff.

"Thanks, man. I'm such a klutz," said Kenny.

The jock's earnest expression made Jesse uneasy at the thought of what was to come, despite the uniform he wore.

Rust pointed to the ketchup dripping out from the fore edge of the notebook, "Dude, what is that?" he asked. "Is that blood?"

Kenny opened the notebook in disbelief, spreading apart the stuck-together pages to reveal the red, blotted pentagram. "Wait a minute. I didn't do that."

The others huddled around as Kenny thumbed through the notebook.

Mal pointed to the pentagram. "People doing weird stuff they can't remember can be a sign of demonic possession."

"Yeah, it's like they're hypnotized under Satan's spell," said Kara.

The color drained from Kenny's face.

Alex jumped on the dogpile with his go-to rap about demonic possession. "My sister went to high school with this kid in the city who killed his parents after being possessed by a demon." He narrowed his eyes into weasel slits as he dealt the killing blow. "It was on *Donahue*."

Rust looked to Jesse who had up to now remained silent.

"It's true," Jesse said. "First it's pentagrams. Then the next thing you know, you wake up in the middle of the night levitating three feet above your bed." He surprised himself at the ease in which he contributed to the torture. "You should probably get to a preacher and get checked out before it's too late."

Kenny held the notebook as if it were a serpent about to strike. "Oh my God, I didn't do this. I swear to *God* I didn't do this." He wound up and threw the notebook as far as he could, landing it near the feet of the on-duty lunch chaperone.

The chaperone blew a whistle that hung from the lanyard around her neck. She jogged up to the scene in her white tennis shoes with the sopping notebook in hand, wearing one of those "Hello, my name is…" nametags that read: MRS. RASMUSSEN.

"Mr. Summers, what on earth do you think you are doing?" she asked.

"I'm possessed by Satan!" Kenny wailed.

IN THE LAIR OF THE ICE QUEEN

The commons fell silent.

Mal took Jesse's hand and bolted through the glass double doors. They made their way through the interior commons before disappearing into the arts hall.

"Holy shit! I can't believe that actually happened," she said.

Jesse's heart was nearly beating out of his chest. "Oh my God. That poor, dumb jock."

"Please. Those jerks deserve much worse." Mal stopped at the end of the hall. "In here."

An unlit DARKROOM IN USE sign hung above the door. Mal produced a key, unlocked the door, and peered inside. The room was dark except for a red safelight that glowed from behind a partition of black plastic curtains that spanned the length of the room.

"Mr. Woods lets me use the darkroom during lunch. He usually goes off campus to eat, so we should be good," she said as she closed the door behind them and locked it from the inside.

Mal guided him through the dark, towards a row of photo enlargers that lined the back counter. A strong chemical smell that Jesse did not recognize hovered in the air.

"I have something for you." She reached up to the clothesline where several photographs were drying out and handed him one. "This is one of my favorites from the practice shoot."

As his eyes adjusted to the scant light, he could see that the photo was a self-portrait. In the background over her left shoulder Jesse could see his likeness playing bass in Alex's garage.

"Can I have this?"

"Well, duh. It's just a test print, but if you like it..."

"It's great." Jesse smiled. "I mean, you're hogging most of the frame, but at least you still managed to get my bass in the shot."

Whether it was the fumes of photographic chemistry that he had been inhaling, or the realization that they were alone together in the dark room, a wave of dizziness washed over Jesse as she stepped closer.

The sound of the key turning in the lock ended the moment.

Mal jabbed Jesse in the shoulder and placed her index finger over her lips for him to keep quiet. The lights went on in the front room as heavy footsteps resounded near the chalkboard.

She pointed through the curtain and mouthed the words *Mr. Woods.*

Jesse nodded, craning his neck to catch a glimpse of the squat, mustachioed photography teacher as he tossed an empty fast food wrapper into the trash.

Mr. Woods stuffed the last bite of a burger in his mouth and wiped his hands on his pants. He then walked to the center of the room, facing the chalkboard, and leaned forward while resting both hands on his hips. The sound of Mr. Woods's ass exploding tore through the silence in the room.

Mal immediately dropped to her knees and covered her mouth with both hands.

They ran out the side door of the darkroom and into the white linoleum-covered hall, bursting with tears. Jesse thought for a moment he might pass out from lack of oxygen.

"Bleh." Mal rolled her tongue off the roof of her mouth. "Now I know what it feels like to get fumigated."

"There you are!" Mrs. Rasmussen's shrill voice paralyzed him. She marched down the hall, still clasping the plastic whistle that hung around her neck. Alex and Rust followed sheepishly behind her. "Mallory Henderson and Jesse Lynn, come with me to the principal's office this instant."

3

Jesse sat with the others in the waiting room of Principal Anderson's office. His thoughts drifted from the darkroom encounter to the look of disappointment on his mother's face when she would learn that Jesse was already in trouble on his first day of school.

A round, middle-aged woman appeared at the desk counter. She scowled at the group from behind a nameplate that read: GRACE JOHNSON, ADMINISTRATIVE ASSISTANT. "Principal Anderson will see you now," she said, clutching the gold crucifix around her neck as she spoke.

The group filed into Principal Anderson's office, who was rifling through a bookshelf behind her desk. Her hair was set in a wreath of tight brown curls that seemed to defy gravity, an attempt at fashion that countered the drab, navy blue power suit she wore.

Jesse felt a sense of dread as he noticed Kenny Summers's ketchup-soaked notebook on her desk.

Principal Anderson took her seat and gestured to the row of empty chairs opposite her desk. She pursed her lips as she read from her notes. "Russell Krokowski, Alexander Brooks, and Mallory Henderson... I heard we had a little incident today during lunch, is that right?"

The group sat frozen in silence.

"I just received a frantic call from Kenny Summers's father, who as we speak is rushing over to pick up his son from school because he believes he is possessed by the devil." Principal Anderson shifted in her chair and folded her arms. "Would anyone care to comment on that?"

"No, ma'am," Alex and Rust said in unison.

Jesse noted the practiced response.

"Is that so?" Principal Anderson sighed as she directed her attention towards Jesse. "And let's see...Mr. Lynn, is it?"

Jesse nodded.

"Well, Mr. Lynn, I'm sorry to see that you have fallen in with the wrong crowd on your very first day at Macomb Springs High. I hope this isn't the beginning of a precedent that you are establishing." She gestured to the large crucifix that hung on the wall behind her desk. "I don't know how they did things where you are from, but I assure you that here in Macomb Springs, we place a high value on our moral convictions."

Jesse looked to the ground, suddenly embarrassed by the situation. Principal Anderson slid a book across her desk towards the group. She tapped her red-polished nails on the cover and waited. Jesse read the title—*Michelle Remembers*—and received a momentary twinge of recognition from one of his brother's anti-establishment tirades. *Rick would flip his lid if he was here to see this.* Jesse stifled a laugh despite himself as he imagined his brother's reaction to the situation at hand.

"You might think this is all a joke, but I have news for you: Satanic cults are real, and nothing to take lightly." She fingered through a neat stack of magazine and newspaper clippings on her desk as she continued. "All over the country, the police and the F.B.I. are encountering occult activity among teenagers just like yourselves. Ritual sacrifice, child abuse, suicide, and worse—some of them are even killing their own parents."

She produced a handful of small rectangular booklets from her desk drawer that she handed out to each of the detainees. "I want you to read through these while you enjoy detention for the rest of the week."

Jesse thumbed through the small rectangular comic strip that depicted a group of teenagers hanging out in the woods. As he turned the page to reveal the next panel, the teenagers were suddenly wearing dark hooded robes and appeared to be in the throes of conducting an animal sacrifice.

"Chick tracts," said Mal. "Really?"

Principal Anderson sat back in her chair and sized up the group. "Mallory, I don't understand why such a pretty young girl would choose to dress like such a hideous ghoul. And to think, you used to be one of our star cheerleaders."

Mal blushed at the mention. "Color guard. And that was like three years ago."

"What your poor parents must think. I feel pity for them, I truly do." Principal Anderson clicked her tongue and shook her head in disapproval. "Such a shame."

Mal's alabaster cheeks turned a deep scarlet hue at the mention of her parents. Her eyes transformed into narrow slits of glacier ice as she leveled her shoulders and spoke in an almost guttural snarl that belied her small frame.

"Lady, you don't know what the fuck you're talking about."

4

By the time the interrogation in Principal Anderson's office had run its course, sixth period had ended. The group were escorted by Grace Johnson to detention hall.

As they entered the classroom, Jesse froze in recognition of the bearded and bespectacled man that sat at the front of the class.

The sex pervert with the weird science equipment.

Unable to visually confirm his suspicion with Mal, who had already covered her head in her arms on her desk, Jesse took his seat with the rest of the group as the strange-looking man began to address the classroom.

"Good afternoon. My name is Mr. Agostino, and I am your new guidance counselor." The words came methodically, though upbeat, and with superb elocution. He seemed happily surprised by each new syllable that formed in his mouth as he toyed with his heavy beard. "In order to get to know some of the students who might best benefit from my services, it has been decided that I monitor detention for the foreseeable future."

Mr. Agostino surveyed each of the students in turn, peering over his circular wire-rim glasses. His eyes beamed excitedly under the mop of dense black curls, which flowed almost seamlessly into the equally dense beard he wore. He lingered on Jesse momentarily, arching an inquisitive eyebrow.

Appearing satisfied with the visual survey of the students, Agostino returned to his desk and opened a worn leather briefcase. "Very well then, one hour of reflective meditation to contemplate your recent turn of fate," he said as he pulled out a paperback from his briefcase.

Jesse passed the hour by examining the illustrations in the Chick tract, all the while watching Mal from his periphery, who sat a few seats over. Her heavy mascara had run down her face in dark streaks, creating thin tributaries of sadness that eroded the landscape of indifference that generally masked her features.

Once Mr. Agostino had announced that the hour had passed, and the students were free to go, Jesse followed after Mal who had already strode out of the room ahead of him.

"Hey, wait up," Jesse called out as he jogged to catch up to her. "Did you happen to notice that our new guidance counselor bears a striking resemblance to a certain—"

"What the fuck does that uppity bitch know about my life?" Mal interrupted.

Jesse thought better of continuing the line of inquiry. "Maybe this can help you find some answers."

He handed her a booklet he had fashioned out of leftover drawing paper from art class. The pages were torn lengthwise into strips and folded down the center to emulate the design of the Chick tracts Principal Anderson had provided to the group. The title read *Spawn of Satan*. The first series of images portrayed Mal and the others being interrogated in the principal's office, which was quickly transformed into an Inquisition-style tribunal.

The next panel revealed Principal Anderson depicted as an evil queen brandishing a sceptre in the shape of a gigantic crucifix. She appeared to be casting a spell on the group who hung from the wall in manacles. A ray of light shot out from the center of the queen's crucifix towards her prisoners.

In the next scene, the students' regular street clothing had been altered into slacks and blazers, and all wore neatly trimmed haircuts.

All but one.

The following panel showed that Mal, unaffected by the evil queen's spell, had broken free from her bindings. She appeared dressed in a dark robe. A maelstrom of fire blazed from her mouth, engulfing the evil crucifix-wielding queen and her minions like a volcanic eruption, spewing molten hot rage down upon her enemies while professing her allegiance to Satan.

The next scene revealed the students of Macomb Springs High fleeing from the school in droves as it was devoured by the flames. The students cheered as the school was reduced to smoldering ruins.

Mal turned the page, smiling, and witnessed a scene that portrayed her as a famous photographer, shooting stageside at a huge arena show. The backdrop banner above the drum riser read HELL PATROL.

In the final scene, Mal was standing on a pile of money surrounded by adoring fans. Jesse stood next to her with his bass in one hand, and the other around her shoulder.

"Solid sympathetic magic." She kissed Jesse on the cheek. "I guess you can walk me home."

5

The woods to the east of the school grounds were a much-needed solace. A void within the surrounding trespasses of civilization, their reach comprised a majority of the small rural township—a pastoral remnant that had only recently been touched by the hand of modernity.

Having grown up mostly in the city, Jesse could get used to a little bit of wilderness. At least Macomb Springs had that going for it.

And *she* was here.

As they walked the wooded trail in silence, Jesse began to dread the moment they would leave the forest. He could feel the outer world threatening to swallow his individuality whole, leaving only the undigestible fibers of his being behind—the stubborn parts of him that wouldn't go down so easy, the parts that made him want to grow his hair long and play loud, heavy shit and wear fucked-up clothes in spite of the friction it caused. Or was it because of the friction it caused? He wasn't sure anymore.

Never mind.

As though sensing the impulse, Mal diverged from their plotted trajectory, leading Jesse through the southern edge of the forest towards the old mine. Despair turned to relief as Mal gripped his hand tighter. Together, they descended down into the forgotten spaces of the Old Townsite—an abandoned industrial venture retooled as sanctuary for the displaced teenage castaway.

When they arrived at the Hell Hole, Mal jettisoned her backpack. She jumped up and down, shaking her hair out.

"Fuck today. Do you ever just feel like you are stuck between worlds?" Her eyes were pleading with him.

Jesse nodded. "Seems like most days, here lately."

"Do you believe in God?" she asked.

Jesse was taken aback by the pointedness of the question. "My brother always says that the only Holy Trinity worth worshiping is Black Sabbath, Deep Purple, and Rainbow."

Mal returned a blank look.

"Because a lot of the same players were in all three bands at one point or another."

"And what about you? What do you think?"

Jesse shrugged. He mostly wondered why people seemed to be so hung up on that question. It was too loaded. The question itself revealed more than the answer.

"I don't know. I guess I don't think anyone really believes. Just something they tell themselves to get through their lives. Something to drown out the fear."

"But if you try to embrace the fear and refuse to go with the flow, you're pushed out into the wild. And here we are." She gestured to the surrounding forest. "I feel like a prisoner. I don't ever want to go back to that shithole high school, or the shithole house I live in. I just want to get the hell out of here."

"Where would you go?" asked Jesse. The question served to momentarily deflect his crumbling vision of the future, a future that he had only just realized he had come to covet.

"My cousin lives in the city. She's basically like my big sister." She tapped the camera case that was strapped over her shoulder. "There's a pretty good photography school not too far from where she lives, off the interstate."

Jesse pulled out the self-portrait she had given him. "You're really good, you know." He held up the photograph as proof.

"You probably say that to all the girls." She stomped out a freshly lit cigarette and held the scene in her eyes. "The lighting is actually perfect right now." Mal pulled the camera out from its case and adjusted the lens. "Go stand against the gate."

The rusted gate groaned as he leaned against it. He could feel the shape of the thin, wrought iron bars as they pressed into his back. Mal took several shots from different angles, calling out various directions to Jesse, who obliged willingly. When she was finished, she leaned against the gate next to him.

They stared up in silence at the barren trees from beneath the stone arch. Silhouetted against the horizon, they looked like great skeletal hands, clawing their way up from the grave. Jesse noted that the imagined scene was reminiscent of one of his brother's album cover sketches.

In addition to being a roadie and a promoter, his brother was also a solid visual artist. Rick had tried his hand at designing logos and putting together flyers for a lot of the local bands on the scene back in the day. Nothing much since the accident aside from the occasional mixtape cover.

Buried beneath the realization that Rick could no longer physically access such blissful wanderings, and the threat of Mal's exodus, Jesse felt like an undead ghoul, torn from the life he once knew. He had awakened from the sweet dream of the living and stumbled out from his gated crypt into a land filled with chaos and uncertainty.

Although the air was still, Jesse thought he saw one of the utmost branches bend slowly towards the ground. He raised his arm to block the glare of the sun. As he was about to dismiss the phenomena as a trick of shadow, he felt Mal's lips brush over his.

The kiss drowned out the world. He could hear the leaves dropping on the stone arch above as he closed his eyes. A brief conversation among birds chimed out somewhere in the distance. Time slowed as he reveled in the touch of her flesh against his.

He leaned back on his shoulder to gain leverage. Together, the combined force of their weight jostled the gate loose from its hinges, causing the pair to tumble backwards through the crumbling brick wall that separated the mine from the outside world.

Mal pulled Jesse up to a seated position, laughing as they looked to the darkened path beyond the gate. The weathered brick seal had disintegrated beneath them, creating an accessible portal into the dormant space.

A pocket of stale, sulphuric air washed over them like an exhale of foul breath trapped in the static bellows of stone.

"Come on, let's check it out," Mal said. She grinned, revealing a crooked bottom tooth that somehow made her smile more authentic. "I'll let you feel me up."

Jesse rushed to fill the silence that came on the heels of the offer.

"Almost everyone on my mom's side of the family have nearly gotten themselves killed down there." He gestured to the darkness beyond the crumbled gate. "They bricked it up after some kid fell down the shaft and died."

"Jimmie Shankly?" Mal shook her head. "That's an urban legend. The real story—the Spring Creek Mine was decommissioned after a terrible accident that happened like over sixty years ago. The workers tunneled into a natural cave system beneath the mine. A large portion of it collapsed and killed the miners—seventeen of them in all."

"Holy shit. I've never heard that before."

She pulled Jesse to his feet and inspected the mine entrance, pointing to the grey springer stones that comprised the arch. "That's why if you count the stones, there are exactly seventeen."

Jesse started to feel uneasy about venturing farther—and not solely for fear of having to confront the growing tension fostered by the presence of adolescent hormones.

"How do you know so much about this?"

Her eyes widened as she recounted the tale. "When I was in fourth grade we had to do a public library assignment on the history of Macomb Springs. It took forever, but I eventually found some original newspaper articles in the *Chronicle* archives that mentioned the mine collapse."

"That's crazy," Jesse shook his head in disbelief. "I'm surprised my mom never told me about that. She grew up here. And ever since my brother's accident she's been *super* overprotective— pointing out every pothole and blind alley across the county."

"Wait, it gets better!" She squealed and punched him in the shoulder. "Nobody knows about it now because the mayor of Macomb Springs at the time, Edgar Winchell, tried to cover it all up. He wanted to prevent the story from becoming national news so the town wouldn't protest the arrival of the coal industry, which was like *the* major economic industry at the time." She took a deep breath and flailed her hands in the air. "I've pretty much been obsessed with the story ever since."

"That's fucked up."

"What's even more fucked up … because the collapse was so deep and widespread, no one was ever able to recover the remains. And Winchell paid off the families to keep them quiet."

"The bodies are still down there?"

Mal nodded. "I know, it's awesome. Eventually, after he died, the Winchell family quietly shut down the mine and bricked up the entrance—out of sight, out of mind." She took his hand and gestured through the archway. "You scared, Jesse?"

6

Guided by the flames of their lighters, the two followed the old rail cart track into the abandoned mine. Mal put her arm under Jesse's and squeezed it tight.

"We're probably like the first people to walk inside this place in years." Her long, black fingernails clawed deeper into his forearm with the utterance of each word.

They passed through the brick-lined entrance, feeling along the natural rock walls of the tunnel for guidance. Wooden support frames were erected every few feet, eventually widening into a spacious corridor.

Shiny black deposits of carbon flickered along the walls and ceiling of the rough-hewn chamber, carved out over a half-century ago.

"Look, there's the service platform for the rail cart track." She pointed to the west wall, where a raised wooden platform ran parallel to the track that snaked deeper into the mine. "So cool."

Jesse turned back to survey the distance from the gate, pushing the rising claustrophobia from his mind. The entrance had receded to nothing more than a pinhole of light surrounded by an impenetrable field of black.

"Is that a door?" asked Mal.

Beneath the soot-lined surface Jesse could make out the unmistakable shape of the large rectangular pair of double doors set within a steel support frame along the east wall of the open corridor. Before he could object, Mal pulled on the handle to the nearest door. To his relief, it remained closed.

"You just gonna stand there?"

Jesse cast aside his reservations and put his hands beneath hers and pulled on the door handle. The hinges creaked in protest, but eventually allowed the door to swing free in an explosion of rust and dust.

"Holy shit—check this out," she said, pulling Jesse through the doorway.

Inside, a bank of modular consoles lined the walls of a large control room. Many had been gutted. All that was left behind were piles of cables and wires that spilled onto the floor like the entrails of disembodied robots (a scene also reminiscent of one of Rick's album cover sketches during his *Somewhere in Time* phase).

Remnants of signage appeared along the walls just above the console banks, indicating the former presence of a rail switching station, lighting control panels, and a two-way radio call box.

"What do you think this one does?" she asked, brushing the dust and grime from one of the large breaker panels.

"Okay, we got inside, now we can go back. There's no way anything still works down here."

"Maybe there's still something connected to the Old Townsite power grid? It still powers all the railroad crossing arms along the old service road."

"How do you know all this stuff?"

"My dad used to work for the railroad before he got off on disability. We'll go back after we see what it does, I promise." She opened the panel and pushed up on one of the main breaker switches.

A shower of sparks erupted from the panel.

The sound of their screams echoed out into the central tunnel and reverberated down into the deeper recesses of the mine.

They stood in silence, listening as the acoustic rumble dissipated. As the echo resolved, what sounded like the call of a deep, bellowing foghorn answered back. Jesse felt a wave of dizziness crawl up his spine as the sound vibrated through the cavern.

"Cool," Mal whispered.

They stepped out into the corridor.

"Hello!" Mal called out into the darkness.

Once again the sound of her voice echoed down into the mine, and once again a deep bellow answered back from its depths like the call of a ship at sea, announcing its presence to the coast.

They steadied themselves against the tunnel wall as the disorienting sound waves reverberated off the stone from all sides.

A pocket of trapped air rushed by, followed by the sound of rocks falling from somewhere deeper within the mine.

"Cover your face, and try not to breathe. There could be blackdamp coming up from below."

"Blackdamp?"

"Bad air, trapped from the collapse."

Though he had never seen it himself, Jesse knew from regional lore that the vertical shaft that led down to the heart of the mine was located near the end of the rail cart track. The sound of the distant rockslide had conjured an image of skeletal miners, still wearing their headlamps and safety gear, scrambling up from the deep towards the sound of their voices.

"We should probably head back. I'm starting to feel a little weird."

"Relax, it will pass," Mal said. She pushed Jesse a step deeper into the tunnel. "Come on, let's go check it out."

Jesse ventured deeper into the abyss alongside Mal.

She called out again into the darkness. This time a voice answered back. Jesse could clearly discern the words as they rattled off the stone walls, raising the hair on the back of his neck.

"HAIL SATAN!"

Mal screamed.

Two silhouetted figures approached from the entrance. Jesse had already drawn his knife before he recognized the familiar cackle that resounded over the lingering reverberations of Mal's scream.

Muffled music rang out from Alex's umbilical boombox as Jesse's bandmates came into view.

"Bitchin'," said Rust. The light from his Zippo revealed the astonishment that bore out on their faces as they explored the forbidden space.

"How did you guys get in here?" asked Alex.

"Goddamnit. Was that you two assholes the whole time?" asked Mal.

"What do you mean? Rust is the asshole. I'm the happy-go-lucky one."

"Shut up. Listen to this."

Alex turned down the boombox as Mal attempted to demonstrate the strange acoustic phenomenon. Her call resounded flatly, absent the deep resonating bellow that had followed from the two previous occurrences.

"What have you guys been smokin' down here, and why are you bogartin' it?" asked Rust.

"Forget it," Mal sighed. "I need to get home anyway."

"Me too. I'll walk you," offered Jesse.

As the group exited, they piled up the loose bricks and propped up the broken gate.

"We gotta promise not to show this to anyone," said Mal, holding out her fist. "If word gets out, they'll seal it off for good. Got it?"

The others formed a circle and put their fists in the center of it, next to Mal's, and swore to uphold the secret of the hidden space.

7

They arrived at Mal's house just as nightfall began to blanket the sleepy town of Macomb Springs.

As they approached, Mal's father was sitting on the front porch downing a beer. He stared at Jesse as he crushed the empty can, placing it next to a dozen of its predecessors that lined the windowsill behind him.

"Hey, I'm home." Mal gestured to Jesse. "Frank, this is Jesse."

Frank shouted back over the blaring volume of the television set that flooded through the open living room window. "You're on your own for dinner. I already ate."

Mal shrugged. "I think I know my way around a frozen TV dinner, but thanks anyways."

"It's disrespectful the way you talk to me, you little jerk. I work too damn hard to put food on the table—"

"Collecting disability isn't exactly a job."

As Mal's demeanor hardened, Jesse suddenly felt transported back to Principal Anderson's office.

"You watch your mouth when you talk to me, little girl. I took that shit from your bitch of a mother, I'm not gonna take it from you, understand?" Frank stood up from the bench, nearly falling back against the windowsill, causing an avalanche of empty beer cans to fall to the porch. "And pick this shit up." He gestured to the spill of empty cans as he leaned on the door jamb. "This ain't a motel."

He stumbled inside, slamming the screen door. The force of the impact caused it to reopen, revealing a similar scene on the coffee table in front of the small color TV.

"That's my Dad."

"You want me to stay?"

"No, it's okay." She forced a smile as her eyes welled with tears. "This is my life. I'm kinda used to it."

"I better head home too. My mom is gonna freak out when she

hears about detention." Jesse gave her a hug and held her for a moment. "Thanks for the Macomb Springs history lesson."

Mal walked up the steps of the porch and turned back to offer a final wave to Jesse.

"Thanks again for the sympathetic magic." She patted the handmade Chick tract that rested in her back pocket.

Jesse lingered until she closed the screen door behind her. As he ventured down the gravel drive towards his familial ranch house, he could still hear the barbed tangle of raised voices through the open window.

CHAPTER THREE

DEEP WELL DOOM

1

Days turned to weeks, and weeks to months as Hell Patrol adhered to a rigorous practice schedule. They were beginning to hold their own, and even won a small cash prize at the Macomb Springs High battle of the bands. Once they stepped foot on that first stage, there was no going back.

Jesse was all in.

They used the prize money to start a fund for new equipment to continue their momentum towards bigger stages and, more importantly, bigger crowds.

Jesse's parents had renovated enough of the old ranch house to allow the Lynn family to move out from the trailer. The empty double-wide provided a dedicated practice space that allowed the band unfettered access to hone their chops. The occasion also presented the opportunity for Jesse to have his own bedroom, which subsequently allowed he and Mal to spend more time together.

In support of their collective musical aspirations, Rust dropped out of school to "Focus on the important things."

All the stars within Jesse's universe were caught in Hell Patrol's gravitation pull.

Even family.

In a rare break from his hermitage, Rick ventured out from behind his books and LPs to lend his industry experience, artistic skills, and encyclopedic knowledge of all things heavy metal to the effort. A vast repository of pop culture accumulated through years of solitude and escapism, Rick's mind was put towards the task of furthering the band's creative development, to which they responded by promoting him to manager.

"I'll give you six months of my life to make something happen," Rick had said. "Try not to blow it."

Finally, in an unforeseen development to further the cause, Alex had somehow managed to convince his parents to decommission one of the old, beat-up Ford economy vans from their church fleet. The band had its first set of wheels.

The name Vanzig surfaced accidentally during a heated argument between Rust and Rick, who were debating the artistic merits of Danzig (solo) versus the Misfits. Rust's slip of the tongue stuck, and a compromise was reached, allowing him to fashion a devil lock from a horsetail wig that dangled from the loudspeaker over the windshield—much to Rick's chagrin.

Overall, the band seemed to be more excited about the functional loudspeaker mounted to the roof of the vehicle than its ability to transport gear.

Armed with space, artistic direction, and the means to travel, the Hell Patrol rock 'n' roll, ride-or-die, heavy metal machine was lurching into motion.

Encouraged by Rick's newfound lust for life, Jesse's parents pitched in by installing a wheelchair lift on the van so that Hell Patrol's manager could attend the handful of small community-driven shows the band had managed to generate.

These early performances were mostly relegated to talent shows, DIY gigs at the local American Legion Hall, and even a failed one-off church-sponsored fundraiser at the Macomb Springs community theatre, hooked up by Alex's parents, where Rust had bitten the head off a fake rubber bat.

After having the plug pulled on them at the community theatre, the band vowed to focus their efforts on playing to the right crowd, particularly one that could appreciate an homage to the *Prince of Darkness* himself.

2

Rick had booked the band at The Deep Well—a local country-and-western dive that had recently put out an ad in the local paper calling for "FRESH LIVE TALENT."

As they finished loading up Vanzig, Rick was giving the group a pep talk to prepare them for their first *true* live experience—one in which alcohol would be served to people of legal drinking age.

"Don't be put off by the vibe of this place. I've made some calls and mailed out some flyers to some of my old street crew to spread the word among our own kind." He folded his hands underneath his chin and bowed his head, almost regally. "Rest assured, Rick the Prick is on the job."

"What if they check our IDs?" asked Jesse.

Rick reached into his chair caddy and produced four envelopes that he distributed to each member of the band. "If anyone asks, you are twenty-one. If they ask a second time, I've taken the liberty of forging notes from your parents, granting each of you permission to play as minors."

"Deception is the most formidable weapon in the rogue's arsenal," Mazes said, looking over his shoulder as he slid the forgery into his tunic.

Rick lined up his chair with the side-door lift. "I'll take care of the venue management, you guys just focus on destroying the stage."

"I'm ready to rock," Rust announced. "Let's go." He jogged in place and slapped himself in the face a couple of times.

Rick turned over his shoulder towards the group. "One more thing … do not, under any circumstances, actually destroy the stage. We don't have the budget for any Ritchie Blackmore antics."

3

Still a ways off from racking up the requisite funding for new gear, Hell Patrol embarked on the pre-show ritual of stopping off at the local RadioShack in order to keep their rag-tag backline of second-hand amplifiers limping along.

Vanzig thundered down the narrow one-way streets of the Old Downtown retail hub, music blaring out its open windows.

Rust promoted the show to many an innocent bystander over the loudspeaker as they headed towards the Plaza on Main, a recently developed strip mall near the North End sprawl. For Jesse, the Plaza consisted of only two shops: RadioShack and Camelot Music. The rest of the businesses within the Plaza could have sold gold-plated dog shit as far as he was concerned.

On the opposite end of the parking lot, the bloated Macomb Springs Church of Christ blotted out the setting sun, casting a gaudy shadow over the newly constructed retail utopia.

"Back in five," Jesse said as he jumped out of the van. Given his proclivity for electronics, Jesse was nominated to run into the store with a short list of audio components that would imbue their sonic implements with the spark of the divine.

Upon entering the shop, Jesse recognized the familiar visage of Mr. Agostino, who stood waiting at the counter in the otherwise empty store. The hirsute guidance counselor gave a nod of recognition as Jesse made his way to the component aisle in search of precious amp-prolonging technology.

Jesse marveled at the long rectangular cabinets, each filled with all manner of noble metals arranged according to their alchemical significance in one of the finest exhibitions of order he had observed within his seemingly random universe. He pulled out his shopping list and began grabbing slow-blow fuses and vacuum tubes from the roll-out drawer cabinets.

An unfamiliar voice called out to the guidance counselor from the back stockroom. Jesse craned his neck to watch as the clerk wrangled a stack of boxes from a pallet.

"I took the liberty of springing for the Russian-made seismographs. I figured you wanted the best, and they invented the damned things." The clerk chuckled to himself as he continued unpacking the boxes. "The old man is going to blow a gasket when he gets the bill."

"Thank you," Agostino said. "I appreciate you going the extra mile." He nodded again to Jesse and offered a polite smile.

"Don't thank me yet. It's gonna be your head when they tally up the equipment expenses for this op—not that we had much of a choice. You and I both know that HQ would still be waiting on the approval routing from the one defense contractor that will still return our calls."

Agostino laid down a crisp stack of bills on the counter. "I'm sure your supervisor will not mind the extra business." Agostino waved Jesse over. "Please apply the young man's purchase to my bill as well."

The clerk emerged from the storeroom and hoisted down the pile of boxes on the counter with a hefty thud. He eyed Jesse warily as he wiped the sweat from his brow.

"Sorry, I didn't hear you come in. Can I help you find something?"

Jesse tried to avoid staring at the deep scar that ran down the right side of the clerk's face. The man appeared to be in his late twenties, maybe older—far too old to be sporting the dense bowl cut that rested above his ears. His muscular frame was barely contained by the comically undersized RadioShack T-shirt. The clerk's nametag simply read CUSTOMER SERVICE REP.

"Is Danny off today?" Jesse couldn't recall the last time he had not seen the gangly teen behind the counter.

"Danny?" asked the clerk. He exchanged a puzzled look with Agostino. "Oh, you must be referring to another employee of this establishment." The clerk's mouth produced a smile that his eyes audited. "He was transferred to another one of our fine locations, elsewhere."

Jesse eyed the tower of parcels that lined the countertop. "You building a radio tower or something?"

"Something like that," Agostino said. He looked at the components Jesse had selected. "If I didn't know better, it would appear
that you are beset to embark on some sort of sonic adventure,
yourself."

"We're about to play a show at some country-and-western dive
downtown." Jesse rattled a bag of fuses. "Our guitar player's amp
blows a fuse if we play for more than five minutes."

"In that case, best of luck."

Jesse held the door as Agostino carried out the stack of boxes.

Rust called out over Vanzig's loudspeaker as they exited the
RadioShack. "Attention Macomb Spring High students! Would
Jesse Lynn please report to detention after final period? It has come
to our attention that Mr. Lynn is unable to refrain from touchin'
himself and must be placed under observation for further study."

The van shook with laughter.

Jesse felt his face turn red. "Just ignore those jerks."

He helped Agostino load up the parcels into a souped up Ford
Bronco outfitted for off-roading. Jesse noted the array of loudspeakers and high-wattage lighting that lined the roof of the
vehicle.

"What time is your set?"

"I think we go on around nine p.m."

"Very good. I wish you the best of luck."

"Thanks again for the parts. See you around, I guess?"

"Absolutely."

Rust threw his cigarette butt into the parking lot and banged
on the roof of the van from his perch on the passenger door.

"Whenever you ladies are done, we have a show to play," he said.

Agostino smiled at Rust.

"Anything I can help you with, professor?" asked Rust.

"Just guidance counselor will suffice." Agostino smiled. "And
I could not help but notice the Baphomet-inspired logo on your
T-shirt."

Rust pulled down his shirt to inspect the logo. "It's a band, dude. They're called Venom—not that you would understand."

Agostino reached into his tweed jacket to retrieve a handkerchief. "And what, pray tell, is your favorite Venom album?" He cleaned his glasses without looking up.

Rust shrugged. "I like 'em all, man. What do you —"

"Personally, I do not like to pick favorites either, but I believe their most *important* album was *Welcome to Hell*, due primarily to its influence on early metal subgenres." The guidance counselor donned his spectacles as he continued. "You will no doubt agree that Venom was very influential to the American thrash scene, particularly the Big Four—Metallica, Anthrax, Megadeth, and Slayer—but it is also often cited as a progenitor of underground subgenres such as black metal and death metal."

Alex's jaw hung open as Rust slid back into his seat. A bout of laughter exploded from all Hell Patrol members except Rust.

"Fuckin' squares," Rust mumbled.

4

Hell Patrol arrived at the venue an hour before showtime, per Rick's instructions, and began to unload their gear.

The Deep Well was located at the south end of the Old Downtown strip, surrounded by an interconnected row of tightly grouped businesses. Each were uniformly red brick and connected by turn-of-the-century, Old West inspired façades that lined both sides of the one-way street.

A simple neon sign flickered above the front door of the venue, illuminating only the first three letters of the word BEER.

An intrusive wash of sunlight preceded the group as they entered the dark space.

Inside, a small triangular-shaped stage was wedged into the back corner of the bar near the restrooms. A shuffleboard and pool table stood opposite the stage separated by a raised dance floor that peeked out from the surrounding polished concrete. The room smelled of stale beer and cigarette smoke, which hung in patches of thick, blue-grey clouds beneath the low-hanging light fixtures.

Rick wheeled up to the bar. After what appeared to be a heated negotiation with the manager—a thick-necked hoss sporting a handlebar mustache and a felt black Vietnam-veteran cowboy hat—Rick returned to the group and motioned for them to follow him back outside.

"What's going on?" asked Jesse.

"Yeah, what gives?" asked Rust. "We loadin' into this dump or what?"

"Okay, couple things. First off, I think the outfits gave us away."

The group looked each other over in the denim and studded leather battle vests that Rick had designed.

"Yosemite 'Nam in there wasn't too thrilled to learn that we were the band that responded to his ad in the paper."

"I thought we were already booked?" asked Alex.

Rick nodded. "Despite the fact that he referred to the band as 'long-haired faggots,' I managed to talk us into playing a half-hour set for fifty bucks."

"We get fifty bucks for just doin' a half hour?" Rust asked. "Right on."

"And that brings me to the next item of business," Rick said. "*We* have to pay fifty dollars in order to play on *his* stage for half an hour."

An audible sigh was collectively uttered by the band.

"I know it's not ideal, but that's the best I could do under the circumstances." Rick peered over his glasses. "Also, they double-booked the show tonight, but have agreed to let us open for the headliner before the regulars show up."

Rust kicked an empty beer can against the side of the building. "Fuck this. We don't have fifty dollars to waste on these hick assholes."

"Look. I don't like this pay-to-play bullshit any more than you guys, but this is how all the greats started out." Rick pulled out a handful of quarters and a black, spiral-bound phone book from his chair caddy. "Only truly great art comes from suffering. You guys set up. I've got some calls to make."

"Fuck it. Let's do this," said Jesse.

"He's right. We gotta start somewhere," added Alex.

Rust looked up at the flickering neon sign. "I guess it beats playin' during the intermission of *Our Town*."

"For glory," Mazes said.

5

As the band finished setting up on the cramped stage, Yosemite 'Nam approached the band stroking his long, handlebar mustache between a pair of yellow-tinged fingers.

"All right boys, I guess we're gonna do this." He pulled out a tactical flashlight from his belt. "When I shine this light, that means you're bein' too loud. If you're too loud, that's gonna run off my customers. If you run off my customers, that's game over, and you critters vamoose off my stage and crawl back under whatever godforsaken rock you crawled out of, comprendo?"

Hell Patrol nodded in unison.

"All right then. When that clock strikes Coors Light, you start your set." He pointed to the neon wall clock that featured an array of beer brands denoting each hour. "When it hits Coors Light-thirty, get your asses off my stage." He sauntered back behind the bar and opened a beer for himself and a squat man in overalls who sat propped up on a barstool.

"Who's got the setlists?" asked Jesse.

"Right here." Rick wheeled up and handed out four copies of the setlist from his chair caddy. "All right, we got twenty minutes until show time. Guitar, bass, make sure you guys are warmed up. Rust, how are the pipes? Feeling good? Did you do your warm-up exercises?"

"I'd feel better if I didn't think I was about to get my ass kicked by everyone in the fuckin' bar," Rust replied.

Rick gave a thumbs up. "That's good, use that nervous energy. Make it work to your advantage." He pointed towards the entrance. "I'll be over at the merch booth if you guys need anything."

"We have merch?" asked Alex.

Rick shook his head. "No, but if anyone asks we tell them we already sold out—creates cachet."

Jesse hopped off the stage and followed his brother over to the empty merch table. He looked over his shoulder to make sure his bandmates were out of earshot.

"Hey man, some people are going to show up, right?"

Rick beamed up at his little brother. "You just worry about the set. Leave the rest to me."

By five-'til-Coors Light, a small crowd of regulars had taken up residence at the bar. The dance floor remained empty. Jesse was pacing in front of the restrooms, inhaling a cigarette, when Alex appeared near the stage carrying a bucket of beer.

"These cowboys are all right—they didn't even ask for my ID." He handed out the beers to the band.

Just as Jesse twisted open the bottle, the front door swung open, revealing an entourage of black-clad, long-haired youths who piled into the cramped bar.

The girls came in last, each wearing dark makeup and skin-tight clothing, with gravity-defying shocks of hair that shot out from their scalps in all directions, assisted in great part by what Jesse could only assume were untold quantities of mousse and Aqua Net.

"Let's hear some fucking Hell Patrol!" someone called out.

A wave of adrenaline washed over Jesse as he took the stage. He could hear his heart beating in his ears while he tried to compare tuning with Alex.

From his vantage point on the stage, he began to witness the mixture of denim, leather, pearl snaps, and polyester as they converged like warring factions on the dance floor battlefield, filling the small room.

Yosemite 'Nam whistled towards the back room and another bartender came out to feed the growing rush at the bar. The beginnings of a crowd had begun to form on the dance floor in front of the stage.

"Fear not, young mage," Mazes said. He pulled out a drumstick from the leather quiver he wore over his shoulder and brandished it over his head like a sword. "Tales of our conquest will spread throughout the realm after this night."

"I think I'm gonna be sick," Jesse replied. "How are you so calm?"

Mazes smiled wide. "Visions of a glorious death visited me yesternight during my slumber." He pulled the second drumstick from his quiver and warmed up with a series of triplets on the closed hi-hat as he continued. "Bearing witness to my awaiting corpse is a fortuitous omen I will not soon forget."

"I'll try to remember that the next time I have a vision of my own death."

Rust jumped up on stage and checked the mic. A wave of ear-splitting feedback resounded over the two wall-mounted speakers that hung precariously over the rear of the stage.

Jesse felt himself leave his body as soon as he heard Mazes give a four count on the hi-hat.

Yosemite 'Nam had already stepped out from behind the bar when the first note rang out on Alex's guitar. Before he had finished the instrumental opener, "Embryo" *by Black Sabbath, from the album* Master of Reality, *released in 1971 on Vertigo Records,* the bright beam of the tactical flashlight trailed across the stage.

Just as the band was about to seamlessly transition into "Children of the Grave," the flashlight was aimed directly into Rust's eyes, causing him to miss his vocal cue. Hell Patrol struggled through an off-tempo, stifled rendition of the cover before catching their breath.

Raucous bouts of laughter and sarcastic applause gave Jesse pause to gather the others in front of Mazes's drum kit. As he looked over the crowd, he saw Mal towards the back of the room, swapping out the lenses on her camera.

"All right, fuck this. Let's just pretend we're back home at the trailer doing our thing, and doing it loud," said Jesse. "Fuck these redneck assholes and the horses they rode in on."

Rust took the mic with renewed vigor and let out a volley of high-pitched vibrato that announced the ambitious next number: "Evil" by Mercyful Fate, *the opening track from the album* Melissa, *released in 1983 on Roadrunner Records.* Jesse saw Alex turn up the volume knob on his amp, and did the same.

Playing in their native sonic environment, the band pulsed ahead with an amateurish, yet blistering set of covers.

Jesse snarled at the audience as the flashlight swept the stage. The dance floor was now packed with an army of heshers who were overtaking the venue.

Yosemite 'Nam looked to the line that had formed at the bar and then back to the band, and opted to sheathe his flashlight in order to contend with the masses who were lining up for drinks.

The half-hour set flew by as the band settled into a rhythm.

Rust was galvanized by the energy of the crowd and began to work the stage. He kicked over the mic stand and wrapped the cable around his neck. Some of the regulars were even getting into the energy and were whistling through their fingers at the end of each song.

Another bucket of ice-cold beer made its way to the front of the stage.

Jesse saw Mal weaving in and out of the crowd, snapping shots and changing lenses. He felt alive; he felt powerful for the first time in his life. He was transformed by the collective sonic ritual whose power was being reaffirmed and reflected in what felt like an endless sea of raised devil horns that penetrated the dingy cloud of smoke that hovered over the dance floor.

"Thank you, Macomb Springs!" Rust called out between songs. "You've been a terrible fuckin' audience." He took a mock bow and reached down for one of the bottles of beer from the bucket at his feet, took a heavy swig, and showered the front row of the dance floor with the rest.

Jesse looked to the setlist taped to the stage in front of him. The words *Hell Hole of Death* etched in Rick's scrawl jumped off the page.

He looked to Mazes, whose wide-eyed grin had transformed into a maniacal grimace. Mazes read the cue and launched into a Scott Travis-inspired intro that heralded their lone original number.

Rust screamed over the mic. "Thanks for comin' out tonight! We are Hell Patrol, and this is our last song." He shoved the mic down the front of his pants and reached for another beer, ignoring the squeal of feedback as he chugged its contents.

An older woman at the bar with long, braided hair cupped her ears as she watched the stage in astonishment.

The intro to "Hell Hole of Death" was executed in near flawless precision. The band's regimented practice schedule was showcased in the original composition unlike the covers that had up to now only enticed the crowd into wanting more.

As Alex took his solo, he approached the front of the stage, sending the front row of the audience into a frenzy.

The song felt like it was already over before it began. As the final notes rang out, a thunderous applause broke out from the crowd. Some of Rick's old DIY metal crew even rushed the stage and tried to lift Jesse over their shoulders.

By the time the headliner took the stage, the metal crowd had dispersed to the parking lot. Two large conversion vans were competing for volume as they blasted metal standards into the night. Rick wheeled up to Jesse and Mal who were watching Rust misfire an attempt at shotgunning a beer, much to the delight of some of the older crowd.

"We did it!" exclaimed Rick. "Yosemite 'Nam totally waived the pay fee—he turned it back over to the band. Said we could even come back if we wanted."

Cheers erupted from the parking lot.

Mal grabbed Jesse by the arms and hopped up and down. Jesse joined her until the bile rose up in his throat; he proceeded to vomit on the custom chrome rims of a midnight blue conversion van.

Before he blacked out, he thought he saw Mr. Agostino climbing into his Bronco from across the parking lot.

6

Jesse found himself alone in the darkness.

A familiar voice echoed from across the empty chasm that opened in front of him. He watched as his brother materialized from the other side. He could hear Rick's voice, distantly, but he couldn't make out the words. Jesse realized his brother was out of his wheelchair, standing on his own, peering over the edge of the pit into the darkness below.

A confused jumble of questions tore through Jesse's mind as he tried to call out to his brother.

Below, a great swirling shape emerged from the darkness of the pit, stirring up the foul air as it rose, obscuring Jesse's vision. A deep, bellowing horn blew from some distant and forgotten place to announce the dark presence that began to materialize between the two brothers.

Jesse awakened to Rick at his bedside.

"Seriously, wake up." Rick said. "We have work to do."

Before Jesse could open his eyes, his feet spirited him to the bathroom, where he proceeded to expel the previous night's indulgence.

"Well, you might play like a pro, but you sure as fuck can't party like one—which is good." Rick cleared his throat as he prattled on. "Nearly sixty-five percent of up-and-coming rock bands are waylaid by substance abuse at some point in their careers. And that's usually after they get swindled into signing their first bullshit record contract. Might as well get it out of your system now, while you're still poor and unaccomplished."

Jesse dry-heaved into the toilet.

"Would it make you feel any better if I told you that while you were blacked out in the van, I was building up your fan base and schmoozing with investors?"

Jesse flushed the toilet and washed his face in the sink.

"Investors?"

"There was a small business owner who seemed open to an investment opportunity, especially after I plied him with a few drinks." Rick smirked as he continued to recount the meeting. "He's a total sleaze bag, likely a child molester, and he'll probably rob us of any profits—he's perfect."

"What kind of small business owner? And what was he doing at that dive bar?"

"He owns the used car lot next door."

"Of course."

"Before you rush to judgment, hear me out. The guy was a walk-up. He heard the band from the street and saw the bar at capacity—you're welcome by the way."

Jesse looked from the mirror to his brother. "Did all that really happen?"

"Oh yes, little bro." Rick grinned. "You guys fucking killed."

"Seriously?"

"Well, I mean the crowd was totally planted, and half your set was out of time and out of tune, but other than that you guys were generally decent—especially the original number." He looked to the small sketchbook that he constantly carried as he read through his notes from the show. "I mean, we have a lot of work do to, but I think we have a shot. But my point is... the investor agrees."

"So what does that mean?"

Rick fished around in his chair caddy and produced a crisp, light-blue bank check. He waved it under his nose as he inhaled deeply. "It means we just got a bankroll for a new backline."

"Are you fucking kidding me?"

Rick pushed his glasses up on his nose. "Remember my ol' buddy Robb-O, the floor manager of the Sound Emporium?

"The guy with the weird eye that you used to roadie with?"

"Yeah. Well, I just got off the phone with him and he said he can have the gear shipped over from the warehouse by Wednesday." Rick turned to a page in his sketchbook and ripped it out. "This is what he has in stock that fits our budget. And before you and little Alex Van Weasel go off the rails, remember it's just an advance. We still have to pay this shit back."

Jesse poured over the list of amps, guitars, and PA gear, all organized by make and model.

"Holy shit. The guys are going to freak the fuck out."

"Robb-O's boss clocks out at six p.m. Just make sure you guys show up after he leaves so Robb-O can give you the employee discount."

Jesse's gear lust faded into disappointment as he added up the cost of all the equipment in his mind. "Wait. So if this guy is gonna want his money back, how do we plan on paying him?"

"While you have been getting your beauty sleep, I've been up making calls." Rick paused to make a note in his sketchbook.

"We're booked next month at Beggar's Banquet Hall on the eleventh. It's a locals night, but the headliner is legit—big up-and-comer on the scene. And it pays."

Jesse's eyes widened at the news. "You got us a show in the city?"

Rick smiled. "Do altar boys leave Rorschach stains whenever they sit down?"

7

Returning to the mundane was a difficult transition after Hell Patrol had taken The Deep Well by storm. The high experienced by being well received on stage offered more than any chemical substance Jesse had ever experienced in his short life.

Almost anything.

Mal was also occupying an ever-increasing expanse within his thoughts.

In contrast, school had become an exercise in tedium, a distraction that seemed to get in the way of the pursuit of conquest for that which sustained him, made him whole. Naturally, Jesse's grades had plummeted and he had accumulated several unexcused absences. The negative report of his academic performance had made its way back to Jesse's parents.

As part of an arrangement brokered by his mother, Jesse was required to meet with guidance counselor Agostino once per week until his grades and attendance improved, or he would risk being excommunicated from the band. He elected to take the meetings during his lunch hour to avoid staying after class to keep his evenings free for practice and spending time with Mal.

When Jesse arrived at the first of his daily meetings, the door to Mr. Agostino's office was already open. He heard what he thought was an acoustic guitar being played. Upon further inspection, the instrument appeared to be a lute, or some other medieval artifact unlikely to grace the cover of one of the guitar rags that

Jesse read. As Agostino plucked the strings, a bouquet of gentle dulcet tones filled the air.

"Please, come in," Agostino said, offering the instrument to Jesse. "Care to play?"

"Thanks, but I'd probably just break it. I don't really know how to play any instruments other than my bass."

"And how is the band coming along?"

"Actually, we just got some guy to invest in a new backline. Finally gonna have some pro-gear. A full PA system too."

"A new backline and a full PA system?" Agostino seemed intrigued by the news. "That is very exciting. Congratulations." He looked to the arcane wooden instrument resting in his lap. "You know, it might help to master your instrument by exploring the iterative forms that preceded its evolution."

"I don't think the other guys would go for that." Jesse laughed at the image in his mind. "Well, maybe our drummer would be into it, but that's a different story."

"It might seem antiquated, but Tony Iommi could not have conceived of the heavy metal genre if his predecessors had not developed the twelve-tone temperament on instruments just like this one."

"How do you know so much about metal?"

Agostino hung the lute on the wall. Jesse's question lingered unanswered while the guidance counselor fumbled through a stack of books on the shelf behind the desk.

"Ah yes, here it is." He produced a leather-bound manuscript and handed it to Jesse. The title read, *A Diachronic Analysis of the Heavy Metal Genre: From Wagner to Black Sabbath*. "My master's thesis."

"You can major in Black Sabbath?"

"Ethnomusicology."

"What's that?"

"Simply put, it is the study of music in a cultural context.

An attempt to explain the impact that music has made among humanity as pontificated by elitist academics."

"Cool. Not sure if college is for me. Besides, I don't think my parents would go for studying something like that."

Agostino laughed. "I can say from experience that you should follow your passions, even if they seem impractical to others."

"Is that how you ended up here?"

"In a manner of speaking."

Jesse pointed to the shelf where a set of pipes were displayed. "What's that one?"

"Pan pipes. Used by ancient Greeks of the Cyclades. Their namesake refers to the pastoral god, Pan, patron of shepherds."

"No, the one next to it, on the left." Jesse pointed to a thin, unassuming instrument with four small holes distributed at equal intervals along its length. Upon closer inspection, the surface of the pipe appeared irregular, like it had been broken to pieces and then glued back together.

"Ah yes. The simple shepherd's pipe—a Neolithic precursor to the Pan pipes—thought to possess a certain acoustic tonality conducive to pacifying the flock." Agostino carefully picked up the instrument and held it for Jesse to observe. "This particular item is an authentic cultural relic, originating from Mesopotamia circa 4000 BCE. It is sort of a family heirloom."

"So they used music to control sheep? I guess that explains Bon Jovi."

"Astute observation." Agostino smiled as he returned the pipe to its resting place. "The expression of certain acoustic wave forms has the ability to affect environments, both organic and non-organic, by manipulating matter through the vibrations of subatomic particles."

"Sounds like my brother. He sits in his room and blasts metal all day, every day. My mom says it's warped his mind."

The guidance counselor laughed a hearty laugh. "And what do you think?"

Jesse's tone took on a somber note as he continued to speak about his brother. "I think that if he didn't have his music, he might not be here." Jesse felt his eyes begin to water. "He was in a bad motorcycle accident. It's pretty much the reason my family moved out here."

Agostino allowed the conversation to breathe for a moment before offering his assessment.

"I think the situation with your brother explains the appeal of certain musical genres to many young people. Those who feel abandoned by a society that they never felt like they belonged to in the first place."

"Yeah, I can see that," said Jesse. He fidgeted with a loose stitch on the *Screaming for Vengeance* patch above the left breast pocket of his jean jacket. "He's always been different, but in a good way."

"Heavy metal music in particular instills the listener with a sense of solidarity among those of us who are turned off by the banality of mainstream society. Your brother sounds like an interesting person."

Jesse wiped his eyes on his sleeve. "Man, you sound a lot different than Principal Anderson," he chuckled, narrowly avoiding choking on the rising lump in his throat. "She thinks me and my friends are Satanists."

Agostino sat back in his chair and spoke with a sigh. "Let us just say that Principal Anderson and I have different pedagogies." He leaned forward over the desk towards Jesse and lowered his voice. "But you should know that anything we discuss here will be held in the strictest confidence."

Jesse nodded and thumbed through the manuscript Agostino had placed before him.

"You can hold on to that. See if it resonates with your musical interests."

"Thanks, Mr. Agostino."

"Please, call me Vincent. And you are welcome."

"No offense, but it seems like high school guidance counselor might be punching a little bit beneath your weight class."

Agostino smiled as he cleaned his glasses with his handkerchief. "This appointment provides certain advantages towards my ultimate research goals."

"Macomb Springs High?" Jesse shook his head. "Must not be a lot of jobs out there for an ethnomusicologist, huh?"

"I am drawn to certain cultural phenomena occurring in this region of the country. This appointment allows access as a participant/observer of the community. Besides, one has to eat."

"This whole town is a social experiment. Sometimes I feel like it's tearing apart at the seams."

"It must be a difficult time to be a young man of your interests."

Jesse pondered the statement. He noticed a curious piece of sound equipment poking out from beneath the tweed overcoat that had been draped over a stack of boxes in the corner of the room.

"So what's with all the gear?"

"I'm conducting an experiment for my —"

"For your research?" Jesse finished.

"Yes." Agostino's smile faded. "That is correct."

"Not to pry, but why aren't you studying at the university?"

Agostino looked to the ceiling as he toyed with his beard. "My adviser subscribes to an unorthodox approach to research design. I have been forced off the reservation, so to speak, in order to prove my worth."

"Sounds harsh."

"Harsh, but effective." Agostino snapped to and opened a binder on his desk. "Now, enough about me. Since our time is almost up, I suppose I must ask—how are the grades coming along?"

"Better." Jesse said, as he handed him a recent grade check summary.

"Good, I'm happy to be able to report that to Mrs. Lynn." Agostino stood and ushered Jesse out of his office door.

"It's Mrs. Reynolds actually. I kept my dad's last name after they got divorced. Not sure why—he's a total loser. I guess it was just easier."

"My mistake." Agostino clasped his hands together and bowed his head. "Jesse, these are indeed strange times. Please feel free to come to me with anything that might concern you." Agostino peered over the rims of his glasses. "Anything at all."

As Jesse left the guidance counselor's office, he caught himself looking back over his shoulder, unsure of what to make of the strange shift in Agostino's voice.

PART II

INTERLUDE

Vincent stood next to his brother Henry's bedside, watching the vital signs that flashed on the monitor for any change. Henry moaned as one of his father's attendants, a hairless man with a strange blue-grey pallor, worked in silence to sew up the dark, bloody gash that ran from beneath his jaw up near his right eye.

A wet thud followed the scratching sound that grated in his ears from down the hall. Without looking, Vincent knew it to be the sound of another corpse being dragged over the shards of broken glass that covered the checkered parquet living room floor.

The monitor chimed an alert as Henry began to convulse, coughing up a mist of blood and phlegm that spattered across the attendant's grey smock.

"Vincent," his father called. "Perhaps you can distract your brother with one of his favorite stories from the *Compendium* transcripts while Rune completes his work?"

Vincent stepped into the hall and followed the sound of his father's voice into the living room.

"Are you sure it is safe?"

"The sun will be up in less than an hour. All the references of this species indicate explicit nocturnal activity. Thanks to you and your brother's valiant efforts, I think we can rest easy for now." He wiped a trail of blood from his forehead with his handkerchief. "How many did you count?"

"Seven—including the big one with the sagittal fin."

"Very good," his father nodded as he counted the bodies. "The murk queen always hatches an even-numbered brood. I cannot say how they managed to track us all the way from Scape Ore, but hopefully that will be the last of their ilk that we see for some time."

"Does this mean we have to move again?"

"See to your brother. I'll finish cleaning up this mess," his father sighed. "Though we're bound to never get the smell out. A pity too. I was rather fond of the decor."

His father stood in front of an ornate marble fireplace fanning his handkerchief in front of his nose. Several bloody corpses were piled up near its opening. The glint of the flames reflected off the shattered glass windowpanes whose sheer drapes wavered freely in the early morning air.

An acrid stench rose from the desiccated reptilian forms as they hit the flames, sending out plumes of greenish-grey smoke through the open windows.

The fishy stink from the South Carolina swamplands followed Vincent down the hall, burning the back of his throat.

He opened the trapdoor that led to the staircase beneath the kitchen. After being granted security access via the optical scanner, he opened the heavy blast door and entered the vault. He scanned through the contents of the dusty repository, filled with all manner of artifacts, weaponry, and his father's extensive collection of early jazz 45s, until he came upon the bookshelf filled with ancient tomes.

He ran his open palm along the spines of the occult volumes until he came upon the familiar shape of the well-worn *Compendium*. As he held the book, he recalled the fond memories of his father reading from the great book when he and his brother were children. It was a different time, when life was simple—before he was burdened with the truth about the family business.

He ran up the stairs with the book and returned to Henry's bedside. The laconic attendant offered a polite bow as he left the room.

Vincent took a seat next to his brother's bed. "In another time we would all have been burned at the stake," he said as he arrived at one of his brother's favorite entries and began to read aloud.

✠ ✠ ✠

Elizabeth huddled beneath the floorboards in the fruit cellar with the twins on either side. She cupped her hands over their little mouths as the shouting grew louder from outside.

A scream erupted from the back of the house, followed by the sounds of footsteps overhead. She knew without being able to see that it was her mother's stilted gait, heavy with child, moving slowly across the kitchen floor towards the front door.

"Charles!" her mother screamed a second time.

Father must be trying to reason with the vestrymen, Elizabeth thought to herself.

The vestrymen had gathered after sunset in the town square, just as the swelling Blood Moon emerged from the horizon. The rest of the townsfolk eventually followed suit, their stern, grey faces cast from the same frowning mold of bitter judgment, and something more sinister.

Once they arrived, Elizabeth's mother had called for her to fetch the twins. "Stay put until you hear different, girl." Her mother had spoken the words as she put the floorboards back in place to conceal the narrow crawl space.

The ground beneath the house was cool and damp, and smelled of mildew and stale earth. The boys whimpered, fighting for air as Elizabeth's hands clamped down over their wet, sniffling faces. One of the twins broke free from her vice-like grip, breaking her concentration as she strained to hear her father's voice as he addressed the gathering throng.

"Benjamin, settle this instant," Elizabeth whispered. She picked up the small child and held him in her lap.

"You smell of cow droppings—I cannot breathe," squeaked the small voice. He held his nose between his two fingers and inhaled through his open mouth.

"Be with your brother in silence before I pluck the very nose from your face." She sat Benjamin next to his brother, Thomas, as she continued. "Then you'll've no reason to complain."

The twins clutched each other, trembling beneath Elizabeth's roughspun dress.

The movement of her mother's frantic pacing stirred up clouds of dust that fell between the narrow gaps in the floorboards, illuminated by the warm candlelight above.

Elizabeth tried to reassure the twins.

"Quiet, now. This is the best hiding spot within the whole of the farm. We will win the game if you are not to give us away."

"I don't want to play this game anymore," said Benjamin.

"Thomas, you want to play with me, don't you?" Elizabeth asked. "We're sure to win because the others will never find us down here."

Thomas nodded at his sister, giving Benjamin pause to rethink his proclamation.

"There's a good boy. See how much fun we are having? Poor ol' Benjamin is going to miss out on the very best game we have ever played, is he not?"

"I have to make water," Benjamin said.

"Then go in the corner, but stay close and keep quiet."

"Mother says not to make water in the house," Thomas whispered.

"It's all right, Thomas, mother won't know so long as we promise not to tell. Can you do that?"

"I promise."

"That's a good boy."

The front door slammed shut.

The sound of her parents' shouting was muffled by the grating of the heavy oak farm table as it slid across the floor towards the front door.

The murmur of voices from outside grew closer to the house.

A lone voice rose above the din.

"Charles Edward Winfield! Produce the girl and save the rest of your lot from certain destruction."

"She's not what you think, McGregor," her father replied. "You'll not harm a child of mine while I still draw breath." His voice sounded fearful despite the strength of his words.

Elizabeth cringed at the mention of the Reverend Stern McGregor. She paired the voice with the image she held in her mind's eye of the minister's birdlike features as his voice bellowed from the crowd.

"Who are you to doubt the convictions of honest Christians, whose almighty God has revealed the devil's concubine in our midst?"

"She is no consort of Satan!" her father shouted. "You have abandoned reason in favor of this fashionable hysteria that sweeps the land."

The crowd jeered in response.

"We stand resolute in the righteous judgment as decreed by our creator!" McGregor shouted.

"If you intend to harm my family, you will first need to step over my corpse—almighty God or no."

After a short pause, the Reverend McGregor called back. "Very well, Charles. Know that you wear the blood of your progeny on your own two hands." His speech quieted as he finished. "And may the Lord God have mercy on your house."

A cold sweat began to trickle down Elizabeth's back as she realized she was holding her breath. She could hear the terror in her mother's voice as she begged to her father.

"She's just a girl, Charles—our girl. You cannot give her over."

Elizabeth heard a loud crash against the side of the house followed by the sound of breaking glass. The smell of burning whale oil filled the cellar as the flames began to climb the walls.

The twins shrieked in unison.

She crawled on her stomach beneath her parent's bedroom, and kicked at a loose board. She eventually forced a small opening and called back to the twins.

"Come with me, I've found a better hiding place."

She sped the twins through the pasture towards the old barn, nearly lifting them off the ground in the process. At her back, a procession of torchbearers circled the house. Bright orange flames rose from the roof of her familial home, sending up a black column of smoke that disappeared into the night sky.

Inside the barn, the horses were startled by the rising commotion. Elizabeth tucked the twins up into the hayloft and threw the bolt across the barn doors from the inside. Satisfied that the twins were safe, she climbed out through one of lesser entrances along the side wall and ran back out into the night.

The air was thick with stinging smoke that stifled her vision as her eyes began to draw tears. She took one last look at the flames just as another torch was thrown into her parents' bedroom towards the back of the house.

Elizabeth ran until she made it to the pump house. Once inside, she lowered herself down into the well, all the way to the bottom until she was standing waist deep in the freezing cold water. She squeezed through the narrow fissure in the limestone casing that opened to reveal the underground stream that fed the well.

Her father had always claimed the aquifer that sourced the well was located in the caves that ran along the river Ipswich before it emptied into the sea. Beyond the river lay the primeval expanse of the Eastern Woods. Once there, it was a day's walk to the adjacent township of Wenham where her cousin Margaret lived. Margaret was worldly and wise, and was married to a prominent landowner. She would know how to sort through this mare's nest.

After what felt like hours of crawling through the narrow portal, she climbed up through an ascending passage that eventually formed into a shallow cavern opening along the bank of the river. Exhausted, she collapsed on the cold stone ground, gazing upon the frothy grey waters of the river Ipswich that tumbled forth to deliver its gift into the frigid Atlantic.

She sat huddled on the floor of the cave, rocking back and forth and wringing out her dress in an effort to get warm. She hummed a familiar tune to calm herself, occasionally breaking out into song. The sweet melody echoed off the walls of the cave, barely audible above the churning river.

Elizabeth fell silent as she heard the bellow of distant horns. She panicked, thinking it the pursuant call of the constabulary

who often used hunting horns to announce their presence to one
another when patrolling the dense forest.

A sliver of moonlight guided her out of the cavern and into the
craggy hillside that overlooked the seashore to the east.

The rumbling of thunder resounded in the distance as Elizabeth
emerged once more into the night. The orange-red glow of the
Blood Moon allowed her to easily find her footing and head up
to higher ground. The bellow of the hunting horns mixed with
the approaching thunder, further masking their origin.

Using the position of the moon as her guide, she pointed herself
towards the direction of town and climbed a tall tree to gain a
vantage point. To the west, the burning of the farmhouse provided
a beacon by which to get her bearings.

Another loud crackling of thunder erupted directly overhead.

A branch fell from above, crashing through the dense canopy
before eventually falling to the forest floor, followed by another.
Elizabeth looked to the sky for evidence of an encroaching tem-
pest; the full moon boasted its dominion over the night sky with
little evidence of storm clouds.

She watched in disbelief as the surrounding trees began to bend
towards the ground, almost as if bowing to an unseen presence.
Fearing a maelstrom come inland, she opted to begin the long,
easterly trek towards the outskirts of Wenham.

Before she could descend from her perch atop the forest canopy,
Elizabeth wavered, feeling disoriented as she heard what sounded
like a discordant orchestra playing disparate notes all at once,
clawing at her ears. She turned, following the sound with her
eyes, until she gazed upon its source.

Silhouetted against the backdrop of the ripened Blood Moon, a
towering shape emerged from the dense primeval forest. Judging
by its position on the horizon, Elizabeth surmised the creature
had to be well over two stories tall. A single spear-like protuber-
ance emerged from the base of its elongated snout.

Paralyzed by fear, Elizabeth was held frozen as the creature emitted a thunderous bellow that sounded like the deep, low blast of a great horn.

The force of the sound caused the tree branch to give way beneath her, awakening her from the paralytic trance as she landed hard on the forest floor. Panicked, she ran with all her might back in the direction of her familial farm.

The sound of heavy footfalls trampling through the forest trailed behind her.

She ran without stopping all the way back to the smoldering ruins of her house. The entire town had gathered to watch the structure burn. With the creature still on her trail, she relinquished any trepidation she had felt among her human persecutors, and fell before the crowd, gasping for breath.

The vestry, surrounded by the town's dutiful magistrates, moved in to apprehend the girl. Before they could don the waiting manacles, crusted in the burned blood of those who had been put to the flames before her, a thunderous blast erupted from the center of town.

An enormous figure appeared, wreathed in shadow despite the abundant torchlight carried by the townsfolk. What she could see of the creature, not veiled in shadow, bore the likeness of a monstrous bipedal equine, reaching out with elongated claws as it strode towards the throng.

As the behemoth neared the house, Elizabeth could feel its focus drawing towards her. The beastly shadow reached out with a pair of clawed talons and plucked the Reverend McGregor's head from his body like the delicate petal of a marigold, holding it aloft for all to see.

Elizabeth's last thought was of the twins as a discordant sonic assault washed over the gathered townsfolk.

CHAPTER FOUR

THE BURNING OF BEELZEBUB

1

Rust exhaled a puff of smoke through the mouth of the rubber demon mask as he read from the church flyer.

"Prizes, games, and a prayer vigil. Sounds like a blast." He tossed the flyer on the floor and sunk back into a bright yellow bean bag chair. "I'm so glad I don't have to deal with that fuckin' school anymore."

"You think Principal Anderson is gonna be at the lock-in?" Alex asked, twirling one of the demonic masks on his index finger.

"She said so on the morning announcements when she declared that all students who attend will be getting extra credit." Mal rolled her eyes. "Desperate much?"

"So this is how we finally get expelled," Jesse said as he surveyed the costumes that were strewn about the practice space.

"Not to mention my parents will disown me and take Vanzig away," Alex said.

"Then we just make sure we don't get caught." Mal grabbed one of masks and pulled it over her head as if to demonstrate. Her voice was muffled under the heavy foam rubber. "People still dress up in costumes for Halloween, right? How are they going to know it's us?"

Jesse grabbed another one of the masks, sizing it up. "Another six months and we'll all be out of that shithole anyway."

He had to remind himself that Rust's status as a high school dropout was a double-edged sword. Sure, it earned him some street cred, but he could also tell it was a source of embarrassment, not that Rust would ever cop to it. Jesse always tried to change the subject whenever the group mentioned events at the high school.

"If we don't get signed before that," laughed Rust. He shot up from the bean bag chair and jumped on Mazes's shoulders.

The drummer had just finished assembling a towering demonic effigy made from foam, pvc pipe, and copious amounts of black gaffer's tape (a stockpile he had rustled up from his Society of Creative Anachronism days).

Mazes stood his creation upright and unfurled its large black wings—an assemblage of garbage bags stretched across a support frame of wire hangers and more gaffer's tape.

Mal removed her mask and tossed it up to Rust, who placed it over the head of the effigy from his perch atop Mazes's broad shoulders.

"Behold!" bellowed Mazes. "A fiend of the Nine Hells walks among us."

Mal grabbed her camera and snapped a photo of the group posing in front of their creation wearing their masks. She took her eye off the viewfinder and nodded approvingly at the scene. "I think it's time we gave these Jesus freaks exactly what they want."

2

Halloween. Today's the day!

Jesse had awakened to the incessant union of hammer upon nail. The familial property had been nearly converted back to its original glory (except for a few lingering cosmetic upgrades), including a complete replacement of the deck planks on the massive wraparound porch that ran the perimeter of the structure.

"Morning rockstar! Happy Halloween!" His mother tapped on his bedroom window from outside. "Sorry to disturb your beauty sleep, but it's almost noon, and Randy could use your help finishing the porch."

"Fine," Jesse grumbled. "Be right there." He rubbed the sleep from his eyes, got dressed, and stumbled out to face the all-too-eager sun.

In the distance, a pair of plump black crows were warding off an encroaching hawk as it glided through the trees that lined the property. Jesse followed the chase with his eyes as they weaved in and out through the lattice of lifeless oaks.

As Jesse laid the planks, Randy hammered in the nails to hold them into place. In typical fashion, Randy executed the labor saying little, only pausing to mark his progress after every ten planks or so by opening a fresh can of beer.

Once they had secured the final plank, Randy turned up the volume on the radio and fell back into one of the patio chairs that lined the deck. Robert Plant's sultry tenor was screeching through the speakers as Randy fished inside the cooler for another beer. He handed Jesse one.

"Job well done, Boss."

Having worked up a thirst, Jesse took the offering despite the early hour, downing a heavy swig.

"Your mother ever tell you about the time we saw Zeppelin at the Myriad?"

"You guys saw Led Zeppelin?"

Randy nodded. "Less than a year after I was out of the service. I was staying with my cousin, trying to get my shit together." Randy paused for a moment, seemingly lost in thought as he surveyed the past. "Any way, his girl was one of your mom's best gal pals."

"Crazy Catherine?"

Randy smiled. "Yep. Little Miss Linda Reynolds was a real firecracker back then."

"I didn't even know she listened to music."

"Welp, she made it through the first half of the set before getting kicked out by security. Her and your Dad had been in some kind of fight, or just separated or some such. I think she was just cuttin' loose."

Jesse fought to contain his astonishment as he took another drink. "When was this?"

Randy wiped the sweat from his brow and reflected on the query as he lit a cigarette. "Spring of '77—the good ol' days. You were just a little bitty thing, probably not even old enough to wipe your own ass. That's when I knew..."

"Yeah?"

"Yessir. She was the finest woman I'd ever seen walk this god-forsaken Earth."

"Okay, okay, let's just focus on the show. How was the band?"

"These guys were somethin' to see." Randy gestured towards the radio. "They don't make music like this anymore."

"Don't let Rick hear you say that."

Randy uttered what sufficed as a laugh. "Speaking of which, when's the next gig, kemosabe?"

"Rick the Prick talked his way into getting us an opening slot on a pretty big show in the city next month."

Randy sat with the news for a few pulls from his can. "Between you and me, it's a good thing you and your brother are doing."

Jesse gestured over his shoulder towards the house. "She think so?"

"Long as you two are together, taking care of each other like you do, she's good."

Jesse couldn't help but notice his own reflection in Randy's dark transition glasses; the visual occurrence forced an uneasy self-awareness. The dark glasses granted a sense of *gravitas* that complimented Randy's stoic demeanor. Beneath the lenses, Jesse couldn't tell if Randy was looking directly at him or combing through some lost desert of memories.

"Just don't do anything to break her heart."

The words carried weight in Jesse's ears.

"She's a strong woman, but she's already had more than her share of misery."

The screen door squeaked open.

"Oh my God! It's like a totally different house." His mother burst out onto the porch. "If only your grandad could see this place."

"Mom. Why didn't you ever tell me?"

"Tell you what, hon?"

"That you got kicked out of a Led-*fucking*-Zeppelin show back in the day?"

"Jesse, watch your mouth." She tried in vain to force back a surfacing grin. "And yeah, we saw Led '*fucking*' Zeppelin." She took a beer from Randy, opened it, and took a slow drink. "And what I can remember of it was incredible."

"Holy shit, it's true," Jesse guffawed.

"You know—you might be surprised to learn that your lame old mom could teach you a thing or two about music. Where do you think you get it from?"

Jesse finished his beer and stood from the patio chair. "Well, that's about all I can handle for today. Thanks for the emotional scarring."

"The Lynn brothers have a gig in the city next month," Randy added. "Maybe we can roadie for 'em?"

Jesse mock-slammed the screen door on his way into the house to the delight of his parents, who responded by turning up the volume on the portable radio.

Once inside, he caught a whiff of his T-shirt, soaked through with sweat, and opted to head to the shower.

Rick's door was ajar. Inside, heavy music and incense lingered in the air.

"Dude. Mom and Randy are freaking me out. Did you know they got kicked out of a Zeppelin show at the Myriad back in the day?"

Rick was reading at his desk. He looked up at Jesse over his shoulder, appearing unfazed by the information.

"*Adventures in Babyshitting.*"

"Pardon?"

"Of course." Rick sighed and turned his chair around. "Why would you be expected to bear the memories of the horrors you have inflicted upon others?"

Jesse shrugged.

"While you were shitting your little infant brains out—sick with some hellspawn stomach bug—your irresponsible young mother was out gallivanting all over town, soaking in the gyrations of overhyped, mediocre, blue-eyed appropriators."

"Whatever, man. Zep rips."

"Do you wanna hear this story or not?"

Jesse settled in, taking a seat on Rick's bed while the tale was weaved. He recalled pieces of the story, but was never one to dismiss his older brother when he was in the zone. Rick had a way of aligning his thoughts with his tongue in ways that Jesse could never muster.

"I was going through my second pack of pampers right about the time Plant's prick was bursting out of his pants on stage."

"Dude."

"What?" Rick shrugged. "That guy wears his wallet mark in the front."

"I don't want to think about mom scoping out some dude's junk. Even if that dude is Robert Plant." Jesse shook his head in disgust. "Also, you sounded like a horny Dr. Seuss just then and it was kinda weird."

"Well it happened, so deal with it." Rick pushed his glasses back atop his nose and began to gesture wildly in the air. "Hour after hour the onslaught continued. I was convinced that you were dying, so in a panic I ran to the phone to call Crazy Catherine's house."

"Wait. This is the shirt story, isn't it?"

Rick raised his hand to ward off the interruption. "By the time I got off the phone you had managed to break out of your crib and crawl through the house, leaving behind a snail trail of hot, runny stink everywhere you went."

"Jesus Christ."

"Oh no, my friend, your precious Jesus was nowhere to be found on this day." Rick did his best Dracula laugh. "Unaware of your prison break, I ran back to your room to check on you, slipped in a stream of shit, and slid down the hall like I was riding an infernal Slip 'N Slide straight to hell."

Jesse frowned. "I think I'm getting sick to my stomach."

"And I never got the smell out of my limited edition *Sad Wings of Destiny* shirt."

"And there it is." Jesse got up to leave. "Clearly you have moved on."

"Not in this life."

"Well thanks for the memories. Speaking of hot stink." Jesse fanned his armpit towards Rick. "I'm gonna jump in the shower before the others get here."

"Wait." Rick held up the bound manuscript from his desk. "Listen to this shit."

A unique feature of heavy metal is the proliferation of a multitude of sub-genres that, while diverse, enable the stability of the parent genre as a whole.

The heavy metal genre is made stable, but not static, by the inherent flux of novel transgressions alongside the incorporation of an early metal pastiche that pays homage to the progenitors of the genre, thereby reaffirming the sonic tenets of tonality and lyrical syntax. These elements, when combined with the visual harmony of semiotics and performative dress, elicit an underlying continuity emblematic of heavy metal as a whole.

"Who the fuck is this guy again?"

"My guidance counselor. Seems like a pretty cool guy, actually. I think you'd like him."

"Like him? He's a fucking genius." Rick looked over the page, shaking his head. "He's clearly missed his calling."

"I think he plays too—had a bunch of weird old instruments, and gets kinda spooky when you ask him about them."

A knock at Jesse's bedroom window alerted him to the itinerary at hand.

"Shit, what time is it?"

Rick examined the black tactical watch on his wrist, turning his chair back to face the desk. "Almost five. Tell Elvira I said hi."

Jesse ran to his bedroom and threw open the window. Mal passed Jesse a large duffel bag before she climbed inside. Once inside, she threw her arms around his neck before recoiling from the embrace.

"Fuck, dude! Sometimes it's actually *cool* to shower," Mal said.

He leaned in for a kiss. "Sorry. I was out front helping Randy finish the deck."

Mal pushed him away and fell back into the bed, feigning unconsciousness. "You can touch me when you're clean."

"All right, all right, I'm going." Jesse opened the door and turned back before closing it. "Rick says hi. He's in his room if you wanna hang out while I take a quick shower."

She offered a fake smile as she sniffed the air. "Take your time, *Smell Patrol*. Be thorough."

Jesse took off the sweaty t-shirt and tossed it on the bed next to Mal, who screamed as she wrestled the soiled garment to the floor.

3

Back at the practice trailer, Rust and Mazes were loading up the demonic effigy and the rest of the loadout into the van.

Jesse and Mal watched from outside as his parents danced across the front windows of the ranch house. Music, laughter, and alcohol flowed freely into the evening like a meandering stream connecting past to present.

"So this is what a happy home looks like?" Mal asked.

Jesse smiled. "This is what a late-afternoon buzz looks like."

"You know what I mean." Mal wiped an isolated tear. "Whatever it is, I don't totally hate it."

Lately, it seemed like any mention of family brought her to tears. He put his arm around her and together they soaked up the scene. The reminiscence of the afternoon had created a celebration of life that by Jesse's estimation would last well into the evening hours.

Before departing, Jesse and Alex seized a couple of the leftover deck planks from Randy's pickup truck and loaded them into the van.

On their way to the church, they stopped at the local convenience store to fulfill the remainder of their plans for the evening. Rick, being the only member of the group of legal age, entered first, followed by Jesse and Mazes.

The clerk behind the counter was distracted by a pair of scantily clad coeds near the soda fountain who were dressed as fairies.

"All right, so that's a keg of Bud and a carton of Camel Lights. Anything else, gentlemen?"

"That should do us," answered Rick.

Jesse moved in to grab the keg.

"You old enough to be handling that?"

Rick cleared his throat. "That's my brother, who is acting as my caretaker, if you must know. As a handicapped member of society, I require certain considerations to enjoy the holiday festivities."

"Apologies, not trying to be a downer. Cops are out in full force on Halloween—you know the drill."

Jesse struggled to drag the keg out through the door. He was quickly assisted by Mazes who heaved the container up over his shoulder.

"Spoils to the victor," Mazes smiled.

Mazes loaded the keg while Jesse assisted Rick up on the lift that loaded his brother and his chair through Vanzig's side cargo door.

Once they were back in the van, Mal handed out the assortment of demonic Halloween masks to the group.

"Not too late to turn back," Alex offered.

Jesse could sense a rising swell of apprehension behind the words. Of all his bandmates, he trusted Alex the most, and could tell the offer was genuine. And while Jesse shared in the apprehension, he dared not submit to the sweet nectar of surrender.

As in the music they shared, there was something invulnerable about the emergent power of the group—a band of heavy metal misfits up against a world at odds with every molecule of their collective being. It was only natural that, on occasion, they give as good as they got.

"Happy Halloween, motherfuckers," said Rust. He donned his mask while helping Mazes secure the contraband.

Once Rick was situated inside the van, he passed a cassette up to Alex. "Here, man. Put this in. I made a Halloween mixtape—it's all cued up."

Alex shoved the cassette in the deck and pressed play as he stepped on the gas. The orchestral influenced counterpoint of "Am I Evil?" *by Diamond Head, from the album* Lightning to the Nations, *released in 1980 on Happy Face Records*, blared over the speakers as they set off towards Old Downtown.

Just after the sun went down, they pulled into the alley that ran behind the shared parking lot between the Plaza on Main strip mall and the adjacent Macomb Springs Church of Christ.

"Okay, everyone know their part?" asked Mal.

"Rick and I stay in the van and keep it running," Alex recited. "If anything goes south, I punch it, and the rest of you jerks are on your—"

Rick interrupted with an exaggerated cough. "That part of the evac strategy was supposed to be classified." He smiled sheepishly to the others, then furrowed his brow at Alex. "Come on, man! We talked about this."

Appearing unsure of who to look at, Alex put on his weasel eyes, swiveling his head back and forth between Rick and the others.

Jesse grabbed Alex by the shoulder. "Do not fucking move this van until we are all back inside of it, understand?" Alex nodded as Jesse continued. "Mal and I will move in first to cut the power." Mal nodded.

"Once the lights go out, Mazes and I will light up Beelzebub," Rust said as he flicked open his Zippo. "Don't forget to give us at least twenty Mississippis before you cut the power."

"Once you light it up, you'll have less than thirty seconds to get your asses back to the van." Rick tapped on his watch as he spoke. "And then we get the fuck out of Dodge."

After they made the circle of fists to seal the pact, the active participants in the plot filed out into the night.

Jesse watched as Rust and Mazes unloaded the effigy and quietly navigated towards the center of the adjacent church lot like a pair of bumbling extras in a bad heist movie.

What could go wrong?

The rest of the group waited until the effigy was positioned directly in front of the winding ramp that led to the church entrance.

Once Jesse saw that Mazes and Rust were erecting the effigy and spreading its wings, he and Mal splintered off towards the rear of the building in search of the main power switch.

It was commonly known to seasoned veterans of suburban mischief that the sole arbiter of power that transformed a lifeless edifice into one filled with electricity was governed by a single, solitary lever. Jesse was no novice. He knew that such a lever was generally found attached to the electric terminal located on the back outer wall of a given building, and made easily detectable due to its red rubber tip.

Jesse and Mal ran down the narrow alley towards the back of the church. As they neared the perimeter of the church building, the muffled singing of a modern Christian hymnal resonated from inside.

"Gah. Why does everything they do have to suck so bad?" Mal asked.

"At least they're consistent."

Jesse pulled out his lighter once they were within sight of the main power console. There within the small radius of light, he saw the rubber red handle protruding from a grey utility box. The box read "ON/OFF," with arrows pointing in either direction.

Jesse counted to twenty under his breath as Mal kept a lookout.

"I wish I could see Anderson's face," said Mal. The words were followed by a grey mist as they exited her mask and struck against the chill night air.

Jesse finished his count. "That's it, I'm killing it." He put his full weight on the switch and pulled it down.

The lever didn't budge.

"What the fuck? Is it locked?"

"I'm pulling it as hard as I fucking can—it's not moving."

Mal added her weight to the lever, which finally snapped down with a loud *crack* that echoed down the alley, causing the two to drop to the ground.

"RUN!" shouted Mal as she grabbed Jesse by the arm.

Jesse's mask had fallen over his eyes. He fought to fix it as they rounded the corner of the church. Through the narrow eye slits of his mask he saw the billowing flames shoot up into the night. The reflection of the orange-yellow glow on the hoods of the cars lit up the parking lot in front of the church.

As they neared the van, he could see Rust's legs floundering from inside the opened rear doors. Just as the reverse lights illuminated the alley, Jesse heard the screams coming from the entrance to the church.

"GO! GO! GO!" shouted Mal as they leapt through the open rear doors.

Mazes pulled them up into the van and slammed the doors shut as Alex tore out of the lot and sped off towards Main Street, heading away from Old Downtown.

Jesse ripped off his mask and gulped down a breath of fresh air. The others had their faces pressed against the windows, fogging up the glass. They watched in silence as the nearly eight foot-tall, wire-framed demon burst with unholy flames.

"Goddammit, man! How much lighter fluid did you use?" Rust pointed to his right eyebrow, which had been singed off, replaced by a boiling red blister. "That shit almost took my fuckin' face off."

As they turned onto Main Street, Jesse could see the crowd of pajama-clad teens that had gathered near the front entrance to the church. In the middle of the parking lot, a handful of adult chaperones were attempting to fight back the flames spewing from the demonic effigy with blankets and a fire extinguisher.

"Holy fucking shit!" Mal shouted the words in ever-increasing volume as the van sped off into the night.

4

Mazes, Alex, and Rust were standing at the bottom of the concrete retaining wall that sloped down to the entrance of the Hell Hole, bracing for the receiving end of their delivery.

"You can do it, man. Just tuck your legs up," said Rust.

"If I could move my legs, I wouldn't be in this fucking thing in the first place, Einstein."

Jesse and Mal stood at the top of the incline where they held back Rick in his wheelchair over the lip of the makeshift ramp. Randy's leftover deck planks were laid out end to end along the steep gradient.

"I don't know how you assholes talked me into this."

The flickering candlelight from inside the Hell Hole created ominous shadows over the features of the awaiting party below.

"You can do it, man!" shouted Rust.

"On my word, I will not allow any physical harm to befall you, Master Rick."

Jesse whispered into his brother's ear. "Don't worry—going down is the easy part."

"You would know," Rick imparted as he drew breath. "Fucking do it."

Free from its anchor, the chair quickly gained momentum as it rolled down the incline, careening over the wooden planks like a loose train car that had just pitched from the tracks. As Rick crashed into the awaiting assembly, Mazes moved forward to catch the brunt of the impact.

The large youth absorbed the momentum by sidestepping the chair at the last minute as he grabbed the handles, leading it into a circular re-entry to slow its inertia. The force of the collision caused the great lummox to knock Rust and Alex on top of each other near the stone archway.

Upon landing, Rick shot up devil horns in both hands and let out an ear-piercing howl into the night.

5

As the festivities gravitated towards the control room, Mal had already sketched out a pentagram on the floor in white chalk. At the terminus of each of the five points she placed a lit black candle, followed by a border of salt that ran around the radius of the pentagram.

"Trying to keep the slugs out?" asked Alex, cradling the boombox in his lap.

"It's for protection. As long as we stay inside the circle, no evil spirits can harm us."

"Evil spirits?" Alex rifled through a half-dozen cassette tapes portioned out among the pockets of his jean jacket. "I think I have just the thing."

Mal finished pouring the salt and lit a stick of incense. "A lot of people died down here—tragically, I might add." She gestured towards the lit candles. "And I'm sure some of them are pissed off about it."

Alex looked around the control room as though suddenly aware of his surroundings.

"Relax. Long as you stay inside the circle, everything will be fine."

He switched tapes on the boombox's cassette player and pressed play. A chorus-tinged bass line volleyed off the walls of the control room as "Lucretia My Reflection" *by The Sisters of Mercy, from the album* Floodland, *released in 1987 on Merciful Release* filled the room.

"Right, relax," Alex chuckled to himself as he rolled a joint on the AM/FM tuner panel that ran the length of the boombox. "I'm on it."

The lure of the music brought in the others. Mazes carried in the keg while Rust helped Rick relieve himself outside.

Jesse and Alex passed the joint back and forth while Mal produced a hand-carved Ouija board from the duffel bag and laid the planchette on the ground next to it, ensuring that it did not come in contact with the board.

Next she pulled out a Manila envelope, spilling out the contents on the board like she was pouring a bowl of cereal. An assortment of obituary clippings and various newspaper articles from the *Macomb Springs Chronicle* surrounded the board; each referenced the historical mine collapse that occurred over a half-century ago.

"Don't forget to tune in next time, on *Scrap Booking with Satan*," Rust said, wheeling in Rick.

Mal selected a newspaper clipping which included obituaries of the mine workers. "Who wants to talk to the dead?"

"I'm in," Jesse called out as he helped Rust navigate Rick into the control room.

Mal had drawn the pentagram wide enough to accommodate the entire group, including Rick's wheelchair. Once seated, they took turns passing around Alex's joint before they settled into the séance as dictated by Mal.

"Man, this place has seen better days," said Rick.

"This place is starting to kill my buzz," said Alex. He brushed a daddy longlegs off his sleeve as he hit the joint.

Mal placed the planchette on the board.

"Okay everyone, shut up. Jesse, Alex, and Rust, I need you three to put your hands on the planchette here with me."

Alex turned down the volume on the boombox and set it on the ground as he moved in closer to the inner circle.

Mal placed her hands around the little glass window in the center of the hand-carved, heart-shaped piece. "The rest of you will be the battery that charges the circle with energy, so that the dead can hear us on the other side." Once the other three joined their fingertips with hers on the planchette, she moved it in a figure-eight pattern. "We'll trace the infinity symbol to warm up the board."

Mal took command of the room as the others fell in line to enact the ritual.

"We come as vessels of peace, seeking visitation with those who have passed beyond this mortal coil. Are there any spirits among us who would like to commune with the living?"

The room turned still and silent save for the flickering of candlelight.

Mal repeated the invitation once more, but received only silence in response, aside from the snickering produced by Rick, who had been nursing the joint by himself. Mal opened one eye to quell the outburst.

"Sometimes it takes a minute," she said.

Jesse brushed his fingertips against hers as she repositioned the planchette. She gave him a sly wink before she composed herself and read the names from the obituaries.

"I call upon your ethereal forms. Are there any spirits here that would like to speak with us?"

The room maintained a silent vigil until the candles began to flicker in unison.

"What the fuck was that?" asked Alex.

The planchette responded by gliding across the board, seemingly of its own volition. It deviated from the figure-eight pattern before spelling out the letters P-E-N-I...

"Very funny," started Mal. "Which one of you dickwads—"

Her words were interrupted by another outburst, this one coming from outside the control room.

A loud, low frequency rumble rose from the depths of the mine. The sound grew louder in intensity as it reached the control room, snuffing out the candlelight as a wave of foul air washed over the central tunnel.

"Fuck this," Alex whimpered as he pulled his hands from the planchette. He grabbed his boombox and headed towards the door just as another horn blast sounded.

Unlike the first rumbling barrage of sound, the crescendo of the second blast was accompanied by a low guttural growl.

"Cute Halloween sound effects, Mal. How long did you guys spend setting that up?" asked Rick. He wheeled up to the control room doors next to Mazes, who had already leapt into action.

Something scurried near the door.

The jarring sound of groaning metal echoed out from the central tunnel just beyond the control room doors. Mazes stuck his head outside the room while gesturing for the others to stay back.

"Everyone keep quiet," Rust whispered. "I think there's somethin' out there."

Click.

The side of the cassette tape had ended, causing the playback head to engage the brake shoe as the auto-rewind function was triggered on the boombox's cassette player.

WHIRRRRRRRRR.

Jesse could hear Alex trying to muffle the sound in the darkness. The noise from the cassette deck had silenced the scuttling and scratching sounds coming from just outside the control room doors.

The others gathered behind Mazes.

"Probably just a stray dog or something," said Rick.

The shuffling of footsteps resounded from down the central tunnel, drawing nearer with each step. Jesse began to tremble despite himself as the somber wail of a young girl echoed off the walls of the central tunnel.

He closed his eyes as the disembodied voice called out, seemingly mere inches from his face, so close that he could feel its breath. He thought for a moment he could smell a hint of wine cooler in the air.

Rust's Zippo clinked open.

The spark of the flame revealed a pair of cat-eye glasses and a mop of dense, curly hair that spilled out above the collar of an oversized military jacket.

"Hey guys! Sorry I'm late," Kara slurred. "Did I scare ya?"

"Jesus fucking Christ, Kara!" Mal shouted as she shoved her friend. "I think I have to change my pants."

Kara jumped inside the control room, latching on to Mal. The two tumbled to the floor in a bout of laughter as the others uttered a collective sigh of relief.

The relief was short-lived, as the stabbing groan of metal on metal called again from the darkness beyond the control room.

Jesse could hear Mal faintly whisper as she pulled Kara to her feet. "Did you come by yourself?"

Kara nodded.

Rust patted Mazes on the shoulder, firmly planting the lighter into his catcher's mitt-sized hand. As Jesse's eyes adjusted to the soft orange-yellow glow, he began to make out the rusted metal outline of the mine cart affixed to the ancient rail cart track.

All eyes followed in the direction of the grating sound as the mine cart rolled slowly along the track, stopping just in front of the control room doors.

Mazes stepped further into the corridor. The others followed suit, funneling out from the control room, with Rick in his wheelchair taking up the rear.

As Mazes raised the Zippo, the glint of the flame was reflected back from a pair of wet, bulbous eyes.

"Totally called it—stray dog," said Rick.

"That doesn't look like any dog I've ever seen," said Rust. "How'd it get in there?"

Jesse fumbled for his lighter.

With the added light, he could make out the broad snout, jutting out urgently from the creature's face like a baboon. Its pale grey flesh was hairless and slick, almost translucent in spots. A barbed, prehensile tail snaked out from behind the beast's large hindquarters.

Jesse stood watching, frozen in disbelief as the thing's tail swayed hypnotically back and forth. A pair of dexterous, clawed hands rose from the shadowy confines of the mine cart, gripping the sides as it hoisted itself up.

As it emerged from the cart, a large fleshy sac began to fan out from beneath its widening jaws as a low rumble gurgled up from its chest. Jesse felt a wave of nausea come over him as the sound began to fill the tunnel.

The creature lunged forward.

Alex swung his boombox by the handle in a wide arc, landing true against the creature's skull. The force of the blow knocked it from the cart where it lay still on the track.

"Run!" Alex squealed. The word trailed behind him as he fled towards the gated entrance with the boombox in tow.

The action spurred the others to follow.

Mal pulled Jesse forward as he stumbled towards the dim rectangle of candlelight at the end of the tunnel.

Rust had stopped ahead of them, doubled over on the ground, vomiting.

Jesse grabbed hold of his downed bandmate, fighting desperately to push ahead through the cacophony of discordant screams that echoed off the walls of the corridor.

Jesse plunged ahead with Mal and Rust on either side. Each step felt more and more difficult to muster, like he was trying to run underwater. Just as he was about to falter, he felt his lungs fill with fresh air from outside. He came to, and found himself with the others back at the Hell Hole.

"What just happened?" asked Kara. Her eyes were welling up with tears as she looked for confirmation from her peers.

Mal moved to console her friend as she looked over the others, dazedly. "Everybody else okay?"

"Where's Rick?" asked Alex.

"I—I dunno man," Rust managed to cough up the words. "I thought he was right behind us."

The question pierced through Jesse's mind like a cold dagger. He looked to the impenetrable darkness beyond the stone archway for any sign of his brother. The sonic remnants of their passage had faded, leaving only a dead silence to fill the night.

He could hear his heart beating loudly in his ears as he ventured back towards the archway. The pulsing of blood gave way to the gallop of heavy footfalls as Mazes's gargantuan form appeared, knocking Jesse aside as he charged through the arch like some medieval juggernaut. In his arms he carried Rick, still seated in his chair, whom he gently sat down just beyond the gate.

"Thanks for the lift," Rick said.

"Discretion is the better part of valor," Mazes panted.

Once outside, they quickly barricaded the gate shut, all the while keeping an eye out for any sign that they were being pursued.

"So let's begin with the obvious question," Jesse started. "What the fuck?"

"Whatever it was, it probably had rabies, or mange," said Rust. He patted Alex on the shoulder. "Lucky nobody got bit, thanks to Mr. Miyagi over here."

"Rabies?" Alex squealed. "That thing made Cujo look tame."

Mal stroked Kara's hair as she sobbed into her shoulder. "Hey guys, I don't wanna be a wet blanket, but I think we need to get this little lady to bed."

"You sure you wanna leave all your stuff?" asked Jesse.

Mal took Jesse's arm as she guided Kara towards the ramp. "We can come back later after we drop her off."

Rust helped Mazes push Rick and his chair up the wooden planks that led to the gravel service road where they had parked the van.

They drove in silence as they headed back to town.

6

After returning Kara safely to her home, the group returned to the practice trailer. Mazes tossed his backpack on the floor and collapsed into the bean bag chair, sending out a small explosion of styrofoam kernels.

"Well, I was wrong," Rick said. "You little shits do know how to throw a good Halloween party." He pulled out two cigarettes from his jacket, lit them both and handed one to Jesse. "That was some real Tom Savini shit. I'm flattered."

Jesse choked on the cigarette, mid-drag, as he attempted a retort. "Dude, that was *not* special effects."

Mal offered a dismissive laugh. "Not to mention you saw our entire production budget burn up in flames in the middle of the church parking lot." She patted Rick on the shoulder as she continued. "It's really sweet that you think we would waste money on showing you such a good time, though."

"I knew that séance was a bad idea," Alex said.

Rust rummaged through the mini-fridge and produced a round of beers for the group. "Worst part about it is, we didn't even get a chance to float the fuckin' keg."

"Fine, I'll bite," Rick giggled as he opened his beer. "Since you are truly going above and beyond—maybe it was just someone's exotic pet that got loose?"

"Since when do they have pet stores in Hell?" said Alex.

"The beast did possess certain Stygian attributes," said Mazes.

A natural silence fell over the group as they contemplated the shared experience.

It was Rust who stepped up first and said aloud what everyone was thinking. "We have to go back. That keg was like a summer's worth of lawns."

"That was a real witchboard too, not some cheap Parker Brothers crap," Mal said.

Jesse piped up, knowing what must be done. "I'll go back with Rust. The rest of you stay here."

Mal jumped on Jesse, wrapping her legs around his waist. "My hero!" she said, kissing him deeply before dropping back to her feet. "Just be careful. And come straight back."

Jesse produced a flashlight from the junk drawer in the kitchen and grabbed a baseball bat from the hall closet.

"This time we go prepared."

Mazes grabbed the bat from Jesse and held it aloft. "I'll not see my brothers in arms ride into battle alone."

7

Back at the mine, Jesse took point with the flashlight, leading the others back into the control room.

"No sign of Cujo," Rust said. "Looks like the coast is clear."

"Probably scared it off for good after Alex smashed its head in," Jesse said. "You guys grab the keg. I'll get the rest of our shit."

"And still plenty of time to get fubared, and salvage this fucked-up night," said Rust.

The control room was all but destroyed. The contents of Mal's duffel bag were strewn about, the console chassis streaked with claw marks. Jesse set to work loading Mal's duffel bag with the Ouija board and her other personal effects, which were left mostly unharmed.

Mazes and Rust were already carrying out the keg before Jesse had finished packing up the rest of their belongings. He surveyed the destruction of the room once more before following his band mates out into the night.

One hell of a stray dog, he thought to himself as he left the mine.

CHAPTER FIVE

WOE TO THE VANISHED

1

Jesse was dreaming about the mine.

He and the others were being chased by an unseen presence as they ran, on and on, trapped within the endless labyrinth of darkness that tunneled beneath the ground. Finally, their path opened into a cavernous hollow in the earth.

In the dream, Jesse was given the knowledge that the cavern he inhabited lay within the natural cave system located deep beneath the abandoned Spring Creek Mine.

Once inside the spacious cavern, he collapsed to the ground, gasping for breath and straining for any sign that they were still being chased. Jesse lay on the cave floor frozen in fear. One by one, his companions fell lifeless to the ground as a great shadow stepped into the center of the cavern. A deep, bellowing call emanated from the shadow; the sound burned in Jesse's ears, ejecting him from his fitful slumber.

He laid in bed listening to the idle chatter of Rick and Randy coming from the kitchen as he got his bearings, and tried to distance himself from the unwelcome vision.

"Two words: David Bowie."

"He's pretty good. But I ain't into that foo-foo shit."

"So he's a gender bender? He's also one of the greatest artists of the twentieth century. See, that's the problem with your generation."

"You tellin' me he's better than Jimi Hendrix?"

"Need I remind you that two-thirds of The Experience were British?"

"What about Alice Cooper?"

"Okay, I'll give you that one. Score one for the Americans. Pretty decent sound for a minister's son."

"Mmm-hmm."

"My next one is a threefer, because in my mind they are all one great incestuous British Triangle. The unholy trinity—Deep Purple, Black Sabbath, and Rainbow. And don't even get me started on the connections to Elf, Whitesnake, or Def Leppard. I could make a Venn diagram that would make your freakin' head explode."

"I do like that 'Smoke on the Water' record."

"Of course you do. Aside from that song, *Machine Head* is a great album."

"But some of that other satanic stuff just gets a little too weird for me, man. I've seen some shit over there, Chief. I don't need a bunch of black magic hippies trying to put the scare on me."

"Satanic stuff? Black Sabbath were Vietnam War protesters—I get it if that's a nonstarter. But don't dismiss them because they were '*satanic*'—that's bullshit. And Dio's only crime was writing one too many songs about dragons."

"All right, all right! Simmer down before you hurt yourself. How 'bout Van Halen?"

"Well played. You're putting me in a tough spot here. For the sake of argument, I'll just say that one amazing record doesn't forgive one of this country's most hedonistic cultural exports since the Big Mac."

"Rush."

"Doesn't count. They're Canadian."

His mother's voice followed the roar of the great white wagon up the driveway as she called for help to unload groceries.

The rest of the house had seemingly gone about their day despite Jesse's lack of participation. He stumbled out into the kitchen to forage for a tonic that would absolve him of his nocturnal sins.

Images from the previous night were beginning to rise to the surface: the burning of the demonic effigy in the church parking lot; the séance and the flight from the mine; the mine cart. *One hell of a stray dog.* The thought resounded again and again inside the pounding walls of his skull.

As he rummaged through the sea of brown paper sacks stacked on the dinner table, he noticed a black-and-white xeroxed flyer peeking out from one of the grocery bags. Jesse digested the heading, writ in bold black letters: MISSING.

The all-American teen wearing his letterman jacket stared back. Jesse immediately recognized the vacant, yet innocent smile.

"Welcome to the land of the living," his mother called. She kicked the screen door shut behind her as she placed another round of groceries on the table. "Isn't that just awful about Kenny Summers?" she asked. "He's in your grade, isn't he?"

Jesse winced at the pronouncement of his classmate's name. "Yeah, some jock kid." He shrugged. "I think I had him in one of my classes."

"Oh hon, I'm so sorry. That must be horrible. You haven't seen him around town the last couple days, have you?"

Jesse shook his head. "Any idea what happened to him?"

"The cashier at the EZ-Buy said his parents last saw him the day before Halloween. He still hasn't made it home." She wagged her finger at Jesse. "I want you and your brother back on the property before sundown until this whole thing blows over."

Jesse could feel his cheeks turn red before the words left his mouth. "I don't get why we should be punished just because some asshole jock stayed out past curfew."

"How could you say that? He's about to be on a milk carton."

"You don't understand, these athletes…they get to do whatever they want at that school. It's probably not any different at home."

"Well, his parents are very worried. And since they're part of the local church community, this is going to affect all of us whether we like it or not." She stuck a magnet on top of the flyer and hung it on the refrigerator. "You can have your friends over at the trailer, but just stay indoors." She rifled through the groceries as she continued. "I know it seems like a small-town oasis, but you have to keep your eyes out for the crazies these days, no matter where you are in the world. Nobody is safe anymore."

Rick wheeled up to the kitchen counter, taking a drink from a carton of orange juice that had been laid out as he scanned the flyer on the refrigerator.

"So just because some rich jock couldn't find his way home from the varsity circle jerk, we all have to suffer the consequences?" he asked.

Jesse's mom stifled a laugh as her jaw was left hanging open.

"Well. I'm glad I won't have to worry about my boys going to any *varsity circle jerks.*"

"Damn straight," said Rick. "Can't speak for my little bro, though. Might wanna keep an eye on him."

His mom ruffled Jesse's hair as she left the room, leaving the brothers to unload the groceries.

Jesse snagged the orange juice carton from his brother and downed a few swallows. "We need to talk about what happened last night."

"You guys were so scared of that stray that you almost cost us a full keg. Bunch of pussies."

"When was the last time you ever saw a dog?"

"It probably had mange or rabies, like Rust said. What else could it have been?"

"Dude, maybe it's time to check your prescription. That was no fucking dog."

"All right, Jim Fowler. I give up. Why don't you tell our viewers at home the name of this mysterious animal?"

2

Alex was pacing around the usual meet-up spot near Mal's locker when Jesse arrived at school. He was licking his lips like a tree frog from the cover of one of those *Ranger Rick* magazines Jesse had when he was a kid.

"What's wrong? You look like you've seen a ghost."

"Anderson's on the war path." Alex gestured around the corner to where Principal Anderson was directing a contingent of uniformed police officers through a locker search. "She's got the cops going through all of our shit after what happened at the lock-in."

"Relax, just be cool. There's no way they know who did it." As the words left his mouth, Principal Anderson turned to meet Jesse's eyes. She pointed at the adjacent bank of lockers and led the officers towards it, never taking her eyes off Jesse.

"Yeah, but who do you think they're gonna blame?" Alex's eyes darted around the hall. "I can't believe I always let you guys talk me into this kind of bullshit."

"Did you leave anything in your locker?"

Alex shook his head. "You?"

"I never even learned the combination."

Alex fidgeted nervously with the straps of his backpack as he followed the police officers with his eyes. "I gotta jet to class. If we get expelled, I'm going to kill all of you."

"Just act normal and everything will be fine." Jesse nudged his bandmate on his shoulder and repeated the mantra. "Everything will be fine."

Jesse waited at Mal's locker until the first-period bell. When she didn't show, he opted to head to class rather than risk adding to his well-curated collection of tardy slips. *She probably just overslept*, he thought to himself. *That girl can sleep like the dead.*

3

Jesse tried to put the looming threat of Principal Anderson's quest for vengeance out of his mind as he headed to physics class, one of his favorite public educational offerings—specially when Mrs. Ford delved into one of her famous in-class experiments. Mrs. Ford was one of his favorite teachers; coincidentally, she was also the only one of his new teachers to remember his name.

As he slunk towards his seat near the back of the classroom, he was surprised to see Mr. Agostino arranging a display of various musical instruments on Mrs. Ford's desk.

A sizable loudspeaker and a microphone were positioned next to a wine glass on the lab table at the front of the classroom. The microphone was connected to a machine that Jesse knew to be an oscilloscope, but he could not identify some of the other modular devices on the table.

"Good morning, class. As you may have heard, Mrs. Ford was involved in a terrible animal attack over the weekend. I will be filling in to the best of my abilities until we find a substitute while she recovers."

A flurry of conspiracy theories were presented for consideration from a few of the more outspoken students in the class.

"I heard she got mauled by a bear."

"There's no bears around here, stupid."

Another student piped up from the back of the class. "Whatever it was messed her up so bad that they were only able to keep part of her brain alive. And now she has to live the rest of her life in a fish tank or something."

The classroom erupted with laughter.

Agostino held his hands up. "I assure you, Mrs. Ford is expected to make a full recovery. In the meantime, I would like to supplement her lesson plan for today with a study of the physics of sound—acoustics."

The guidance counselor approached the lab table, producing a box of protective headphones which he passed out to each student.

"Most of us tend to think of sound as an invisible force, but it actually requires a physical medium to travel through in order to form, such as air, water, stone, or even glass." Agostino switched on the loudspeaker and gestured to the equipment on the lab table. "Once generated from a sound source—such as this signal generator—sound vibrates through the surrounding medium as it travels from the source and forms a sound wave."

Jesse applied the clunky headphones and watched as Mr. Agostino tapped the wineglass with a metal rod. As the glass sang into the microphone, a corresponding waveform rippled across the oscilloscope's rectangular screen.

"All physical matter has a resonant frequency—a natural threshold that determines how it is affected by vibrations of sound waves. By exposing an object or medium to its own resonant frequency at a high enough volume, we can cause the catastrophic failure of that object."

Mr. Agostino replayed the tone through the signal generator and increased the volume of the loudspeaker until the glass cracked.

"And that is how sound can manipulate matter. Pretty impressive, yes?" He picked up a bizarre looking implement: a round resonator fashioned from a cured gourd, with a row of thin metal tines affixed to its surface. He held the contraption for all to see as he continued. "And since you seem to be interested in grim tales, let us take a closer examination of the lives of the ancients through an exploration of their traditional instruments."

The classroom settled into a steady hum of hushed conversation as Agostino lectured.

"In an earlier, more superstitious time, some ancient cultures believed that singing—particularly in the form of an angelic chorus—channeled the voice of the gods." As Agostino passed around the instrument, melodic chimes filled the air as the students manipulated the metal tines. "In contrast, it was also believed that musical instruments, fabricated by the fallible hands of humans, could be used to speak to the spirits of their ancestors." He lifted a beat-up, old violin and plucked its strings. "Some were even known to conjure up the devil."

"Is it true that if you play some records backwards you can summon Satan?" asked a frizzy-haired girl in purple overalls who always sat in the front row.

"It's called backmasking. My brother showed me on one of his KISS records," said a pockmarked boy with rubber-banded braces.

"I think you mean Knights In Satan's Service," corrected another student.

"Or AC/DC—Antichrist, Demon Child. They all worship the devil," said another.

Jesse watched as the classroom devolved into a frenzy of pop culture sound bites and regurgitated urban legends. He felt bad for the guidance counselor who seemed to be fighting a losing battle.

Agostino began to bow the violin, softly at first, then creating strange dissonant chords that sprang from his fingertips. A group of the more curious students began to gather around the desk to examine Agostino's musical offerings.

Something about the chord Agostino played and the strange tones that seemed to rake against the air left Jesse thinking about the recent experience in the mine. He replayed the scene in his mind's eye over and over, and realized he was growing more curious as to Mal's whereabouts.

He was already on his feet when the class bell rang.

"Mr. Lynn, could I have a quick word?" asked Agostino.

Jesse sighed internally and did his best to focus his attention on the request.

"Sure. What's up?"

"I noticed you have not made it to one of our appointments in a few days." Agostino parted his mustache between his thumb and index finger as he spoke. "Is everything okay?"

"Yeah, sorry." Jesse was beginning to become annoyed with his guidance counselor's perceptiveness. "I've just been busy with band practice after school. We have a pretty big gig coming up."

"Is that so?" He probed Jesse with his dark eyes. "Then I believe congratulations are in order."

"Thanks." Jesse tried to curb the impulse to flee into the hall to resume his search for Mal.

Agostino began to reassemble the various instruments on the desk in preparation for his next class. "I do not mean to keep you, but I do hope that we may catch up soon." He gestured to the open door. "Sometimes, at your age, it does not take much to feel like your very world is being torn asunder."

"That part about being able to use music to summon forces from the netherworld...you believe that?"

"It does not matter if I believe it, but the sentiment—or perhaps 'wish' is a better way to think about it—may serve as an indicator that there is something within the collective human consciousness that wants it to be true."

Jesse felt sheepish in continuing the line of questioning, as he had yet to articulate his own thoughts on the matter. Despite his unease, something within the back of his mind prodded him to delve further.

"In your research, the ethnic music—"

"Ethnomusicology," corrected Agostino.

"Yeah. In that research, did you ever read anything about people actually summoning demons?"

Agostino squinted his eyes and looked to the ceiling as he pondered the question.

"History is rife with widespread accounts of agents of the netherworld being summoned to do the bidding of their vengeful, power-hungry human masters."

"But was there ever any proof or evidence that they actually did?"

"The passage of time makes it all but impossible to discern factual accounts from myth and legend."

"Seems like that's almost all anyone talks about these days when it comes to music."

Agostino nodded as he chewed on the corner of his mustache. "Fascinating times. I would hazard a guess that not since the Salem witch trials, or the various European inquisitions that preceded them, has there been such widespread social hysteria regarding the attribution of demonic or satanic influence on contemporary American society."

The second-period bell rang out over the hall speakers.

"Speaking of demonic music," said Jesse, "I better run to class. Thanks for the info."

"My door is always open."

4

Jesse took the long way to his second period class, hoping again to catch Mal at her locker. With no sign of her, he sprinted to class to beat another tardy bell.

As he turned the corner, he ran smack into a dense wall of letterman jackets. The pungent scent of Drakkar Noir filled his nostrils as he looked up to meet the gaze of a tall, neckless youth sporting an overgrown red flat top.

Flat Top pushed Jesse against the lockers and yelled in his face. "I thought I told you to watch where you're going, freak!"

Flat Top's spittle rained down on Jesse's face. He recognized the fire-engine red rectangle that sat atop the round, freckled face, giving him the appearance of a flabby exclamation point—the jerk-off who knocked over his chili dog on the first day of school.

Jesse mentally prepared to face off against what appeared to be the entirety of the varsity football team. He felt a species removed from the army of robust, muscle-bound specimens towering above him.

At least he wouldn't die a virgin.

"Hey, isn't that one of those stoner asswipes who was fucking with Kenny?" someone asked.

A chiseled-face jock with black, swept-back hair emerged from the pack and stuck his nose in Jesse's face. "So you and your scummy little friends like to sit around and worship Satan, is that it?"

"I'm just trying to get to class," Jesse smiled.

"You think it's funny?" asked Flat Top. "You think it's cool to worship the devil?"

Jesse retreated behind his smile, which was beginning to grow stiff.

Black Hair shoved his finger into Jesse's chest as he spoke. "Yeah. What's your deal, man? You can't get laid so you and your little *faggot* friends go out in the woods and get each other off, listening to your shit music?"

A familiar voice cut through the verbal assault just as Jesse was being squeezed against the wall of lockers.

"Who says he can't get laid?" Mal appeared, pushing her way in between Jesse and the amassing jocks. She slapped a flyer against Black Hair's chest. "While you and the rest of the boys are chasing each other across the field wearing those cute little tights, Jesse and his band will be rocking the Beggar's Banquet Hall next Friday night." She gave Jesse a deep kiss, and took his hand as she strode past the group of jocks. She turned back, sticking out her tongue between her index and middle finger. "And they make all the girls cream their jeans."

The football team were a mix of jeers and dropped jaws.

Once they were out of earshot he pulled her close. "Perfect timing. Where the hell have you been? I can barely function in this place by myself."

She offered a meek smile as they ventured down the hall.

"Everything okay?"

"There are just so many fucking assholes in this world."

"Yeah, I know." He looked over his shoulder, relieved to see an empty bank of lockers. "I can't believe people like them exist in real life. Thanks for saving my ass."

She looked through Jesse as she wiped her eyes.

The tardy bell rang.

After a deep breath, she let out a low guttural growl and proceeded to put a dent in one of the lower tier lockers with a heel of her Doc Martens. She grabbed Jesse by the collar. "You wanna get out of here? I'm not in the mood for this fucking place."

5

A fresh rain began to fall as they ran, hand in hand, down the wooded, leaf-littered trails that meandered away from the school grounds towards the newly built housing additions to the east. As the rain came down harder, they ducked under the patio roof of one of the empty model homes.

"It's fucking pouring. Should we go back?"

Mal gestured towards the back door. "Let's see if it's open."

"Truancy *and* breaking and entering? Busy day."

"No one lives here, yet. Besides, we're soaked, and it's coming down harder. You want to catch pneumonia out here?" Mal tried the back door. When it didn't budge, she pulled out her driver's license and forced the latch open.

Inside, the newly built model home was sparsely furnished and pristine white; the carpet and walls practically glowed in the shadows. Jesse flicked the light switch in the kitchen to no avail.

"Electricity probably hasn't been turned on yet," he said.

Mal had already kicked off her boots and was in the process of peeling off her shirt and jeans. She draped the wet clothes over the chairs that surrounded the kitchen table.

"You'll catch your death," she whispered as she pulled off Jesse's shirt.

"What if somebody comes in?"

She left the question unanswered as it resonated within the empty house. The bare white walls volleyed the insipid utterance over and over like a loose tennis ball that Jesse longed to recapture.

He followed her up the stairs and into the master bedroom. The bed was neatly made and covered in throw pillows.

"This clean-sheen, cookie-cutter bullshit is really getting on my nerves." Mal tussled the bedclothes and threw the pillows on the floor. "That's better," she sighed. "Now, let's do something dirty in it."

The warmth of her mouth contrasted against the cool wet skin of her body. She smelled like patchouli and burnt sage. Goosebumps marked her naked flesh as she called for the warm press of his body against hers. Their love was quick and heated, feeling somehow like the answer to a question that was never asked.

After they finished, they lay side by side staring at the ceiling.

"So let me get this straight," Jesse started. "When Hell Patrol makes it big, and I buy you a big, beautiful house like this one, you'd be disappointed?"

"That's so sweet." Her eyes transitioned from somber grey to icy blue as her face lit up.

He wondered what she saw when she looked in his eyes, and if it was anything like this.

"You want to lock me up in a suburban death cage, drowning in credit card debt, while you and the kids choke down what passes for meals that I learned to make from my only friend, television?"

"It's not all bad. You can also self-medicate with alcohol and Xanax to mask your inevitable depression." He shrugged his shoulders as he finished the thought. "Which will be severe after you've put aside your promising photography career to wait on me and the kids hand and foot."

"You paint such a beautiful picture—how could I refuse?" Mal laughed in contagious little bursts. She kicked him over onto his side and placed her cold feet into the small of his back. "When hell freezes over, Jesse Lynn."

They held each other in silence for a long time.

"I know this is going to sound fucking stupid, but do you ever think about Halloween?"

"Only like every day of my life." She traced the skin around his shoulder as she whispered. "It's my favorite holiday."

"I meant this last Halloween," he said. "Like less than a week ago—in the mine? I keep having these weird dreams."

"I've been trying not to think about it," she said, suddenly turning cold. She sat up and started putting on her bra. "I already feel crazy enough just dealing with my own shit."

"Hey." Jesse pulled her back to the bed. "Eventually you're gonna have to tell me what's going on."

Mal looked to the floor. "It will all be over soon." She forced a smile and pulled at him to get up. "Can we just talk about something else until then?"

"Message received." Jesse stood and rested his arms on her shoulders. "Next chance we get we should go back to the mine. Just you and me, okay?"

She nodded.

"And your camera."

6

Jesse ran into the house to grab a quick bite to eat before setting up the trailer for practice. Skipping the majority of the school day, and therefore lunch, had stirred a formidable hunger. He threw together the contents of a sandwich, more utilitarian than visually appealing, and downed it with a frothing glass of ice-cold milk.

Randy and his mother passed through the kitchen on their way out the front door. His mother was arguing with Rick, who wheeled into the kitchen behind them.

"These *pillars of the community* you are so desperate to fit in with are the same people that are driving these kids to the edge," said Rick. "I mean, just take a look at this one." He nodded to Jesse, who flipped him the bird, and then proceeded to spin around in circles to deflect the impending rebuttal from his mother.

"These are nice, churchgoing people," she said. "They're just trying to do their best to understand what's going on with their children. You can't blame them for wanting to come together during their time of need. There was another missing persons case reported this morning, Rick. This isn't a joke."

Randy tucked in his shirt and grabbed a set of keys from the counter. "Come on, man. Don't get your mother all riled up before we leave the house."

"I'm sorry that it's not as easy for those of us with actual functioning brains to avoid falling into the trappings of the holy church and its eons of inquisition and genocide."

"Where are you guys going?" asked Jesse.

"They're going to be indoctrinated into the world's most well marketed death cult."

"If they're so well marketed, how come I've never heard about any death cults around here?" said Jesse.

"Thank you, Jesse," his mother said.

"Very funny." Rick shook his head. "You might have heard of it. It's the one that still worships a magical baby whose working-class father was cuckolded by a narcissistic creator deity?"

"We're going to a community vigil at the church for the missing boy, Kenny Summers," his mother said.

The name sat heavy in Jesse's ears as he tried to finish the glass of milk. "Oh yeah?" he mustered. Kenny's annoying face had been making the rounds inside Jesse's carousel of guilty thoughts of late.

"We moved to this quiet little developing community outside of the city to try to provide a better life for you boys." She pointed to both Jesse and Rick as she spoke. "And God forbid we show some support for our new neighbors."

"No thanks," said Rick. "This place is a fucking joke."

A dark silence filled the room as the words left Rick's mouth. Jesse braced against the encroaching tension. *Five more minutes,* he thought to himself. *Five more goddamn minutes and I would have been out the door and on my way to practice.*

His mother locked eyes with Rick.

Beneath her furrowed brow was a contorted mask of anger and hurt that Jesse found hard to behold, despite not being the intended target.

Rick returned the gaze without expression. Jesse recognized the blank stare. The oversized metal frames that rested atop his nose obscured any hint of emotion in his brother's dead eyes. After what felt like an eternity, Rick let out a burst of comically loud flatulence, seamlessly incorporated into his exodus as he propelled his wheelchair down the hall towards his room.

Jesse's mother had already stomped out through the front door before the screen door slammed shut behind her.

Randy held up his hands in defeat as he looked to Jesse, who could only shrug in response.

"There's a frozen pizza in the freezer for you guys to share," said Randy. He stepped out and held the screen door open as he called to Jesse. "Try to teach your brother some goddamned manners before we get back."

Jesse barged into Rick's room. "What the hell was that about?"

"Just trying to educate the masses." Rick glanced down at the large tactical watch he wore on his wrist. "Aren't you supposed to be at practice?"

"You know, our lives would be a lot easier if you guys could get along."

"Keep your mind on the show and let me worry about the little things. I've put a lot on the line for this gig. At this point my credibility is all we have."

Jesse stood his ground; Rick raised his eyebrows as if to ask, *Anything else?* The expression tapped a wellspring of anger that

Jesse didn't realize he had harbored towards his brother.

"You don't have to be such a dick to mom. She's been through a lot." Jesse inadvertently gestured at his brother's chair as he made the comment. He froze, unable to rewind the moment. Instead it played on, one agony-filled second after another.

Rick responded in the coldest way possible: by turning his back on his brother without another word.

CHAPTER SIX

PRISONERS OF FLESH

1

Jesse stared up at the stage.

The headliner's backline of Marshall full stacks loomed above the drum riser like the black monolith in Kubrick's *2001*. The comparison felt true as he stared up at the visual spectacle like a lesser being, unable to fully comprehend its meaning. A team of stagehands handled the heavy stacks of flight cases, each bearing the white spray-painted, stenciled letters "P.O.F."

Still mesmerized by the volume of the sound check, Jesse watched as the headliners, Prisoners of Flesh, strolled towards the bar as they left the stage. They seemed calm and collected, almost bored by the tedium.

A disembodied voice called over the loudspeakers. "All right, thanks guys, sounded great. Gimme about twenty minutes to setup for the support and opener line checks."

"This is intense," Alex said.

"That sounded fuckin' awesome," said Rust. "P.O.F. rules."

One of the members of P.O.F. smirked at the audible mention of their band in passing, causing Jesse to feel a twinge of embarrassment.

"I heard they just got signed to Metal Midnight," Alex added.

Jesse felt a heavy hand on his shoulder as Mazes' wide-eyed grin loomed from above. "It would seem that our banner rides in good company."

Rick wheeled up behind a tall, wiry middle-aged man adorned with a clean-shaven scalp. He called to the assembled members of Hell Patrol as he approached the band.

"Guys, fall in. This is Blasto, he's the tour manager for Prisoners of Flesh."

Blasto sized up the group with a scowl as he stood, arms crossed. "Jesus Christ, are you girls even old enough to bleed?"

Rick wheeled in between Blasto and his band. "Like I told the booking agent, all of our papers are in order. We are a professional outfit, and this isn't our first rodeo, so please—"

Blasto shot Rick a look fierce enough to cause his chair to wheel backwards, seemingly of its own volition.

"Please continue," Rick finished.

Blasto stepped forward and cleared his throat while tugging on his genitals in one fluid motion.

"All right ladies, this ain't no talent show. You got five minutes on either side of the set—which is exactly twenty-five minutes long—to get your shit on and off our stage. You go one minute over, and I will personally cut the power to the stage."

"Yes, sir," Alex said, licking his lips nervously.

Jesse gave Alex a slight elbow to the ribs to steady his bandmate. It felt like everywhere they went someone was trying to get them off *their* stage.

Blasto gestured towards the stage. "One more thing. See those pyro pots along the riser?"

The group nodded collectively.

"Don't even go near those," said Blasto. "They cost more than you are likely to make during the rest of your *professional* career."

Before the insult could set in, Blasto left to join the members of Prisoners of Flesh, who were sitting at the bar ordering their first of many drinks.

"What's up his ass?" asked Jesse.

"Don't let him get into your head," Rick said. "Baldness is upsetting. He's on the losing end of the hair-to-happiness ratio."

"Hair-to-happiness ratio?" Jesse asked.

"Name one bald, middle-aged dude who seems happy, as opposed to those with a luxurious head of hair?"

"Dude, you're almost as bald as that dude, and you're like half his age," said Rust.

"And do I seem happy to you? Why do you think they call me Rick the Prick?"

Rust shook his head.

"That's what I thought. But thanks anyway for the observation, Seinfeld."

2

The doors to the Beggar's Banquet Hall opened promptly at eight p.m., allowing a slow trickle of early arrivals to mill about the nearly three hundred-capacity venue.

Jesse was pacing in front of the Hell Patrol merch booth when he heard a familiar voice call out near the stage. He turned to see Mal, dragging Kara in tow, as they crossed the sparsely filled room. Her camera dangled by the strap that hung over her shoulder as she threw her arms around his neck. She held him as she took in the view of the stage.

"Well this is quite a step up. Did I miss the sound check?"

"Five steps up." Jesse pointed to the staircase on the side of the stage. "And yes, you missed all thirty seconds of it, but it's totally cool."

"Uh-oh. You're nervous aren't you?"

"Why?"

"You always make those kind of jokes when you're nervous."

"Okay, fine. I'm about to shit my pants if you must know." There was no use denying the obvious. She could see right through him.

Jesse wasn't very experienced with relationships; Mal was his first serious girlfriend. If you didn't count getting a handjob from Tracy Stephens in her tent last summer during a weekend campout at Lake Keystone, Mal was his only girlfriend.

He knew enough to know that she could read even the faintest residue of his inner dialogue just by looking into his eyes.

One glance from those witchy orbs and she had him dead to rights. Despite her being one of the few humans he treasured on this planet, he made a practice of never lying to someone who could read auras and seemed to know what he was thinking before he did.

"Just remember not to suck when you get up there, and you'll be fine."

"Thanks."

Rick regaled the new arrivals with the tale of the tour manger's dressing-down of the band while doing his best Blasto impression. The imitation was nearly discovered as the tour manager passed by Hell Patrol's merch booth.

"Five minutes," Blasto said. He tapped on his wristwatch.

As was his custom before any performance, Rick ushered the group to fall in for a brief pep talk. "Okay, so we're in a rough spot on the lineup, no bones about it. Nobody gives a shit about your set—it's the first of three on the bill—and no one has ever heard of you."

The group looked at each other uneasily, save for Mazes, who nodded in affirmation after every few words.

"The good news ... because of the many factors that I've just laid out, the pressure is off." He pushed up his large wire frames as he looked each band member in the eye. "You've already been written off, so relax and have fun. This is just another stop along the highway to hell. Now put your fists in and tear it up."

Jesse found that he was actually breathing easier after the initial sting of his brother's words had faded. He could see that the others were getting a little looser as well.

"Wish me luck up there," Jesse said.

Mal pulled him in for a kiss and whispered in his ear. "Knock 'em fucking dead."

Jesse followed the others to their dead space—a stockpile of empty guitar cases and drum covers stashed at the rear of the stage. He picked up his bass and threw it over his shoulder, warming up his fingers on the fretboard as he surveyed the sparse crowd.

The house music went down and so did the lights.

Mazes took the stage first and got behind the drum set. He stepped on his hi-hat pedal a few times as he pulled his sticks from the leather quiver on his back and adjusted the drum throne to his satisfaction.

Jesse hoped this throne would last through the set. Mazes had already burned through four of them since the band's inception. A fair portion of the band's backline funds had been put towards backup gear for the unwieldy giant. It was worth every penny. Jesse had never seen anyone play with such power and stamina.

"A band is as only as good as their drummer," Rick had said.

Jesse followed suit, taking his usual spot at stage right. He plugged in his bass and took his amp off standby. Across the floor, the sound man was giving the thumbs up from his booth.

Jesse returned the gesture and took a deep breath. *You can do this. Highway to hell and whatnot.*

"Hello, Beggar's Banquet Hall," Rust began. He threw off his shirt into the front row and shook his mane in both hands as he yelled into the mic. "We are Hell Patrol, and we'd like to thank Prisoners of Flesh for havin' us on the bill tonight." Rust pointed to the side of the stage as he continued. "And we'd also like to thank their tour manager, Blasto, for the warm reception." He carried the mic stand around the stage as he spoke to the crowd, narrowly missing one of the pyro pots that lined the drum riser.

Blasto extended his middle finger high over the audience. Jesse could see the sheen of the stage lights bouncing off the top of his shiny bald head.

Rust planted his foot on one of the wedge monitors à la Bruce Dickinson, and the band began to play.

Unlike their previous shows, Hell Patrol was now able to play mostly original songs with only a couple of choice covers peppered in throughout their set. The sonic alchemy of the set's composition had seemed to work. A small but enthusiastic crowd had lined the front of the stage by the time Hell Patrol was halfway into their set.

The rest of the set flashed by in a haze of lights and sound.

The instant the last song ended Jesse had already started to dismantle his gear. The stagehands were already hovering like vultures to wipe them clear of the stage. It had been drilled into him by his brother that only posers fuck off on stage after their set (unless you're the headliner).

He looked back at Mazes, who carried his entire drum set under one arm and Alex's guitar amp in the other. As the stage cleared, Jesse felt like the entire ordeal lasted mere seconds (after subtracting the weeks of preparation and anxiety).

To the side of the stage, Rick and Kara were busily fulfilling merch orders while Mal took shots of the action.

"Great job, rock star," Mal said. "I think I got some really great shots." She brandished her camera like it was a pistol, blowing away the imaginary smoke from its lens.

He wiped the sweat from his brow and feigned a smile. "How terrible was that?"

"Honestly, that was probably the best you guys have ever sounded."

"That's not saying a whole lot."

"I should know. I've been to all of your shows." She nudged Jesse on the arm with her fist. "Seriously, you guys killed it."

"Okay, cool," Jesse sighed. "I just felt kinda off tonight."

Mal pointed to the merch booth. "I think you actually managed to make some fans, too."

Jesse followed the line at the merch booth with his eyes.

"Hey man, good set. Where are you guys from?" The question came from one of the guitarists from Prisoners of Flesh who appeared in his field of view. The guitar player's face was partly obscured by a shock of waist-length black hair that he fanned aside as he spoke.

"Macomb Springs." The words were almost lost in Jesse's throat as he tried to recall the fundamentals of human speech.

"Hell Patrol from Macomb Springs, right on," he said, reaching for Jesse's hand. "I'm Travis."

Jesse fought for breath as he clasped the studded-leather gauntlet on Travis's forearm. "Thanks for having us, great stage."

"This place is a shithole," Travis sneered. "You should come out with us on the road sometime, then you might see a decent stage."

"Seriously?" Jesse asked. His eyes widened as he looked to Mal for confirmation that the conversation was really happening.

"Yeah, fuck it. Why not?" Travis replied. "Fucking record label is burying us with tour dates since we got signed. We can always use some fresh meat for the grinder. You got a booking agent?"

Jesse gestured to Rick, who was making change for a T-shirt order. "That's our manager—I mean he's also my brother. He does all of our booking."

Another member of Prisoners of Flesh called for Travis at the bar.

"Let's talk after the show. You guys are gonna stick around, right?"

"Yeah, definitely."

Travis ambled back towards the bar, stopping periodically to visit with friends and fans that seemed to hang on his every word.

Mal shot Jesse a look of concern. "Jesus, Jesse, are you hard?"

"Dude, that was the guitar player from Prisoners of Flesh. Alex said they just got signed to Metal Midnight—they're like one of the biggest bands on the scene." Jesse took a deep breath. "And they want us to go on the road with them."

She put her camera up in its case and tucked the strap under her arm. He felt the warmth of her fingertips as she slid her hand beneath his jeans.

"Oh my God, you are totally hard."

"Thanks for that." He laughed and gently deflected as he felt himself blush. "Come on, we should celebrate."

Mal gave him a gentle squeeze before relenting. "I hate to be a downer, but I have to get Kara home before curfew."

"But the second band hasn't even played yet, and I was really looking forward to us hanging out."

She edged up closer and pouted her lips. "I know, I'm sorry—I can tell. I promise to make it up to you. You wanna meet at the Hell Hole when you guys get back?" Her breath was warm as she whispered into his ear. "I'll make it worth your while."

"Is that cool? I know it's lame, but now I pretty much have to stick around to see those guys or they're going to think we're assholes."

"It's okay, I promise—I'll still be up." She looked down to his crotch. "And so will you, by the looks of things."

"Real funny. I'll bail now if you want… it's just that this could be a big thing for us."

"Seriously, enjoy yourself. You've earned it. Plus, I feel bad about dragging you through all my drama, lately. You've been really good to me, and I just want you to know that if you weren't around, I honestly don't know what I would do."

"That's not something you'll ever have to worry about."

They locked eyes for a moment.

"I'll see you later, just you and me, okay?"

"I'm right behind you."

She gave Jesse a parting hug and disappeared into the amassing throng.

3

Hell Patrol spent the majority of the second band's set in the back parking lot sharing kudos and a few lukewarm cans of beer that Rust had managed to pilfer from Prisoners of Flesh's green room.

Jesse relayed the conversation he had with Travis to his bandmates and Rick, who reprimanded Rust. "Knock off the bush league antics and focus on the four-octave range. We might actually have a shot at this thing here if you guys don't fuck it up."

When they returned to the stage, the crowd had gathered en masse to witness the headlining act. The lights went down as Jesse fought his way to the front row with his bandmates trailing behind him.

The restless crowd cheered in unison as the tension began to build.

A lone spotlight pierced through the darkness to reveal an elaborate stage dress depicting a post-apocalyptic prison scene. Four prison cells, comprised of spray-painted styrofoam, were erected on the fog-filled stage.

The light illuminated Travis at stage left who appeared chained to the walls of his modular cell. He appeared alone in the cell with his guitar, which he used to play a solemn chord progression, plucking the strings lightly with his fingers. Up on the stage he appeared like a Greek god, looking down on the audience from Mt. Olympus.

A second spotlight revealed yet another manacled guitarist at stage right, producing a single high note that sustained above the airy chords of Travis's rhythm guitar.

As the dual guitars built to a crescendo, a third stage light revealed the bass player within his cell. The thunderous low end pushed out through the speakers, causing the chained shackles that bound his wrists to fall apart. Jesse could feel the deep pulsing rhythm in his chest as the drums answered the call.

Finally, the lead singer emerged center stage, dressed like a skeletal prison warden, and belted out a soaring high note that swelled with vibrato until the lights went dim once again.

By the time the opening number had come to a climax, each member had broken free of their chains, and kicked down the walls of their cells.

As the stage lights came back on, the band lumbered into a tight, technical number devoid of the theatrics of the set opener.

Jesse was beside himself with how rehearsed the band sounded and their seemingly effortless musicianship.

He felt Mazes's arm wrap around his shoulders. The lumbering teen's eyes were like saucers as he howled with excitement. Jesse felt himself get lost in the moment, his life's cares washing away under the sonic assault.

Live music was the closest thing in Jesse's life that could be compared to a religious experience. He had seen his share of shows even at his young age, thanks to Rick; though for the first time in his life, he began to perceive some of the themes that he had read in Agostino's master's thesis from the perspective of a participant observer.

Through Agostino's words, he could see that all the ritual elements were present: the performative dress; the dynamic relationship between the audience and the sonic mystics who gallivanted upon the raised dais; the creation of an alternative universe that allowed all participants to transcend from the mundane, transforming the venue into a sacred space.

It was a gathering of worship in the purest sense, absent gods or kings. Just people—united together in their commonly held love of perhaps the one benevolent creation humanity could offer the universe: music. And for Jesse and his friends, that music was *heavy fucking metal.*

He felt healed. He felt complete. But more than that, he knew in his heart of hearts that he was now tied to the mast on the sonic odyssey that would define his life's journey.

4

Back at the Hell Hole, Jesse found Mal's instructions scribbled on a note that was wedged in between the bars of the wrought iron gate. ROCK STAR GROUPIE, THIS WAY.

He passed through the mine entrance and followed the soft glow of candlelight into the control room. Inside, a sleeping bag was stretched out in the middle of a fresh chalk pentagram. "Black

No. 1 (Little Miss Scare-All)," *from the album* Bloody Kisses *by Type O Negative, released in 1993 on Roadrunner Records*, was playing on a small, blood-red cassette/FM-radio player set atop the bank of gutted consoles.

Jesse found an unused candle that lay on the floor next to Mal's backpack. He lit the candle from one of the half-melted others that made up the points of the pentagram, and headed back out into the mine's central corridor.

Seeing no sign of Mal between the entrance and the control room, Jesse decided to follow along the rail track that snaked through the central tunnel. The air was stale and damp as he headed farther along the track.

The cart was still there, and much to Jesse's relief, empty. He tried to shake the memory of Halloween night as he ventured deeper into the mine.

As he passed the rusty metal cart, he called out for her, half expecting to see the flash from her camera answer back. Instead, the empty tunnel echoed her name drenched in the growing desperation of his voice.

He ventured deeper still, towards the beginnings of a noticeable descent in the track when he heard a slight rustling coming from up ahead.

As he took another step forward, the flickering candlelight revealed a grey, scaly tail that quickly slithered away into the darkness. Jesse uttered a sigh of relief as a rat squealed in protest of his pursuit.

As he came to the end of the track, the soft, orange glow from the candle reflected off a small, silver object at the edge of the light's radius.

He could hear the hum of the battery-operated flash charging up on the camera as he drew nearer. The lens cap had been removed, but was still held attached to the lens by its lanyard. He slung the camera strap over his shoulder and continued into the darkness that lay ahead.

"Mal! I got your camera. Where the hell are you?"

The track dead-ended at the mouth of a large chasm surrounded by piles of rubble and fallen debris. Jesse was suddenly reminded of the dream he had had about Rick standing across the mouth of a similar opening in the ground without the aid of his chair.

A towering winch apparatus was stationed next to a crumpled shack that stood on its last legs across from what remained of a rail switch station near the end of the track. The winch craned over the edge of the vast opening, whose depths reached well beyond the light of the candle.

"Very funny," Jesse said. "You can come out now, you got me." The words were tossed into the abyss of the dark pit below with no response, as before. No longer amused, Jesse headed back towards the entrance.

He searched the woods surrounding the mine and everything in between the Hell Hole and the control room three times before he decided to search elsewhere. The pale moon guided his path as he hurried through the woods that separated the Old Townsite from the rural parcel of land that defined his grandparents' homestead to the north.

After a quick search of the practice trailer proved fruitless, Jesse scratched out a note to Mal and laid it on the kitchen table next to her camera.

He sprinted all the way from the trailer to Mal's street.

Her house was dark, save for the flickering of the television set through the living room window. He could see Frank's silhouette stationed at his usual post on the couch.

The kick drum in his chest started beating a little faster as the incessant knocking on her bedroom window went unanswered. He pushed up on the outer windowpane, which eventually relented, and crawled inside the room. Inside the darkened room he fumbled for the lamp that he knew to be near her bed.

The room was empty.

He searched the rest of the house with no sign of Mal. Finally, he stormed into the living room. The theme to *The Tonight Show Starring Johnny Carson* was blaring at full volume. Frank was slumped over on the couch with a beer in his hand.

"Frank," Jesse called. "Hey Frank!" The words were lost in the noise of the television and the snoring coming from the couch. "It's Jesse. I'm trying to find Mal. I think something might have happened to her."

Jesse threw an empty can at the pile of beers that circled the TV tray in front of the couch, causing an avalanche of aluminum to fall into Frank's lap.

Frank shot up, knocking over the TV tray, and lunged towards the intruder. He began screaming incoherently at Jesse, who despite all efforts to calm the man, was pushed aside as Frank reached for the wall-mounted shotgun above the mantel.

The TV was knocked on its side in the scuffle. A burst of applause from the studio audience rang out as the TV flickered on and off, creating a strobe-like effect that cast disorienting shadows across the living room walls.

Jesse was reaching for a light switch as the sound of the shotgun blast filled his ears. The kickback from the weapon's discharge sent Frank careening backwards over the coffee table.

A burst of high-frequency sonic needles stabbed Jesse's ears with such intensity that he almost didn't notice the dull, creeping pain in his right shoulder. Out of the corner of his eye, he could see a ring of chrome BBs lodged in his jean jacket, illuminated by the light of the television set. It was the last thing he saw before his vision faded.

5

Jesse came to when the cops arrived. They had stormed into the living room and placed him in cuffs before he could say a word.

He winced at the throbbing pain in his shoulder as they donned the restraints. Luckily, the birdshot had not fully penetrated the denim of his jean jacket, but it still hurt like hell.

Frank was snoring audibly, his legs draped over the coffee table, the shotgun across his chest.

One of the officers, a rotund specimen with a thinning comb-over, was rifling through Jesse's wallet while he talked into his shoulder-mounted radio handset. "Officer Jenkins to dispatch. Dispatch, we're on the scene of the shots-fired call. Looks like we got a home invasion at the Henderson place out on Scissortail Drive. One seventeen-year-old suspect in custody, last name Lynn."

"Dispatch confirmed. You need backup, Marcus?" the voice responded over the radio.

"Negative dispatch, situation under control."

"Looks like one of those punk kids from the high school," said the other policeman, who appeared to be Jenkins's junior by several years. Jesse could make out the last name WARREN on the name tag pinned just above the right-breast pocket of the officer's uniform. "Lucky he didn't get his head blown clean off."

"Might be one of the perps that lit the fire at the church by the looks of him," Officer Jenkins said. "You wouldn't know anything about that, would you son?"

"I was just looking for my girlfriend. This is her house," Jesse managed. "Please, her name is Mal—Mallory Henderson. We were supposed to meet up tonight, but she didn't show, and I think something happened to her."

Officer Jenkins was trying to rouse Frank with smelling salts. "Save it for the judge, kid."

Officer Warren hoisted Jesse up off the ground and marched him into the squad car that was idling out front.

Muffled shouts came from inside the squad car that appeared to already be occupied.

"Must be the full moon," laughed the younger officer as he opened the back passenger door. "I'm sure you two have a lot to talk about."

Jesse was shoved next to a disheveled-looking man in the back seat who reeked of alcohol. A secondary stench emanated from the vagrant who, in a spate of worsening fortune, appeared to have recently soiled himself.

"That's how they hypnotize you, man. They hypnotize you with that noise," he said. "The sound is power—raw power used to keep you down, man." He gestured despite his bindings to the pair of headphones draped around his neck. "They couldn't get to me because I know how to fool them."

The smell of the vagrant's breath directed into Jesse's face caused his stomach to turn as he waited for the ride to the station.

6

After several hours of interrogation, Jesse managed to avoid a slew of felony charges including, but not limited to breaking and entering, burglary, and criminal trespassing. Luckily, the Reynolds name still retained some measure of respect in the small community of Macomb Springs; a community that Jesse's grandparents had helped to build.

Randy was pacing in the station's waiting room when Jesse was released from custody. His mother was too upset to wait inside. She sat in silence on the drive home.

When they arrived back home, Randy was visibly shaken. He grabbed Jesse by the wrist, hard.

"You're not off the hook, young'un. You and I are gonna have a nice long talk in the mornin'."

It was the first time Jesse could recall Randy ever laying a hand on him.

Jesse went to his room without another word and succumbed to the exhaustion delivered by the night's events.

7

In the days after the news of Mal's disappearance—one of now six missing persons that had been reported within the community—Macomb Springs High had undergone many changes.

Principal Anderson had unveiled a new dress code forbidding any articles of clothing affiliated with the Parental Music Resource Center's (PMRC) filthy fifteen—a list of "porn rock" recording artists deemed vulgar and obscene by the organization.

Jesse was intimately familiar with the list; it included some of his favorite artists: Judas Priest, Mercyful Fate, Black Sabbath, Venom, etc. It was one of Rick's favorite anti-establishment topics. Jesse had been subjected to many of his brother's tirades detailing, at length, the many transgressions of Tipper Gore and Susan Baker, founders of the PMRC.

Another equally nauseating development of Macomb Springs High's newfound austerity was a regular morning prayer given by MSCOC's own Pastor Seth Roberts. Each morning, the prayer was piped into each classroom over the school's intercom system to a captive audience of increasingly anxious teenagers.

Jesse cringed at the cadence of the canned speech, whose contents would often detail upcoming events at the church that targeted his peers.

He was particularly alarmed at the mention of a "Community Cleansing" that was to be held in the church parking lot over the upcoming Thanksgiving holiday break. The pastor encouraged the students to join members of the church in bringing records, tapes, and clothing deemed to possess satanic influence to be publicly destroyed.

Between classes, Jesse noted the appearance of several posters detailing the church-sponsored call to action that had been placed throughout the school.

He found Kara poring over one of the Community Cleansing flyers that had been stuffed into each students' lockers.

"You believe this shit?" she asked, handing him the flyer. "The whole town has gone batshit fucking crazy."

Jesse nodded as he stared blankly at the flyer.

"Hey." Kara's voice lowered as she put her hand on Jesse's shoulder. "How are you holding up, Jess?"

He shied away from her change in tone and the obligation of making direct eye contact. Sleep had not come easy in the two days since Mal had disappeared, and he knew he must look the part.

"Actually, I could use a favor." Jesse pulled out Mal's camera from his backpack. "Can you develop what's on here?"

Kara's smile faded.

"Oh Jess, whatever is going on with her, it's not about you, I promise. Like I already told you—this is total Mal, like to a tee." The arc of her smile lined up with the corners of the cat-eye glasses she wore. Jesse felt almost convinced by her words the more she spoke. She shooed away the camera, taking a step back. "Not to mention she would murder me if I ever touched her baby."

"I know we've already gone over it, but were you able to think of anything else she said that night that seemed out of the ordinary? Anything at all?"

Kara shook her head sympathetically. "Like I told you, she seemed fine when she dropped me off after the show, but that can change really quickly with her. Especially lately."

"Look. I'm not trying to freak out, I promise." Jesse's voice began to falter despite himself. "It's just getting a little hard to ignore all the fucked-up shit happening around here."

"It's not the first time she's ditched. She'll be back. She probably just needed to blow off some steam." Kara slammed her locker. "If that asshole was my dad, I'd have checked out a long time ago."

"I know—I get it. But leaving the way she did doesn't make any sense. Not like this." He held up the camera once more for emphasis. "You and I both know she wouldn't leave it behind. What if something happened? Something out of her control?"

"Jesse…"

"Just humor me, will you? I'm losing my fucking mind, here." He handed Kara the camera. "Maybe something on there can give us a clue."

Kara hesitated, then finally relented. "Okay. But just because I'm helping you get some peace of mind doesn't mean anything bad has happened to her, all right? I'm not ready to go there yet." She held the camera with reverence before gently tucking it into her backpack. "I have darkroom time during fourth period. Meet me in the studio during lunch."

"Thank you."

Kara tugged on his sleeve as she was about to part ways. "You need to know that she is totally into you. I've never seen her so happy. Like genuinely happy for the first time in, like, forever."

The ring of the class bell emptied the crowded hall.

Jesse felt an incredible weight pushing him down with each step he took towards his next class. He decided under the circumstances that it was better for his sanity to skip the next two class periods. Kara ought to be done developing the film in Mal's camera by then.

8

A lone security guard patrolled the edge of the school property bordering on the surrounding forest. Jesse watched from the edge of the student parking lot until the coast was clear.

Unsure of his destination, he found himself walking through the woods towards the Old Townsite, recalling the treasure trove of private moments he and Mal had shared as they searched for an escape from the outside world.

Everywhere, a ghost of her memory.

When he reached the gravel drive that overlooked the mine, he stopped to pack an unopened soft pack of Camel Lights before making his way down to the Hell Hole.

He was relieved to hear Rust and Alex's voices as he approached. Alex was running his hands over the short bristles that lined his scalp. His long, shoulder-length hair had disappeared overnight. A stiff cardigan sweater and brown corduroy pants completed the ensemble.

"Holy shit," said Jesse. He tossed down his backpack as he stared at Alex in disbelief.

"You believe this shit?" Rust threw his hands up at Jesse. "Fuckin' square-cut here is gonna make us look like a bunch of dopes at our next show."

"I told you, man! There's not going to be a next show." Alex nervously bit his bottom lip with his large front teeth as he spoke. "My parents flipped out and threatened to kick me out of the house if I don't straighten up."

Jesse felt crushed beneath the weight of his crumbling universe; it seemed hell-bent on collapsing further on top of him with each passing moment.

"Dude, you make straight As," Rust said.

"I just have to put up with their shit until graduation. Then I'll be out of here."

"What about the band? What are we gonna do without a guitar player, or a van? We're supposed to hit the road with P.O.F. in like three weeks."

"What do you want me to do? I can't just drop out of school like you."

Rust lit a cigarette and paced around the archway. "That's a fucked-up thing to say, man."

"Maybe they'll chill out when all this blows over," Jesse said.

"This ain't gonna blow over, man. There's already a half-dozen people in town that are either missing or dead, not to mention two of them used to go to our school." Alex grimaced as the words left his mouth. He looked up at Jesse. "I'm sorry, man, I didn't mean —"

"It's okay," finished Jesse.

The three lingered in silence for a time.

"It's not the first time she's run away," said Rust.

"That's what everyone keeps telling me."

Rust offered Jesse a nod of solidarity before turning his attention back to Alex.

"This is a once-in-a-lifetime opportunity to hit the road with those guys." Rust knelt directly in front of Alex and forced him to meet his eyes. "Are you gonna be able to look back when you're on your deathbed, years from now, and be cool with the fact that you bailed on us because you were worried about what your fuckin' parents think? You think you can live with that shit?"

Jesse felt cast off from the shore, slowly circling in a massive whirlpool that threatened to drown all that he held dear.

"I love playing music with you guys, but this shit is getting out of hand." He wiped his runny nose on the sleeve of the cardigan sweater. "Besides, maybe I've got other shit I want to do with my life."

"So—what? The band is over? We're calling it quits? You're not even eighteen years old! What's the rush? Don't buy into the bullshit, man. Like Rick always says, it's just hysteria whipped up by these Jesus freaks to bring more people into the church so they can fill their coffers."

"Then why are all these people missing? Why the fuck don't we know where Mal is?" Alex asked. He stood up and threw his boombox against the iron gate. Shards from the unit's grey plastic body splintered into the air. Alex pointed through the gate as he looked to the others. "And what the fuck happened to us down there?"

"I don't know, but I'm going to find out," Jesse said. He grabbed his backpack and set off to make the trek back to the school.

9

Jesse made his way back to Macomb Springs High just before lunch. As he approached the photography lab, the red warning light above the door was turned on.

Kara's voice answered back as he knocked on the door.

"Just a minute," she said.

Just as the door to the photo lab cracked open, he was pulled inside by his jacket collar. He heard the door lock behind him.

"This way," Kara's voice called out from the dark.

Once his eyes adjusted, he followed her to the back of the room as she guided him through the heavy plastic partitions.

As Jesse stepped into the safe light, he could see that Kara had been hard at work. Several prints were line-drying above a row of trays filled with chemical solutions. Even in the faint red light, he could clearly make out the images from the night of Hell Patrol's Beggar's Banquet Hall show.

Kara reached to stop a buzzing timer while she passed a developing print from one tray to another with a pair of tongs.

The acrid smell of the chemicals hung heavy in Jesse's nostrils.

"Okay, so I just finished developing the photos from your show—which, turns out, was most of the roll." She hesitated. "There are still a few frames left, but I couldn't make anything out from the contact print, so I'm not holding out much hope."

"Thanks for doing this. I had to be sure."

"I'm developing the last of the prints now." She spoke while trying to force the usual lilt in her voice. "We'll be able to see them in just a sec."

They watched together as the image slowly materialized on the pristine white photographic paper.

At first, Jesse had difficulty orienting the frame in his mind.

"Wait a minute," Kara said. "This looks like the inside of the mine. At least what I can remember of it. Drunkest Halloween, ever."

"That's the control room," said Jesse as he pored over the image. Mal had taken the time to document the room she had made up for them—the place where they were supposed to be together after the show. It meant something to her. So much so that she had taken a picture of it, to preserve the moment. *Why didn't I just leave with you? Just please be okay, and I promise I'll never do anything that fucking stupid or selfish again.*

"That's weird," Kara said. "What time did you say it was when you got there?"

"Probably around one in the morning." Jesse shrugged. "Why?"

"She dropped me off just after eleven p.m. I'm sure of it because my parents are Nazis about getting home an hour before curfew."

"What's your point?"

"Look at the candles."

The candles that comprised the pentagram were recently lit, having not melted down at the time the photo was taken.

"When I got there they were still lit—melted down at least a few inches. I remember lighting a candle off one of them so I could go look for her."

"So we know that she must have stayed up there for at least a little while before you showed up. It's not like her to leave a bunch of lit candles lying around. She spends a fortune on those things."

"Good catch."

Kara left Jesse to inspect the print as she moved it from the second tray labeled STOP BATH to the third and final tray labeled FIXER.

"How many frames are left on the roll?"

"Just two more. Shouldn't take long."

Jesse examined the prints that were drying on the line while he waited. He felt envious of the young man that bore his likeness. The fleeting moments enjoyed by his former self stood frozen in time, mocking him from the safe harbor of the past.

Being able to chart the passage of time made life seem so delicate. So unpredictable. He had moved to this new place with no aspirations, simply adrift on the cosmic winds that propelled him forward. And now he had everything to lose.

Images of the past projected onto the surrounding canvas of darkness—an overflow of despair that tumbled forth from his shattered mind. The first time he saw her in the shadows of the derelict ranch house; the first kiss; the endearing, but bullshit séances that he didn't quite buy into; the first time they made love. All the missing pieces that made the uncertainty of life tolerable, and without that anchor, the ballast that kept him on course within a churning sea of chaos, there was only shivering, cold madness.

"Here's another one from inside the mine," Kara reported. She transferred the print to the sink to rinse off the chemicals.

In the image Jesse could make out the mine cart in the foreground and the portion of the rail cart track beyond that led deeper towards the descending vertical shaft.

"Looks like she was using the flash on this one," she said as she positioned the safe light a little closer.

In the upper half of the frame Jesse could make out little pinpoints of light that stood out against the surrounding darkness.

"What the hell is that?"

"I dunno. Could be some kind of overexposure caused by the flash, or a lens flare," Kara said. She fished out the print once it was processed, shook it dry, and handed it to Jesse.

He rotated the image, desperate to make sense of the anomaly. Once fully inverted, the image revealed three distinct shapes that emerged from the visual noise of the dimly lit photograph.

As his mind ordered the information, Jesse could see that the pinpoints of light were actually several pairs of eyes reflecting back the camera flash like the eyeshine of a cat, or a skunk, or some other nocturnal creature caught in the headlights during a nighttime drive.

"Stray dog, my ass."

"What is it?"

"You tell me." He held the photo up to the safe light, pointing out the distinct outlines of three impish, simian-looking creatures, climbing upside down on the tunnel ceiling above the rail cart track.

"Oh my God."

"Quick. What's on the last frame?"

Kara set up the enlarger for another print. After a brief exposure of light through the mounted negative, she placed another piece of photo paper into the first tray and began developing the last image Mal had taken with her camera.

Again they watched with bated breath as an image began to form from the layer of emulsion that lined the paper as it soaked in the tray.

Kara huddled over the image as she ran it through the succession of chemicals and water bath.

"I can't see shit," she said, holding the image up to the red safe light. "Let's take a look at this one under the glass." She turned on a nearby light box and ran a magnifying loupe over the image.

"Something did happen to us down there," Jesse said as he paced back and forth. "I fucking knew it."

Kara furrowed her brow as she examined the image. "Oh Jesus Christ, Jesse," she muttered, visibly shaken. She pushed away the loupe as though it burned her skin, and turned to Jesse with a look of disbelief.

Jesse jumped to take her place, scrambling to line up the loupe on top of the photograph.

From the dark abyss, a discernible shape had materialized within the void of the mine shaft. An almost imperceptible shadow exhibited the grotesque profile of a great horned beast that emerged from the surrounding darkness. The light from the flash reflected off the tip of what appeared to be an ornate crown that rested atop the figure's skull.

"What the fuck do we do?" sobbed Kara.

He gathered up the photographs and put them in his backpack. Before leaving the darkroom, he placed both hands on Kara's shoulders and looked her dead in the eyes. "You can't tell anyone about this," he pleaded. "Not until you hear back from me, okay?"

Kara nodded, dazedly. "Where are you going?"

Jesse turned on his heels as he passed through the doorway. "I'm late for an appointment with my guidance counselor."

10

Jesse left the darkroom and waded into the bustling corridor that had filled with students returning from lunch hour.

"Mr. Lynn." Principal Anderson's voice stopped him in his tracks. "I think it's about time we had a little chat."

He turned to see the principal flanked by two police officers. He recognized Officer Jenkins and Officer Warren from the night he took a shell of birdshot from Frank's shotgun.

A throng of onlookers had gathered to watch as Jesse was escorted to the principal's office. The procession cut through the crowded hall amid a wash of whispers and slack-jawed stares.

As Jesse entered the school's administrative suite, Grace Johnson stood from her seat behind the front counter and made the sign of the cross as he passed.

Principal Anderson ushered the escort into her office and closed the door behind them. Officer Jenkins stood with his back against the door; Officer Warren hovered over Jesse as he took a seat in front of Principal Anderson's desk.

The principal spoke with the beginnings of a wry grin. "I've had the honor of being principal of this school for over fifteen years." She let the words linger in the air before she continued. "Sounds like a long time when you say it out loud, doesn't it?"

Jesse stared straight ahead, trying to ignore the police officers' piercing gaze.

"During this time, I've worked hard to cultivate a sense of community that extends beyond the walls of this fine institution." She opened her arms to gesture towards the police officers who stood idly by. "And I think we have achieved that."

The officers nodded.

"I would do almost anything to see that legacy preserved," Principal Anderson said. "Right now, ours is a community in crisis. But that's where you come in, Mr. Lynn. I think you can help this community a great deal. Would you help us, Mr. Lynn?"

As Jesse looked around the room, he suddenly began to feel like a sick gazelle, caught out in the open savannah, surrounded by a pride of hungry lions.

"I suppose by now you must have heard about the incident at the Macomb Springs Church of Christ lock-in that took place during the evening of October thirty-first?"

Jesse nodded.

"What you might not have heard is that Pastor Seth Roberts is planning on pressing charges on the perpetrators of these crimes." She turned to Officer Jenkins. "Please remind me of those charges again, Marcus?"

The heavyset officer looked down at Jesse as he pushed back his combover. "Malicious mischief, for starters. We're also looking at attempted fourth-degree arson, among other things."

"These are very serious charges, Mr. Lynn. We will not tolerate this type of behavior here at Macomb Springs High," Principal Anderson scolded. "If any of our students are found to have any involvement with these heinous acts, they will be expelled immediately."

Jesse returned a blank stare.

"Mr. Lynn, do you know anything about this incident?"

"No, ma'am."

"What about the whereabouts of Mr. Russell Krokowski?"

"Last I heard, he dropped out of school."

Principal Anderson opened her desk drawer and pulled out a crumpled flyer. Jesse cringed when he saw the Hell Patrol logo. It was a play off the *Priest...Live!* album cover, designed for the Prisoners of Flesh gig at the Beggar's Banquet Hall. Rick's idea.

"It has come to my attention that you and Mr. Krokowski are more closely acquainted than you are leading us to believe. In fact, it looks as though you even play together in some sort of satanic rock band. Would that be an accurate assessment of the facts?"

Jesse felt his skin turn hot. "Look. Nobody really worships the devil. Satan sells. And you'll be happy to know that the band broke up." Jesse threw his arms up in the air. "I don't know where Rust—where Russell is, okay? Can I go now?"

"I'm happy to hear it." The principal looked to the two officers and then leaned back in her chair as she continued the interrogation. "Given your recent brush with the law, and the fact that you are now a person of interest in not one, but two missing persons cases, I would be sure to be on your best behavior, Mr. Lynn. We'll be keeping an eye on you."

11

Jesse found Mr. Agostino in his office, engrossed in a book as he chewed an apple. The guidance counselor looked up from the page and scrambled for his glasses as Jesse burst into the room and slammed shut the door behind him.

"Mr. Lynn! To what do I owe this pleasant surprise?"

"I have to show you something, and it's going to sound crazy, but I have nowhere else to turn."

Agostino picked up his glasses from the desk and began to clean them on his sleeve. "Please, call me Vincent."

"Vincent." Jesse slammed down the handful of photographs on his desk. "You said I can come to you with anything, right?"

"Of course," Agostino absently replied as he shuffled through the stack of photographs.

"Well, right now I need someone to tell me what the fuck is going on around here. And I think you know."

PART III

EPILOGUE

Vincent and his older brother Henry were sparring in the weapons room when their father entered, carrying a heavy book under one arm and leaning on a cane with the other.

"Pardon the interruption to your training, but it is time for a reading. Now that you are both of age, I am prepared to reveal a more advanced synthesis from the *Compendium*—one with more *adult* themes."

"If this is the one I think it is, you're a little too late," Henry laughed. He bobbed and weaved in front of his brother. "Vinny reads it to himself every night before he goes to bed, if you catch my drift."

Vincent punched Henry in the gut, sending both brothers wrestling to the ground.

"That's enough!" Vincent's father shouted. "I'm trying to teach you to become men, so stop acting like boys." His cheeks reddened and he became short of breath, taking a seat on a cushioned weight bench.

The brothers rose to their feet.

"Soon the fate of our organization will rest on your shoulders. Such a great responsibility cannot be trusted to children. There is too much at stake."

"Sorry, dad," Henry said, removing his sparring helmet. "I was just messing around with Vinny."

"Apologies, father," Vincent said. "Is everything all right?"

Vincent's father sat the book on the bench and removed his glasses, squeezing the bridge of his nose between his thumb and index finger.

"A quickening is on the horizon. It is my belief that all the prognostications and prophecies that we have been researching up to now all herald this event. We must be prepared to contend with what may very well be the greatest threat we have faced in our history."

"We'll be ready. Ready to kick some ass," Henry said as he threw a one-two combo into the air.

Vincent nodded.

"I hope you are right," Vincent's father said. His eyes became distant as he appeared to size up the two brothers. "All right then, enough lamentation," he said as he opened the book in his lap. "More than mere hormone-inducing masturbation fodder, this is a story of accepting the responsibility of one's true calling, and following it wherever it leads."

Vincent blushed as he met his father's eyes.

"To do so requires one to shed the skin of adolescence, and to don the mantle of manhood. Do you understand?"

"Yes, sir," the brothers said in unison.

"Very well," said Vincent's father. "Try to refrain from indulging your baser instincts, and, instead, focus on the ultimate message of the synthesis."

☩ ☩ ☩

Seth fidgeted in his desk as his younger sister, Laura, read the final verse of scripture. Her slow, faltering speech grated at his ears as she fumbled over the words of the sacred texts.

"'I will n-never again p-pass by them. The high p-places of Isaac sh-sh-shall be made desolate, and the sanctuaries of Israel shall be l-laid waste.'" She swung her feet as she read, creating a pair of identical ovular depressions in the dirt floor beneath the hand-carved school desk from which her legs dangled. "'And I will r-rise against the house of Jeroboam with the s-sword.'"

Seth loathed the fact that being the eldest of seven meant he was the last to conduct a divine reading. Having to endure several hours of his younger siblings butchering the scripture was one thing. It was another to do so while confined to the half-century-old hardwood desk that pushed the ill-fitting brace up over his shoulders, causing burning hot embers of pain to smolder between his hips and shoulder blades.

The brace was provided by one of the visiting missionary doctors who had passed through Temple's Bend when Seth was a child.

One of the last of the "outsiders" allowed entry to the mission, the doctor was a small, shriveled man who wore the same frumpy linen suit day after day. Seth could recall the doctor's kind eyes, often filled with pity when they fell upon him.

Since the Revival, the mission had retreated into itself, shuttering its doors to the outside world. Seth was forced to contend with the aging lattice of steel rods and leather straps that ran the length of his spine—an arcane device he had long outgrown since entering adolescence.

He could weather the pain; he had lived with it most of his life. Although his body had succumbed prematurely to an earthly affliction, his primary concern was the ultimate destination of his eternal soul.

The words carry no comfort today. No meaning. Only pain, Seth thought to himself.

The words are false. Better to rip the crooked tongue from her mouth and end it now than spend another minute trapped in this fucking torture device. The voice whispered to him from the deepest and darkest recesses of his mind—a place he had not known to exist until recently.

"Well done, Laura." The words came from his father, a stern-faced man with deep, sorrowful lines etched beneath his eyes and mouth. He stood from his chair at the head of the sweltering classroom with the help of a cane. Droplets of perspiration trickled down his brow, saturating the unruly thickets of his eyebrows. "Your tongue is feeble, but your memory is strong." He took the Bible from her desk and placed it in front of Seth.

Seth opened the well-worn tome to his prescribed reading, marked by a purple ribbon. Each of the children were assigned their own colored ribbons based on their age and ascendancy on the path to righteousness. He set aside the frayed piece of cloth and read aloud from the passage. The words REVELATION TO JOHN were writ in bold black letters at the top of the page.

He continued to read, regurgitating the passage until he came upon the final words marked REVELATION 22:21.

Seth cleared his throat and held his father in his gaze as he recited the final words from memory. "The grace of the Lord Jesus be with God's people. Amen."

His father gave a solemn nod. "Thank you, Seth. The Lord has blessed us." He bowed his head and led a prayer. "Today marks an auspicious end to our eldest son's journey through the scripture among his kin. Please continue to guide our righteous flock into your kingdom, Amen." The old man stood and retrieved the heavy, leather-bound book, tucking it under his arm. "Now, run and clean yourselves in the bend, and be sure to lend a hand with the chores before supper."

"In Jesus's name," squeaked Michael, the youngest of the brood.

The outburst was followed with a resolute "Amen" from all in attendance.

The youngest siblings had already breached the wood-plank door by the time Seth was able to stretch his legs from the confines of the ramshackle school desk. He exited the schoolhouse with his father and latched the door from the outside.

"A penny for your thoughts?" asked his father.

Seth felt the intrusive words burn through his thoughts like molten steel before he could douse them with reason. *I'd like to run a prod up your ass for every time you've laid hands on me, you rotten sonofabitch.*

Enough. The man is our father.

Seth weighed his truth in his mind for several moments before uttering it aloud. "I believe I am experiencing a crisis of faith."

"We wouldn't be men of faith if we didn't experience doubt from time to time," his father said. "Let us witness."

After a silent prayer, Seth felt obliged to continue. "I have had moments of doubt, father. This is different." Seth felt his eyes take on water. "Sometimes I feel a presence inside me—a dark presence, one that questions my faith and drives me towards temptation and unclean thoughts."

"Have you acted on these compulsions?" asked his father.

"No, sir."

Lies.

Seth's father sighed with relief at the news. "We've tried to teach you children that Satan is a powerful force. I know it can sometimes be difficult to fathom that such evil can exist in the world, especially when you are looking out from the safe haven of Temple's Bend." His father spoke in slow, deliberate phrasing—a convention developed from his many years as pastor. "We must remain vigilant in this war, my son. The devil is on the hunt for our very souls, and he never tires or falters in his quest." The elder masked the glare of the sun from his eyes and gestured down the hill towards the bend. "Go mind your flock, eldest. We can talk more after supper if you like."

Seth traversed the well-trodden dirt road that ran from the hilltop compound—an infrastructure consisting of three familial residences, a communal barn for livestock, a school house, and a tall, though narrow, white-walled chapel erected on the highest point of the hill.

Several of the mission wives were gathered on the edge of the river bank. Rows of woven baskets lined the bank, each piled high with dirty linens. The mission wives shared the news of the day as they washed, all the while keeping a watchful eye on the younger children who bathed in the bend. Seth enjoyed listening to the wives' idle chatter in the same manner he enjoyed listening to the birds sing, though he would never engage in such excessive speech.

The children cleaned themselves in the soapy runoff of hand-washed linens that radiated out into the bend from the bank. Seth joined in the watch as his siblings tore off their hand-stitched garments and immersed themselves in the tea-colored water.

Seth's youngest brother, Michael, was already fast at work chasing a cluster of dragonflies as they deftly maneuvered between the row of cypress trees that emerged from the shallow depths of the bend.

He abandoned the urge to scold his brother, as bathing in the gentle shallows of the bend were one of the rare outlets for play within the mission. Few things could withstand the strictures of mission life. A child's indomitable spirit was one of them. He took off his hard leather boots, rolled up his britches, and decided to indulge in the cool waters himself.

Today he had completed a momentous rite of passage.

Seth recalled the tales of traveling missionaries who regaled his kin with stories of modern conveniences such as refrigeration and air conditioning. The crisp waters of the Trinity River were all the respite from the oppressive summer heat he would need—a gift provided by God's bountiful earth.

Why not fully embrace your God's bounty? Just slip beneath the waters, and spare yourself a life of pain and suffering.

A shrill cry perforated the sound of splashing and gleeful laughter that filled his ears. Mary, his second eldest sister, was jumping up and down and pointing frantically downstream. Before he could comprehend her movements, he saw his youngest brother Michael, bobbing up and down in the murky waters, gasping for breath.

Seth ran out farther into the bend until the waters reached above his waist. He flailed his hands and called out to his little brother. "Michael! Move your arms! Swim to the other side!"

He knew that if his brother, barely more than a toddler, could not cross the waters soon there would be trouble. Michael was being pulled into the outflow. Soon he would be lost in the swifter-moving currents that defined the middle course of the Trinity River.

Seth lost sight of his brother in the ensuing chaos.

He wrenched off the cumbersome back brace and dove head first into the body of the river where he had last seen Michael. As he rounded the calmer waters of the bend, he could feel the force of the current sweep him out farther downstream.

The act of swimming was unbearable, though nothing would compare to seeing the pain in his mother's eyes if Michael was swallowed by the Trinity. Because of his ailment, he had not swum the river in several years, a fact his atrophied muscles could attest to as the pull of the current became stronger.

Stop fighting. It is better this way. End it now!

The words, no longer a whisper but a shout, clawed from the darkness and raked against the walls of his skull as he fought for breath. He sank deeper into the greenish-brown murk where he found himself surrounded by an impenetrable darkness. With limbs frozen in fatigue, his mind raced with a panic that filled every molecule of his being, desperate to stir his broken body into motion.

It is better this way.

The voice was calm. Almost peaceful.

Seth felt himself drift away just as a strong, vice-like grip pulled him to the surface, sending explosions of pain down his crooked spine as he was lifted from the waters and carried towards the bank.

He expelled the sour, fishy water from his lungs and fell on his back, crawling away from the river's edge. A figure stood over him, casting from beneath the glaring sun a silhouette of a man wearing a long beard and long, flowing hair.

And now, the time of your judgment is at hand, sinner.

The silhouette was soon joined by several others who stood huddled over Seth. One of the figures spoke as a hand was extended towards him. "Thought we almost lost you there, man."

Seth took the young man's outstretched hand and was pulled up into a seated position.

His eyes immediately went to his brother Michael, who was being held in the lap of a sun-kissed young girl, barely older than Seth, wearing cut-off jean shorts and a bikini top.

Another woman, some years older and wearing a long, flowing bandana, was rubbing a towel over Michael's hair. She stopped periodically to kiss him on the cheek and offer a soothing whisper. Seth could see the outline of her bare breasts beneath the open robe she wore.

Seth looked on in shock as women were joined in the waters by young men who brandished their genitalia openly, almost proudly, as they jumped off the rocky cliffs that lined the opposite side of the river. Everywhere he looked, the waters were teeming with scantily clad youth.

Strange music exploded from the open windows of a parked van whose side door was ajar. Through the beaded curtain that lined the open doorway, Seth caught a glimpse of a couple having intercourse. He watched as they continued their lovemaking, hypnotized by the pounding rhythm of their flesh as it intertwined, oblivious to the others that had gathered to observe the newcomers pulled from the river.

The surrounding voices echoed through his ears as though from a distance.

Seth gathered his wits and realized he had not been deposited at the gates of heaven, but had instead washed upon the shores of a modern-day Sodom and Gomorrah, a hedonistic bacchanal, rife with wanton carnality.

"Hey, dude, are you all right?" asked one of the gathered throng.

"We need to get him some dry clothes. He's probably in shock," another voice called.

Bolts of electricity shot across his back as someone slipped a T-shirt over his head. He looked down at the shirt, too numb to recoil from the image of the five snarling faces that stared back. The figure in the center foreground held a barbed tail in his hand

and appeared to possess horns that protruded from his forehead. Above, the words HIGHWAY TO HELL seemed to claw at Seth's very soul, confirming his intuition.

"Hey, man, where'd you all come from? Do you live around here?" asked one of the silhouettes.

"I think they might be from that mission upriver that Riley was telling us about."

Seth turned his attention back to his brother. The sun-kissed girl in the bikini top and her robed companion looked at Seth uneasily as they conversed in hushed tones.

"Oh, shit, you mean like one of those Jonestown cults?"

"Yeah man. The place is a freakin' time capsule, totally cut off. Should we go tell someone?"

An empty beer can was hurled against the side of the van as someone called out, "Hey give it a rest, will ya? We got kids out here."

A voluptuous female parted the beaded curtain, whipping her long, blonde hair back over her shoulders as she cupped her breasts for all to see. She cast a devilish grin towards Seth, flicking her rose-pink nipples with her thumbs in an erogenous display. Seth felt himself blush as she slammed shut the door to the van from the inside.

Then the Lord rained on Sodom and Gomorrah brimstone and fire from the Lord out of heaven, and he overthrew those cities, and all the valley, and all the inhabitants of the cities, and what grew on the ground.

Ghoulish laughter filled his ears.

Fool. Now you've gone and done it, the voice chuckled from inside.

Even the women who had helped Michael were now giggling. They stood, shielding their bodies as they helped his youngest brother to his feet.

"I think he's going to be fine," laughed another voice.

Someone tossed a towel into his lap.

Seth looked down, suddenly aware of his folly, and wrapped the towel around his waist to conceal his body's wickedness. He pushed through the circle of fiends that preyed upon him and grabbed Michael by the arm as they stumbled through the biting milkweed and into the solace of the surrounding forest.

The sun began to set on the brothers as they traversed the dense foliage. Michael proceeded with an onslaught of questions as they marched wearily ahead. "Who were they?" he asked. "Are we lost?"

"Quiet, I need to think."

Seth had become disoriented in the thick brush after being cast so far downstream beyond the safety of the bend. The added trauma of nearly drowning was still very much a factor inhibiting his sense of direction, yet somehow it paled in comparison to the sting of the heretics' laughter still ringing in his ears.

You are filthy and unclean, and the others know. That is why the river tried to wash you away.

After what felt like several hours of hiking through the dense woods, Seth opted to find shelter for himself and his brother before nightfall. He cleared the brush near the mouth of a narrow rock shelter and laid out the towel for the brothers to sleep on as the sun sank below the horizon. Seth could no longer hear the rush of the river, and knew they would fare better in the light of day.

After Michael fell asleep, Seth was alone with his thoughts. He tossed and turned, recalling the embarrassment on the riverbank and the filth he had witnessed...the filth that sought to transform him, to lure him into a realm of wickedness. Had he stood his ground and emerged victorious against the temptations of Satan? Or had he been cast out of Eden into the wilderness?

The events of the day played over and over in his mind as he tried in vain to ward off the dark voice from surfacing. Unable to sleep, Seth pulled himself to his feet. He felt along the rock walls of the shelter and out into the moonless night so that he might relieve himself. He nearly doubled over in pain at the act of standing without his brace after such an ordeal.

After he finished, he supported himself against the cool, hard stone and felt along the walls of the shelter to find his way back to his brother. With the absence of light, he relied on his memory of the space to find his way.

He pushed his broken body forward to find another handhold on the wall of stone, and instead found himself falling forward, tumbling end over end into perpetual darkness. He landed hard against the rock floor below and rolled to his side.

The darkness around him seemed to move of its own volition as it crawled beneath the earth. Dismissing the phenomena as some trick of the eye induced by the fall, Seth continued his search for a way out, and headed deeper into darkness.

As he ventured further, Seth thought he heard the distant bellow of a deep horn blast that seemed somehow to vibrate the very stone beneath his feet.

Gabriel's trumpet. The end at last.

Ignoring the voice, Seth plodded ahead by feeling along the surface of the rocky enclosure. Rather than attempt to climb up the sheer rock face at his back, he opted to follow the path ahead in the hopes of finding a more suitable exit. In the distance, a shimmering tendril of darkness within darkness beckoned.

Guided by the strange phenomena, he followed the snaking shape down a narrow passage beneath the ground until it opened into a wide central chamber. In the center of the chamber, he could more clearly make out the inky shadow's source—a swirling vortex that rippled through the air.

Thinking it a possible egress towards the surface, Seth entered the vortex. Once inside, he found himself standing inside a great cavernous hollow beneath the Earth. A network of shimmering tendrils reached out from the darkness in all directions, connecting to a central nexus set within the surrounding arcade of symmetrically placed vortices.

A great, shadowy figure emerged from the central nexus, which began to shimmer and pulse as it grew. The snaking tendrils seemed to manifest from the heart of the ominous shape, which appeared to move of its own volition, although its form was fluid.

Seth watched, awestruck as the amorphous shape gradually shifted into a terrible, horned beast of enormous stature. The beast pointed its great horn towards one of the portals and emitted a deep, resonating blast of sound that caused a shower of dust and debris to fall to the cavern floor.

A beam of shimmering particles emitted from atop the shadowy titan's singular horn, crashing like a wave against the cavern wall. Seth watched in horror as another vortex opened in the stone from where the blank rock face once stood.

Behold! The Beast.

Seth summoned his last reserves of strength and stumbled back down the tunnel, through the open vortex that he had moments ago entered. He managed to climb his way back to the surface, where he eventually found his brother and set off once more into the woods.

After several hours of marching through the dark forest, Seth fell to his knees and began to pray aloud. His words were cast into the air as loud as his voice would carry, until he could speak no further.

A wash of lantern light broke from the darkness across the ridge, just visible in the breaking of day.

Just after dawn, the weary brothers were finally discovered by the mission's search party, and escorted back to the safety of Temple's Bend.

Upon their safe return to the mission, Seth recounted the trials he had faced: the river, the heathens who openly fornicated near its waters, and the vision he had received in the cave. Seth weaved the tale tirelessly, despite his lack of sleep and the physical toll taken on his broken body. Despite it all he felt rejuvenated, validated by a renewed conviction in his faith that had allowed him to persevere through the harrowing events of the previous day.

The mission elders conferred for several days before calling to witness in the chapel.

On the morning of their emergence, Seth was brought before the congregation and was presented with a bus ticket, one hundred and fifty dollars in cash, and a modest care package that included clothes, homemade bread, and the familial Bible that bore his mark—a solitary purple ribbon placed within the final passage of scripture. Seth held the generations-old tome that was as much a talisman as it was a sacred text, and felt its power surge through his fingertips.

His father addressed the congregation as Seth stood upon the dais. "Our beloved son. You have been chosen by the almighty God as a righteous emissary of Temple's Bend. You will go out from this sacred space, and into the lands of darkness that shy from His light. You will speak the words from His great book and prevent the will of Satan from being carried out among the forsaken cities of man." His father raised his arms high in the air as though addressing God himself. "You will return the children of God back to the arms of the Almighty, and destroy any and all trappings of Satan that appear before you on your righteous journey."

Seth accepted the offerings and was ushered out of the chapel in song and many a warm embrace as he set off for the road that led into town.

He watched out the window of the passenger bus that plodded along through the expanse of endless scrub brush and red dirt. For the first time in his life, away from the safety of Temple's Bend, Seth felt truly alone—a fact he was thankful for. The gnawing whispers and bleak prognostications of doom broadcast from the hidden recesses of his mind had ceased.

I am reborn.

After a sleepless night in a dingy roadside motel, Seth embarked for his destination: a bustling shopping center in the middle of the city's urban center. He watched in amazement at the steady throng of consumers who buzzed about mindlessly in pursuit of filling their empty lives with material goods.

He followed a group of black-clad, long-haired teenagers into a small department store. The store's windows were bedecked with a ghastly assortment of images all appearing to bear homage to the Dark Lord himself. Seth steadied himself as he recalled the encounter in the cave, and entered the store.

"Welcome to Sam Goody. How can I help you today?" a voice called out.

Seth followed the voice to the checkout counter and approached a blank-faced, middle-aged man wearing a dangling dagger earring. The man bore the likeness of the Grim Reaper on his forearm.

Seth reached into his pack and held out the sullied black T-shirt given to him by the river fornicators.

"Do you sell these?"

"All band tees are ten percent off this week. What size do you want?"

Seth reached into his pocket and laid out a crumple of bills on the counter left over from his traveling money. "How many will this afford me?"

The clerk raised an eyebrow. "Seriously? That's like ten shirts. You want them all to be the same?"

"Yes."

"Suit yourself," shrugged the clerk. "Big AC/DC fan?"

"No. I'm not a fan at all."

The clerk fetched the shirts from beneath a grid wall display. "What are you going to do with all these, if you don't mind me asking? That's a lot of AC/DC shirts for someone who doesn't like AC/DC."

  "I'm going to release the world of these graven images," said Seth. A few of the shoppers gave pause to gaze upon the young man at the counter, who was brandishing one of the AC/DC T-shirts over his head as he began to shout. "I'm going to bear witness to the flames as I burn these articles of Satan in the righteous and cleansing fire of the Lord God Almighty!"

CHAPTER SEVEN

INVADERS FROM HELL

1

Several days had passed since Jesse had revealed the contents of Mal's film roll, along with his own account of the incidents surrounding the mine, to Mr. Agostino.

Agostino had left town shortly after, during the Thanksgiving holiday, to "Confer with my advisor regarding the recent events at Macomb Springs."

Curiously, he seemed unperturbed by the narrative Jesse had presented, a fact that troubled Jesse in hindsight; however, Agostino did seem interested in particular details, such as the precise locations of events and their chronology. Jesse felt some measure of relief in sharing his burden, and was doubly reassured in doing so by Agostino's fastidious attention to said details, which the guidance counselor logged in one of the numerous leather-bound notebooks crammed within his briefcase.

At the conclusion of their meeting, Agostino promised a swift return with a decided course of action, along with several cryptic remarks that further cemented Jesse's impression that Agostino knew more than he was letting on about the happenings in Macomb Springs.

"These developments are concerning, but we must not be hasty in our response. The timing must be right," Agostino had said. "Until we meet again, stay above ground. And if you must leave the house, travel in groups."

In the meantime, Jesse languished in solitude as he tried in vain to stave off the impenetrable darkness growing inside himself. The cold abyss of the mineshaft was hungry, swallowing up his every thought. He found himself gazing into the chasm beneath the winch house no matter where he deposited his physical body.

He was lying on his bed looking at the self-portrait Mal had given him when Rick entered his room. Rick appeared in full regalia, wearing his battle vest and the FUCK PARENTAL ADVICE T-shirt that he had ordered from an SST Records catalog.

"Come on, Jess. Wheels up in five, and you're not even dressed yet."

"I told you, I'm not going."

"So you're just going to let those opportunistic Jesus freaks capitalize on a community tragedy? You're gonna let them censor artistic expression? Freedom of speech?" He made a fist and pounded the gauntlet against the field of pyramid studs on his vest. "Where does it stop?"

"Sounds like you have it under control," said Jesse. He laid down Mal's self-portrait and stared up at the ceiling.

"Look, man, I know what you're going through." Rick wheeled closer to the bed and picked up the photograph. "When I lost Julie, I didn't want to go on. I didn't want to sleep, or eat—I didn't care if I lived or died. And I'm not trying to sound like a tough guy. I just didn't have the will to care anymore. It wasn't a choice."

"How did you get over it?"

Rick handed Jesse back the photograph. "I didn't. But it got easier. It took a long time, but it got easier. And the thing that helped me through it—not the counseling, not the Prozac, and certainly not fucking God or prayer. It was music. Heavy-fucking-metal music. And I'll be damned if I'm going to let the Tipper Gores and Susan Bakers of the world decide what I can listen to. Not just for me, but for all the other broken, miserable bastards out there who need to get on with their miserable lives."

"I keep waiting for her," Jesse said. "I just sit and wait at all the places we would go just to be together. Any place we could pretend we were somewhere else."

"We're gonna find her, man. Even if it's just you and me."

Jesse wiped his face and sat up in bed. "I feel like I'm going fucking insane."

"Stop crying, pussy." Rick laughed out the words through his own tears as a snot bubble exploded from his nose. The brothers shared a much-needed laugh before settling into a shared silence.

"There's something else," Rick said.

Jesse looked to his brother.

"Goddammit, you're gonna make me say it, aren't you?" he sighed. "There's something else you need to know about how I got through the accident."

"What?"

"It was you, dude. I could never admit it because it killed me inside. I was supposed to be your big brother, your protector—the mighty Rick. Instead, *you* ended up taking care of *me*. And I'm finally in a spot where I can return the favor." He held out his hand to Jesse. "So let me do my job for a change, and let's get out there and fuck with some Jesus freaks."

2

The Lynn brothers, along with Mazes and Rust, arrived at the church in Mazes's beat up '81 Honda Civic hatchback. The vehicle pushed its way through the crowded lot like a small silver fist. Spectators of the Community Cleansing circled around a large roll-off dumpster where a controlled burn was being supervised by the local fire department.

Peppered throughout the crowd were several individuals parading as caricatured, costumed devils. An array of colorful props and informationals lined the front entrance of the church, adding to the convention-like atmosphere.

"And, of course, there's the P&G lunatics." Rick gestured out the window towards a large exhibit detailing the evolution of the Proctor & Gamble logo through time. "They really missed the plot on that one. Even Satan could learn a thing or two about evil from corporate America."

They parked the Civic next to a tight circle of cars at the far end of the expansive lot in front of the adjacent Plaza on Main businesses. Jesse felt a mixed sense of relief upon seeing that the site of the counter-protest had already been established by the half-dozen alternative kids Jesse recognized from school. A genre rift between the two cliques had exposed a mutual disinterest in one another, but having allies in this fight was a numbers game—the more the merrier.

As he helped his brother exit the vehicle, Jesse noticed that a handful of employees from Camelot Music were shuttering the doors and windows as they eyed the gathering taking place across the lot.

The muscled clerk with the bowl cut from RadioShack had also emerged from his storefront. He eyed Jesse as he leaned against one of the red-brick columns that supported the plaza façade. Unlike his fellow retail jockeys, there was something different in his manner— something almost relaxed, despite the already tense atmosphere.

"Here we go," Rick said. "It's showtime."

All eyes were on the podium that had been erected at the base of the steps leading to the front entrance of the church. Jesse watched with the others as a handful of MSCOC community organizers took their turn on the bull horn.

After the opening remarks, Pastor Seth Roberts stepped up to the podium with his giant saucer-shaped eyes and wide, beaming smile. He brandished an unlit torch over his head in one hand and a megaphone in the other.

"God is great," said Pastor Roberts.

The crowd echoed the utterance in unison.

"God is smiling upon the community of Macomb Springs, whose believers and steadfast worshippers have turned out today, seeking

Divine Providence, in such amazing numbers." Pastor Roberts waved the torch overhead as he chuckled into the megaphone. "I hope to see such a wonderful turnout this Sunday too, y'all." The crowd returned a playful laugh at the remark.

The pastor's smile faded. "In all seriousness, thank you for bearing witness to the almighty power of our lord, Jesus Christ, as we band together to ward off the forces of Satan, who even now seek to infiltrate our community."

Jesse wanted to puke his guts out.

Pastor Roberts gestured at the counter-protesters gathered at the opposite end of the parking lot. "For those in league with the lowly outcast, Lucifer, I would also invite you to bear witness as we destroy these satanic articles that are corrupting our youth. Watch as we release Macomb Springs from Satan's grip. Watch as our community is reborn in the cleansing flames of Christ, our lord!"

Pastor Roberts stepped down from the podium to sustained applause. He moved gingerly, walking with a stooped posture as he made his way towards the site of the impending burn. As the torch was lit by one of the attendees, Pastor Roberts dropped it into the dumpster. Once the controlled fire began to blaze, a crowd of parents and children lined up behind the pastor carrying boxes, milk crates, and garbage bags full of various and sundry items deemed to possess satanic influence.

One by one, they dumped cassettes, vinyl LPs, CDs, T-shirts, and posters into the fire. The crowd roared with each devilish deposit as the flames rose higher and higher.

"Holy shit." Rust pointed over the circle of cars towards the line of parents and children leading up to the dumpster. "It's Alex."

Jesse stood aghast as he watched Alex approach the dumpster. Still barely recognizable in his short hair and conservative dress, their former guitar player looked to the contents of the box he carried and hesitated. Alex's parents prodded him along as Pastor Roberts whipped the crowd into a frenzy, rejoicing as the young man emptied the contents of his prized cassette collection into the fire. The flames rose higher and licked at Alex's hands as he tossed out the few remaining tapes that clung to the bottom of the box.

Rust climbed up on the roof of the Civic and tried to shout over the din of the crowd. "Jump in, you fuckin' traitor! Fuckin' kill yourself!"

He kicked over the radio antenna mounted on the roof above the front driver window before jumping down off the car. Jesse thought for a minute that Mazes might tear his arms off, but instead the gentle giant simply patted Rust on the shoulder as he cast his eyes away from the flames.

By nightfall, the fire had burned through the contents of the dumpster, filled to the brim with the church community's sacrificial offerings. Pastor Roberts led the gathering in a rendition of "Just a Closer Walk with Thee" to close out the event. The official portion of the ceremonial cleansing had come to an end. Unofficially, Jesse could sense that the God-fearing citizens of Macomb Springs were just getting started.

Many of the counter-protesters had turned up their car stereos in an attempt to drown out Pastor Roberts's sing-a-long. The discordant aural onslaught was maddening.

A group of parishioners led by Stan Summers—father of the missing Kenny Summers—marched across the parking lot, pushing through the counter-protest towards the adjacent strip mall. The mob lined up in front of Camelot Music and began banging on the windows and doors, demanding to be let inside. Jesse heard a loud crash as one of the store windows shattered, an act which added an ear-splitting security alarm to the sonic fray.

Droves of looters streamed inside the store, emerging with armloads of CDs, LPs, and cassette tapes destined for the cleansing flames of the dumpster. A few moments later the red-and-blue police sirens were flashing near the entrance to the parking lot.

"Let's get the fuck out of here," Jesse said to the others.

A clap of thunder rolled overhead, followed by a gust of wind that picked up one of the large Community Cleansing flyers and lodged it between the spokes of one of Rick's wheels.

"Look at this shit," Rick said as he removed the flyer from his chair and held it aloft. "Can you believe the amount of money these fuckers put into their propaganda? We need a production budget like that." He gestured towards the church entrance as he continued. "I mean, shit, take a look at those props."

The group hymnal erupted into a chorus of screams as a great black shape emerged from the shadows on the edge of the smoldering fire. A bestial form swelled within the cocoon of shifting darkness, rising above the group of arm-locked parishioners who stood paralyzed in fear. Even from his distant vantage point, Jesse could see the agony on their faces.

He watched, unable to take his eyes off the horror as it began to materialize near the entrance to the church. The glint of the dying flames reflected off the crown of the beastly figure as it loomed over the crowded lot. A great horn pierced through the veil of shadow, rising from its head like a spiny, segmented spear.

A pack of quadrupeds emerged from the vortex of living darkness that seemed to transport the colossal being. They looked like the result of some kind of half-baked genetic experiment that tried to cross a hairless ape with a king-sized dog. Jesse immediately flashed back to the creature from the mine cart. The thought that Mal had been down there alone with these things just before she disappeared made him sick.

Fucking stray dog, my ass.

Following behind the pack of hairless fiends were a handful of larger, bipedal humanoid forms who, unlike the pack, ambled slowly and methodically towards the crowd of onlookers. The latter arrivals appeared in all manner of historical dress, looking like a bunch of *Night of the Living Dead* extras that had wondered into the wrong wardrobe department.

A chill ran down Jesse's spine as he began to intuit some mechanism of cooperation among the amassing horde.

"I don't think this is part of the production." Jesse grabbed the back of Rick's wheelchair and called to the others as he tried to push his brother through the crowd. "We need to get the fuck out of here—*now*."

Mazes and Rust nodded without taking their eyes from the scene.

Pastor Roberts was one of the first to break ranks at the sight of the otherworldly legion. He tried to run, arms flailing, towards the inner sanctum of the church. Before he got to the entrance he was stopped by a pair of the lesser imps that snapped and snarled at the Pastor, backing him down the church steps towards the shadowy presence that lingered at the edge of the fire.

The hellish minions had corralled the remaining church goers at the foot of the abominable being, rallying around the monstrosity like trained hounds.

In unison, the pack unhinged their swelling jaws and emitted a low sonic pulse that Jesse could feel in his chest, even from across the parking lot. The parishioners were rendered immobile by the paralytic call, tumbling to the ground, unconscious.

Mazes forged a path through the counter-protest, allowing Jesse to get Rick inside the car while Mazes and Rust loaded the wheelchair into the hatchback. Others were already fleeing in their vehicles, creating a logjam at both the lot's two main exits.

"Oh my God! They're taking them!" someone screamed.

The group of nearby counter-protesters had taken to the roofs of their cars. Screams and blaring horns mixed with the loud music being played from the circle of trapped cars.

Jesse followed suit and climbed on top of Mazes's car. From the roof of the Civic he could see the great beast as it idled in an amorphous flux of shadow that seemed at times to phase in and out of existence. It continued to loom motionless over the lot as the slow-moving humanoid forms worked in concert with the pack of corralling minions to immobilize dozens of the Community Cleansing participants.

The slow-moving lurkers appeared to kneel over the fallen, quaking in convulsive fits as they performed some unseen rite of dominion. After a few passing moments, the townsfolk each came to, standing of their own volition. They stood passively in wait until they were marched by the lurkers in a ghoulish procession towards the dark void that surrounded the towering horned beast.

As the last of the fallen disappeared into the abyss of shadow, a deep, baleful call resounded from the heart of the vortex and shook through the night. The force of the call shattered the windows of the church entrance and any vehicle caught within the call's blast radius.

Jesse slid down from the hood as the pack drew nearer. "Mazes, start the car."

"It's no good, man—we're trapped," Rust said. "We have to go on foot."

"We *can't* go on foot," Jesse snarled between clenched teeth. He gestured at Rick, who sat in the back passenger seat of the Civic.

"Hey guys?" Rick called. He pointed out the window towards the approaching pack. "They're getting closer."

"Get in the car," Jesse repeated.

They jumped in the car, locked the doors, and rolled up the windows.

"What's the plan?" asked Rust. "We're sittin' ducks here, man."

"Why aren't they going after those cars?" asked Jesse. He pointed to the remaining counter-protest vehicles, whose passengers were still standing on the roofs of the cars, blasting out music from their car stereos.

A baby-blue Chevy pickup truck sped through the lot towards the exit. The tires squealed as the truck crashed into another car, stalling out. Two young men exited the vehicle from the passenger-side door. They made it about twenty yards before a few of the pack splintered off and ran them down.

"Mazes, turn the music up," Jesse said.

Mazes started the engine and obliged by turning up the volume on the car stereo. The cassette deck engaged, and the chorus of "Don't Bring Me Down" *by Riot, from their album* Fire Down Under, *released in 1981 on Elektra Records*, blared over the Civic's stock speakers.

"Louder," Jesse urged.

Mazes turned the volume knob as far as it would go, rattling the speakers and causing them to distort as they fought to contain the music.

Rust turned to Jesse from the front passenger seat, screaming inaudibly over the speakers as he cupped his own ears.

"WHAT?!" yelled Jesse.

Rust put his mouth up to Jesse's ear, close enough to where he could smell his rank breath. "LAST SONG." He pointed to the cassette deck. "WE GOTTA SWITCH SIDES."

"NO TIME." Jesse shook his head and tapped at the pretend watch on his wrist. "RADIO?"

Rick punched Jesse in the shoulder and pointed out the window towards the broken antenna that hung limp from the roof.

"FUCK," shouted Rust.

The deafening garble of the car stereo came to an immediate halt as the tape stopped.

Jesse watched as one of the encroaching minions began to sway its barbed tail above its head while it snapped at the air, eying the Civic and its inhabitants hungrily.

Mazes turned to face the backseat. "It has been my honor to accompany each of you on this final journey," he smiled.

Another low-frequency blast broke above the chaos of the church parking lot. The pack retreated back to the shadowy portal through which their master had emerged. Jesse and the others watched as the last of the otherworldly legions returned to the darkness from whence they came, along with several dozen of Macomb Springs's population.

3

Jesse had witnessed first-hand how traumatic events could do funny things to people, how they are forever changed when life pulls back the curtain to reveal something they were never meant to see.

Right after Rick's accident, Jesse's mother had been pulling double duty between work and waiting on Rick at the hospital for nights on end. The event had created a shockwave of pain and misery that rippled through the lives of all those who were caught in the existential blast radius of the crash.

It was the final straw that ended his parents' marriage. That had been a long time coming; things hadn't been good for a while. In the end Jesse's dad—his biological father—had used Rick's accident to make his chicken-shit exit. He couldn't hack it and he bailed.

Turns out his real dad was a real asshole.

Around that time, Jesse had gotten into a couple of fistfights back at his old school. One day, his mother was called in to pick Jesse up after a particularly nasty scuffle, one that left him with a swollen black eye and a gash on his forehead requiring seven stitches.

The principal, a Mr. Jones (who was coincidentally always eating a sloppy hamburger every time Jesse was called into his office), had asked his mother how everything was going in Jesse's home life since her recent divorce.

"Is there a father figure in these boys' lives?" Mr. Jones had asked, a glob of mayo in the corner of his mouth. "Young men need discipline. And above all, a happy, healthy home so they can thrive."

Jesse's mother turned to stone for several moments before bursting out in a hysterical fit of laughter. She laughed all the way out
of the school building and all the way home (which was on the
complete other side of town) where she locked herself inside her
bedroom without saying a word for three days.

He couldn't imagine how she would have reacted to seeing a
thirty foot-tall shadow monster materialize out of thin air, but he
imagined that after seeing her firstborn pinned under a flatbed
truck next to what remained of his late girlfriend's headless torso,
she could handle it.

Jesse could only try.

Once they returned to the practice trailer, Rust passed around
a twelve pack of beer to the others as he talked to himself in
hushed tones.

"I gotta get the fuck out of here," he muttered. "I got a buddy
that lives in the city, said I can crash in his garage whenever I
needed."

Jesse felt his mind splintering under the weight of what he
had just witnessed. No longer capable of letting his innermost
thoughts fester privately in his mind, he decided to come clean.

"I have to tell you guys something," he started. "And it's going
to sound insane—or at least it would have before tonight—but I
just really need all of you to hear me out."

His companions returned a blank stare.

As Jesse addressed the group, he noticed for the first time he
could recall that Mazes was no longer smiling. "It's about Mal.
It might explain all of this."

The room fell silent.

Jesse relayed the events surrounding the photographs he and
Kara had found on Mal's camera. He told them again how they
were supposed to meet after the Prisoners of Flesh show, and
everything that had happened since. "What happened that night
in the mine is somehow connected to everything that is going

on in this town—the missing people, the animal attacks, the shit that happened tonight at the church. All of it."

"Connected how?" asked Rick. "Through LSD in the water supply?"

Jesse rummaged through his backpack and presented the stack of photographs that Kara had developed from Mal's camera.

The group crowded around the small circular table in the trailer's kitchenette and watched as Jesse fanned out the photographs.

"Is anybody else sick of trying to pretend what we saw down there in the mine was normal?" He watched as their weary faces scanned the photographs. "There's something happening in this town and it's about time we face up to it."

Rick picked up one of the photographs. He stared at the image that depicted the shadowy figure rising out from the abyss of the vertical mineshaft.

"This is it," Rick said.

"Finally." Jesse breathed a sigh of relief. "Are you starting to get it now?"

Rick held the photo up to the light. "This is the fucking album cover for our first record."

Jesse plucked the photo from Rick's hand and threw it back on the table. "These are the last images on Mal's camera. That camera was her life—she wouldn't have left it behind. She saw something down there, and then she was taken, just like the others tonight at the church."

Mazes leaned in next to Jesse and clasped him firmly on the shoulder. "I would like to name the architect behind the nefarious plot to pillage the fair township of Macomb Springs as witnessed tonight."

"I've told you everything I know," Jesse sighed, falling into one of the chairs around the kitchen table. "Agostino said that he would have answers when he gets back."

"You're putting a lot of stock in the words of a high school guidance counselor," said Rick.

The screen door to the trailer opened.

All eyes followed the sound of the booming voice that preceded the wild shock of dense black hair and heavy beard that erupted from the top of the tweed overcoat.

"Actually, I prefer to think of myself as an ethnomusicologist," Agostino said as he let himself in the trailer.

"Mr. Agostino!" Jesse jumped to help him inside. Agostino was carrying a rolled map and a briefcase under his arm.

"Speak of the devil," Rick said.

"Nice to see you again, Professor Venom," said Rust. "The town really went to shit while you were away."

Agostino nodded politely to the group as he entered. "I heard the radio chatter on the police scanner and came as quickly as I could."

Rick looked quizzically at the new arrival. "How did you know where to find us?"

"I took the liberty of locating your home address from Jesse's school records—I hope you don't mind the breach of privacy, given the circumstances." He sat his briefcase on the table with a hefty thud. "I saw the light on in the trailer on my way over, and here we are." Agostino took a breath as he surveyed his audience. "Did you brief the others?"

"We were just getting into it," Jesse replied.

Agostino set to work by removing his overcoat and wiping the table clean of ashtrays and empty beer cans. He unfurled his map. "How many were there at the church?"

"How many what?" asked Rick.

"Demons, devils, denizens of the netherworld—all misnomers of course. I actually prefer the term visitors, or the more technical *sonopods*."

"Sonopods?" scoffed Rick. "Has everyone gone insane?"

"Lay off, man. He's here to help," said Jesse.

"Maybe like fifteen or twenty hell hounds, a half-dozen of the zombie lurkers, and one main boss," Rust said.

Agostino shook his head and appeared deep in thought as he muttered under his breath. "Sentinels, drones, *and* a Rift Lord," Agostino continued to speak to himself as he undid the brass hasps on his briefcase. "No doubt preparing for the passage of an entire hive legion."

"Can we back up here just a minute, Professor?" Rick asked.

Agostino unrolled the sepia-colored map, placing a half-empty beer can on each corner to hold it in place. Various geographical regions were circled in red, including Mesopotamia, Western Europe, and the Northeastern United States. Scribbled annotations and strange, arcane symbols littered the map.

"Hey, that's us." Rust pointed to the large red circle plotted on the southern center of the North American continent. "Why the hell is Macomb Springs circled on this map?"

All eyes watched as Agostino traced his index finger over the map. "Throughout history, certain cultural phenomena marked by localized mass hysteria—typically of religious origin—have coincided with reports of demonic visitation and satanic influence." He absently took a drink from one of the open beer cans on the table as he continued. "The Maqlu rituals of ancient Mesopotamia, various European Inquisitions, the Salem witch trials, and the current rise of 'Satanic Panic' throughout the United States are but a few of the more infamous examples."

"Look, man, in case you hadn't noticed, we're not exactly the churchgoing crowd," said Rick. "So you can save the Armageddon fearmongering for the squares over at the mini-mall."

"On the contrary," Agostino said, "my interest in the end of the world is purely academic."

"Did you find out anything from your adviser?" asked Jesse.

Agostino nodded. "Perhaps we should start at the beginning. You should first know that Macomb Springs is not the only populace to encounter such events." Jesse noticed a faraway look in the guidance counselor's eyes as he continued. "And secondly, it might help you to prepare for what is to come if you opened your minds to the possibility that *Hell,* as referenced in the Judeo-Christian religious tradition, is indeed a real place—though not exactly as it was described."

"No issue there," said Rust.

"All right, you're starting to freak everybody out," Jesse said. "Just tell us what's going on, please."

"It is part of our working theory that the entities you witnessed tonight, these so-called demonic forces, are attracted to certain biochemical resonating frequencies which manifest in humans as the fear response."

"*Our* theory?" asked Rick. "What are you, some kind of Fortean witch doctor?"

"I belong to a specialized research group who have been monitoring similar events throughout human history," Agostino shrugged. "I suppose you could call it a family tradition." He looked to his watch and raised a thick, black eyebrow. "Unfortunately, that is a conversation for another time."

"We can trust him." Jesse nodded to his brother. "He majored in Black Sabbath."

Rust raised his beer in solidarity.

Jesse attempted to steer the conversation back to its plotted course. "So you're saying that what we saw tonight were actual demons? From Hell?"

Rick belched an interjection. "I've been to anti-Halloween fright nights with twice the production budgets of that bullshit." He continued to belch periodically as he spoke. "It's all smoke and mirrors paid for by the collection plate to scare young people into the arms of God."

Agostino gestured to Jesse. "To answer your question: yes and no." He rummaged through his briefcase and presented several diagrams depicting a menagerie of fantastic-looking creatures. "As depicted in the *Ars Goetia* of the *Lesser Key of Solomon,* the physical characteristics of demons—horns, barbed tails, chimeras with heads of beasts, and so on—were described long ago by ancient scribes and preserved in what would later become humanity's most prominent religious texts." He passed around the diagrams as he continued. "Little did the future stewards of these texts know that what had been preserved were actual, first-hand accounts of extraterrestrial contact—warnings veiled in scripture that described these visitors who had come to our world to feed."

"World eaters from the Nine Hells of Baator," said Mazes.

A low grumble resounded through the kitchenette.

"Sorry." Rust grabbed his stomach. "I know this is bad timing, but I'm freakin' starving." Rust elbowed Jesse. "You got anything to eat in here?"

Jesse nodded towards the pantry from beneath a furrowed brow.

Agostino pulled a copy of the American Psychiatric Association's DSM-IV from his briefcase. "There are no biological organisms on Earth that are capable of generating as much fear and anxiety as human beings." He fanned the pages of the weighty tome beneath his thumb as he continued. "In this manner, we are more or less self-contained, high-octane, psychosexual batteries, outputting unprecedented levels of biochemical energy that is somehow observable to these sonopods—emitting like a sonic beacon, or perhaps more aptly, a dinner bell. Especially when—"

"Especially when we get freaked the fuck out," finished Rust. The wiry frontman spoke over his shoulder as he foraged through the sparse pantry. The loud crinkling of a pastry wrapper brought all eyes upon him. "So people are basically, like, anxiety-filled Twinkies to these alien-demon things?"

Agostino ran his hand through his beard, presumably calculating the proposed scenario. "I suppose that is one way to look at it."

"So when that douchebag, Pastor Roberts, was up there at the pulpit preachin' hellfire and brimstone, he was really talkin' about these visitors?"

"Unwittingly."

"Well, there's no shortage of hysteria around here," Jesse said. He smoothed out a crumpled up Community Cleansing flyer from his jacket pocket and dropped it on the table. "That dinner bell is ringing loud and clear right about now."

"Which brings me to the bad news," said Agostino.

"Wait. Bad news?" asked Rust.

"Yeah, so all that stuff before about us being snack cakes for some interdimensional assholes...that was the *good* news?" asked Rick.

The guidance counselor rifled through a stack of newspaper clippings and magazines in his briefcase. "Due to the advent of modern media, namely television, what might have once been geographically isolated outbreaks of social hysteria are now readily experienced by an entire nation—and in real time."

"Fuckin' Geraldo," said Rust.

Agostino placed his fingertips together as he spoke. "Reports of Satanic Panic throughout the country over the past few years indicate that we are currently witnessing one of the most widespread episodes of mass hysteria ever recorded in human history. And so we have an observation." He pulled his fingers apart and looked through them. "The hypothesis ... Macomb Springs appears to be the staging ground for the next sonopod feeding. A feeding on the grandest scale that humanity has ever witnessed."

"Great. That's just fuckin' great," said Rust. "Just when we were about to blow up."

Jesse turned towards Agostino and met his eyes. "Okay, so now that we're all caught up, what the hell do we do about it?" asked Jesse. "Mal is still missing."

"There is cause for concern, I'm afraid."

"Please," begged Jesse. "If there's still a chance...I have to find her."

Agostino pointed to the red circle at the center of the map. "I believe I have discovered the location of the nexus between worlds—a gateway that connects our world and theirs."

"The gateway to the Nine Hells," whispered Mazes.

"More aptly known as the Spring Creek Mine," Agostino corrected. "Ultrasonic and seismographic readings conducted over the last few months confirm the existence of a natural cave system beneath the mine. Perhaps one of the largest uncharted cave systems discovered in recent history. Somewhere within that cave system, a point of entry into our world is being torn out of the fabric of space and time from the other side."

"The other side of what?" asked Rick.

"That much remains unclear." Agostino shrugged. "A parallel universe? Or a dimensional axis we have yet to discover? Possibly an intergalactic civilization that has evolved the ability to travel vast distances seemingly without the use of technology—at least one that we would recognize."

Rick whistled and looked to his watch. "Okay, that's it for me." He stifled a yawn. "Call me when the movie comes out, I'm going to pass the fuck out."

"Hold on, let's hear him out," said Jesse. He looked to Agostino. "It's been a long day. Please, go ahead."

"It may sound far-fetched, but nature has set a precedent for similar adaptations. For example, bats, as well as many species of marine mammals, utilize sound waves—echolocation—to navigate their habitats in order find food."

"Far-fetched is a good start," said Rick.

"By our best estimates the universe is a hearty fourteen billion years old. In contrast, Earth has only existed for 4.6 billion years of that time." Agostino's voice became more emphatic as he explained. "Imagine how many planetary civilizations have come and gone during this differential, not to mention what kinds of novel adaptive traits and social orders have evolved among them, elsewhere in the universe—things we have never even conceived of."

"This isn't *Star Trek* or *The Twilight Zone*, man. This is Macomb Springs. You can't even get MTV out here. This kind of shit just doesn't happen in places like this," said Rick. "Jess, I'm sorry, man, but this is beyond the pale."

"Just let him finish," Jesse growled.

Agostino shrugged. "While the mechanism remains uncertain, it is possible to imagine an organism that, over vast eons of time, has evolved a sophisticated adaptation to sound—an adaptation which conferred the ability to attenuate or overload the resonating frequency of matter, which has somehow allowed them to gain access to the very fabric of space and time. An adaptation that enables the passage to other worlds, thereby increasing the chance of survival beyond the confines of their native habitat."

"He's right," Jesse said. "All objects have their own unique resonating frequency—like the wine glass experiment."

"Precisely," Agostino said.

"But instead of some parlor trick, they're using subatomic vibrations to somehow crack open a door between worlds." Jesse repeated Agostino's synopsis aloud as he reasoned through the logic. "But if they can open a door to our world, there has to be a way to close the door from our side, right?"

Rick repositioned his glasses over his nose as he directed an inquiry to Agostino. "Okay, say I were to buy into this cocka-mamie story—why Earth? What's so special about this planet?"

"In a word, sustenance." Agostino gestured towards Rust who was working through his second Twinkie. "We are potentially looking at a cyclical subsistence strategy that likely began as soon as anatomically modern humans, i.e., Twinkies, evolved on this planet."

"If this has been going on for that long, why haven't we heard about it before now?" asked Rick.

"Maybe we have. As a wise man once said, 'Hell was a warning.' The very concept of shadowy denizens escaping from the underworld to wreak havoc on unsuspecting humans is as old as time itself."

Jesse's mind was reeling from the information overload. "The ones we saw tonight…they just came out of nowhere, nabbed a couple dozen Bible thumpers, and vanished into thin air. Where are they taking them?"

"What you witnessed tonight was just the beginning. A scouting party sent to siphon energy from the citizens of Macomb Springs in order to build a bridge from the visitor's home world. Since the nexus is not yet powerful enough to sustain their passage in substantial numbers, the sonopods will likely begin harvesting the energy of the townsfolk in close proximity to the point of entry to our world."

"The mine," Jesse said.

Agostino nodded as he met Jesse's eyes. "If there are any survivors left, we would likely find them near the nexus. And likely alive. The good news is that we might still have time. The sonopods are using the townsfolk as fuel cells, but they will need many more to finish building the nexus. The bigger the battery, the stronger the bridge between worlds."

"And how do we vanquish these foes?" asked Mazes. "What are their vulnerabilities? Silver? Frost magic? Perhaps an aversion to sunlight?"

"Music."

The word came out definitively, with no approximations or speculation.

"That's it? Just music?" asked Rust.

"It is a little more complicated than that. In short, a very specific overloaded acoustic waveform could disrupt the visitors' gateway, thus dislodging their foothold on the entrance to our world. We have a recipe for such a waveform, but until now we have lacked the means to make it operational."

"Now hold on just a—" started Rick.

"We find the resonating frequency of the nexus and shatter it, just like the wine glass," Jesse interrupted.

"Piece of cake," laughed Rust, his mouth full of Twinkie.

"Professor Venom, I see where you're going—" Rick continued.

"I understand the band has recently come into the possession of a new backline and PA system?" Agostino smiled. "First, we will need to transport the equipment to my lab. There I can further demonstrate an experiment that my colleagues and I have been working on which seems quite promising."

"Now wait just a minute, Professor." Rick held his hands up in front of him, his voice raised. "We haven't even paid off that gear yet. And now we're just supposed to risk destroying it all over some fool's errand?" asked Rick. "No offense."

Agostino bowed his head.

"We have to do *something*," said Jesse. He crossed his arms as he shot a stern glance at his brother. "All of you have seen what's going on around here, even if you're too afraid to admit it."

Agostino continued despite the confrontation. "We can use the backline to create a dislocation—an amplified sonic pulse emitted at extremely high decibels, preferably something involving a sustained tritone." Agostino rifled through his briefcase as he continued. "I was able to fabricate a prototype."

"You want Hell Patrol to play a show down there in the mine?" asked Rust. "How the fuck are we gonna pull that off?"

"If my theory is correct, there is some probability of success, albeit a low one, but it needs to happen soon."

"How long do we have?" asked Jesse.

"After tonight's harvest, the visitors' gateway will soon become powerful enough to allow for the passage of an entire hive legion. However, transferring that much energy from their captives will take some time. According to the energy signatures we are reading from the mine, we should have at least twenty-four, maybe forty-eight hours to destroy the nexus before the arrival of the hive legion."

Rick wheeled back from the table and addressed the room. "Okay, I've heard enough. I'm calling a band meeting, right now."

The three reunited members of Hell Patrol and their manager huddled in the corner of the room. "I'm just the manager of this outfit. It's your call." He nodded towards Agostino. "Do we call the white coats in from the asylum? Or just knock him out and leave him in the woods?"

The three band members looked to each other and then to Agostino, who brandished a handheld electrical device above his head. The apparatus consisted of an assortment of wires and cables that ran from a silver parabolic resonating dish mounted to an augmented rifle stock. Jesse recognized the familiar shape of the Sony Walkman that was duct taped to the butt of the stock.

He waived the gadget in the air and called out to the group. "I call it the 'Hand of Doom.'"

Rick raised an eyebrow towards Jesse and shook his head.

"Quit being such a dick. You're just as stubborn with your skepticism as those Jesus freaks are about their Bible," Jesse said. "If even a fraction of this is true, it means there might be a chance to find Mal and bring her back. As long is there is a chance, no matter how small, I have to try. I don't expect you guys to understand. It's just something I have to do."

Mazes and Rust exchanged a look of solidarity.

Rick shrugged, turning his chair towards Jesse. "Looks like we're getting the band back together."

Agostino passed the Hand of Doom to Jesse. "If anything not of this world gets in your way, switch on the device, aim, and pull the trigger."

"All right, what do we do next?" asked Jesse. He held the strange contraption aloft, fearing it would go off in his hand.

Agostino tapped on his watch. "I have some final preparations to attend to." He scribbled on a piece of paper and handed it to Jesse before picking up his belongings. "In the meantime, rest and prepare yourselves accordingly. Bring the gear to this address just after sundown, tomorrow."

Jesse held the note to the light. 8512 RTE. 12 NE.

"Professor Venom, we're going to need some roadies to help hump all that gear in and out of the mine," Rick called out. "This is not a very desirable venue for the band that I represent. We're gonna need a bankroll."

"I suppose any help would be useful, but know that we will be putting anyone who ventures into the mine in mortal danger. My colleagues and I will cover any expenses you deem necessary."

"I've got this." Rick grabbed the phone off the kitchen wall and started dialing. "Rick the Prick is on the clock."

"Only one problem," said Rust. He flicked open the switchblade comb and ran it across his greasy curls. "We don't have a van to move the gear since our guitar player quit the band, on account that he's a fuckin' square."

4

After their meeting with Agostino, the three bandmates jumped back into the Civic and headed once more into town.

The streets were empty in the aftermath of the Community Cleansing, allowing the group to swiftly navigate through town. A squadron of police cars had surrounded the church parking lot, whose entrances had been taped off. Jesse stared at the flashing red-and-blue lights as they headed east towards the residential district.

As they arrived at their destination, Mazes parked the car a few houses up the street to avoid detection. They proceeded on foot, passing through the row of open backyards towards their former practice space.

Jesse picked up a hefty piece of mulch from a nearby flower bed and lobbed it up to Alex's second-story window.

The bedroom lights flashed on and off.

A few moments later, Alex emerged from the side door that led out from the garage. "What are you guys doing? My parents will go apeshit if they see you here." Alex looked over his shoulder as he whispered. "The whole town has gone crazy. They fucking stormed Camelot."

"Yeah, we saw," Jesse replied.

"Oh." He looked down at his feet. "You guys were there? I guess I didn't see you. My parents took me home right when the mob started up."

"Alex, I know it feels like everything is falling apart," Jesse started. "And trust me, we all feel it—"

"Somebody wanna give me a fucking smoke? I haven't had one in like three days."

Rust tapped out a cigarette from his soft pack.

Jesse lit the smoke and held the lighter up towards his face. "Look, man, we don't have a lot of time. I know there's a lot going on with your parents, and I can't go into everything, but we need you for one last show."

"After tonight?" Alex asked. "Are you fucking crazy?"

Rust shoved Alex back against the house. "You think *you* had a bad night? We've been chased by fuckin' *demons* all over town." Flecks of spittle flew from Rust's lips as he spoke. "There's more goin' on than the free haircuts your bullshit church is givin' out in between book burnings."

Alex looked to Mazes and Jesse for explanation.

Mazes spoke first, stepping closer to Alex. "Master Rust's words ring with the truth of clashing steel. A great evil walks the land."

"We have to play a show at the mine," said Jesse. "I know it sounds crazy, but it might be the only way to get Mal back."

"Here we go." Alex squinted through the dark. "How fucked up are you guys?"

"Stone-cold sober," said Jesse.

"Mostly," added Rust.

Alex shook his head. "Dude, I'm sorry, but Mal's gone. She was probably the only smart one out of all of us. She saw what was happening in this town and got the fuck out."

Before Jesse could stop himself, he had grabbed Alex by his shirt collar and was snarling into his face. "She didn't leave. She was taken."

Mazes intervened and separated the two.

"All right, look—long story short," Rust said. "Professor Venom, your guidance counselor, thinks that the town is being overrun by demons. Except they're not, like, *Exorcist* demons. They're like, for real, *Alien* demons. And they have come to Earth to eat humans—their favorite food—because we are basically anxiety-filled Twinkies."

Alex stepped back towards the house.

"Oh, okay. Why didn't you say so in the first place?" He stomped out the cigarette as he continued. "Just gimme a second to tell my parents." He proceeded to have a conversation through the open garage door. "Hey, mom? Dad? I have to go out and play a show in the old abandoned mine because the town is about to be eaten by demons." He turned back to face the band. "Hey, guys, how long do you think it will take? An hour? Maybe two?"

"All right. We don't have time for this shit," said Jesse.

"What? Do you think I'm fucking insane?"

Rust threw up his hands. "We don't think you're insane. We just think you're a fuckin' asshole. You ditched your friends, and your band, right as we're gettin' off the fuckin' ground. We're supposed to be on tour with Prisoners of Flesh in less than three weeks, for fuck's sake." Rust took a breath and paced back and forth. "Jesus Christ, man, you're almost eighteen years old. Why don't you sack up and stand up for somethin' for a change, instead of being the clone your small-minded parents are forcin' you to be?"

"What do you want me to do about it, man? Drop out of school? Sleep in my cousin's backyard, like you?"

"It's a fuckin' pop-up trailer, you little rich prick. I ain't sleepin' in the yard like a dog."

"I guess the pop-up doesn't have a shower, because from here, you sure as fuck smell like one."

Rust pushed Alex against the wall again and made a fist. Mazes grabbed his arm and held it back.

Jesse motioned for Rust to back off. "Let's go. It's not worth it. We can't change his mind if he's already made it up. Maybe he's not the person we thought we needed." Jesse turned to walk towards the Civic. "The person we used to know."

"You guys just think I got it so easy," Alex squealed. "You don't get it."

Jesse turned on his heel and found himself standing nose to nose with Alex. "The Alex I knew wouldn't have been forced into burning his prized tape collection, or cut his hair, or allowed himself to be taken out of the band that he loved—the thing we'd all worked so hard for." Jesse tried to lower his voice as one of the downstairs lights came on. "And you know what sucks the most? We were actually pretty fucking good, and on our way to becoming even better." Jesse shook his head and spit on the ground in front of him. "The Alex we knew is gone. I don't even recognize this person. I just see a coward who doesn't have anything left worth fighting for."

Alex slumped to the ground and held his head in his hands.

"Forget this square. Let's get the fuck out of here," added Rust.

As the others left through the backyard, Mazes turned back towards Alex, and lowered his head. "I am most disappointed with your lack of honor, Master Alex."

CHAPTER EIGHT

THE FORGOTTEN ORDER

1

The following afternoon, Jesse found himself escorting his mother and Randy to the station wagon.

"Have fun at Aunt Nancy's, and don't worry about us, we'll be fine," Rick called out from the porch.

"We have a whole weekend planned," Jesse added.

Rick grinned and gave a thumbs up to their parents. "Brother stuff—you know."

Jesse's mom stood next to the passenger-side door as Randy loaded a cooler into the back. "It's just not like her to call out of the blue like this," she said.

"She's probably feeling sentimental since grandma and grandpa passed away. Making up for lost time and all," Jesse said. "At least that's how she sounded when she left the answering machine message." He grinned sheepishly. "Before I accidentally erased it. Sorry."

She stifled a follow-up to Jesse's convenient explanation as she shifted her attention to the police helicopter that hovered overhead in the distance.

"I'm not sure it's such a good idea to be leaving you guys alone here with all the crazy stuff going on in this town." She pointed at the helicopter. "They still haven't caught those protesters that assaulted all those people at the church."

Rick and Jesse exchanged a wry look.

"Besides, shouldn't we wait to talk to her just to be sure? It's such a long drive."

"Come on, Mom! You know better than to believe in the collective hallucinations of the religiously compromised." Rick laughed.

"It's just another pathetic PR move put on by the church and their big money PMRC backers." Rick waved his hands in the air wildly. "A little smoke and mirrors to stir the fear of God into the populace. What better way to line the pews, not to mention their pockets?"

"When he's right, he's right." Jesse shrugged. He did his best to maintain a look of sincerity as his mother eyed the brothers warily. Clearly, she knew they were full of shit, but for all the wrong reasons. He hoped she would forgive him if the worst happened. *At least they'll be safe.* "Besides, a weekend on the lake sounds like the perfect distraction."

Randy climbed into the driver's seat and pointed out the window towards his truck. "I marked Bessie's odometer. If you so much as look at her while we're gone, I'll have you singin' soprano alongside Pastor Roberts's church choir."

Pastor Roberts might be a little tied up at the moment, Jesse thought to himself.

"I just feel so weird showing up without talking to her," his mother said. "Things haven't been exactly easy between us since mom and dad passed." She put her purse in the car and turned back towards the house. "Maybe I'll just try her one more time to double check?"

Jesse groaned dramatically, conveniently ambling between his mom and the deck stairs. One stroke of luck had somehow managed to keep his aunt from answering a call from his mother earlier.

A second call would almost certainly compromise the plan.

"She said they were heading down to the dock for the day, and for you guys to just head straight in and join them." Jesse waved her back into the car.

Rick chimed from the porch. "Besides, you guys deserve a break. You haven't had any time to yourself since finishing up the house."

His mother narrowed her eyes. "If I didn't know better, I would swear you two were trying to get rid of us."

Rick guffawed. "Of course we are. You're the parents," he said, offering a preemptive goodbye wave from the porch.

"We're on a tight schedule," Jesse said. "Lots of band stuff."

Randy honked the horn.

Finally, his mother relented and got into the vehicle. "We'll be back first thing Sunday. Until then I don't want you guys to leave the house."

"Don't worry about us. We have it all under control," Rick promised. "Enjoy yourselves."

Jesse joined Rick on the porch as they watched the tires on the great white wagon kick up the dust on the gravel drive.

"How pissed do you think she's going to be when they find out Aunt Nancy never called?"

"Doesn't matter," Jesse spoke out of the corner of his mouth as he waved at his parents. "By that time they'll be nearly four hours away from town and safe from what's about to happen."

2

"I think we missed the turn," Rick said, navigating from Randy's well-worn road atlas. "Should've taken a right back there."

"Are we still on the road?" Jesse asked. He tried unsuccessfully to wipe off the layer of condensation that had formed on the interior windshield. "I can't see shit out here."

Bessie lurched down the narrow strip of gravel with Hell Patrol's full backline in tow. The meandering ribbon of grey cut through the rising topography of the northern hill country, barely visible within the surrounding sea of darkness.

Mazes and Rust held tight to the gear as they rode in the back of the pickup.

Rick grimaced as a rogue piece of gravel bounced off the side of the vehicle. "Randy is going to fucking kill us. And all thanks to that buck-toothed little weasel." He shuffled the atlas in his lap as he tried to help Jesse with the instrument panel. "Switch on the high beams—second knob to the left of the steering wheel."

Jesse complied, sighing with relief as the high beams cut through the night. The relief was short-lived as he slammed on the brakes just in time to prevent Bessie from careening down a sharp decline in the road ahead.

Mazes and Rust slid forward as the truck came to a halt in the middle of the road.

Rust knocked on the roof of the cab. "Everything okay in there?" he asked through the opened back glass.

Jesse turned to give a thumbs up. Rust's cocky half-smile faded into a scowl as his eyes became fixed on the patch of road ahead.

"Oh, shit. Check out Farmer John over here," said Rick. "Dude looks drunk as a skunk."

Extended visibility provided by the high beams revealed a rotund, middle-aged man who appeared on the side of the road, climbing out from the barrow ditch.

The man staggered into the headlights, clutching his right shoulder; a trail of fresh blood spilled out from beneath his hand, trickling down the straps of the overalls that cradled his oversized belly. He appeared to call out, but his words became lost in the mighty hum of the truck's engine.

Rick pointed past the injured man, towards the pack of canine-like forms that materialized from the darkness beyond the headlights. Jesse recognized the unnatural gait of the creatures as they swarmed the man.

Hell hounds.

The fiends recoiled from the headlights, forming a perimeter around their prey just beyond the radius of the high beams. Two of the hell hounds flanked Farmer John, unhinging their jaws in unison to reveal the swelling sac-like organs that gurgled up from their insides. The sound of the low-frequency sonic pulse the creatures emitted was barely audible over the idling engine, but it was enough to cause a wave of nausea to wash over Jesse's body. He watched in numbed horror as Farmer John slumped to the ground.

Rick shot back in his seat as one of the hell hounds jumped up on Bessie's hood. The creature appeared to be the alpha of the pack; it was much larger than the others, easily the size of a great dane, or even a small horse. A series of bony protrusions crested the slick, grey flesh that ran along its spine, amassing in a symmetrical wreath of horns that spanned the circumference of its skull. It pulled off one of Bessie's windshield wipers and examined it curiously before tossing it into woods.

"Get it off! GET IT OFF!" Rick shouted as he shrank back against the headrest.

Bessie jostled back and forth as the creature postured on the hood of the truck. Jesse fumbled for the radio controls as it thrashed the barb of its prehensile tail across the hood. The hell hound's aggressive display culminated in the exhibition of a large, fleshy sac that began to swell from the creature's abdomen.

"Cover your ears!" Jesse shouted as he cranked the volume of the radio dial as far as it would go.

As the radio blasted through the interior of the vehicle, the alpha leapt from the hood and bounded off into the forest.

Jesse instinctively rolled down the window to avoid puking inside the cab.

As he leaned his head out the window, he could hear the rising swell of a sustained horn blast that bellowed in the distance. The sound was reminiscent of one of the ubiquitous tornado sirens one might hear in the spring time, but the pitch was much lower.

He had heard the sound twice before: in the mine and at the church during the horrors that followed the Community Cleansing. An image of swirling darkness adorned by a golden crown filled his mind as he put the truck in gear.

"Hold on!" he shouted to the others in back.

A rising wind rustled through the trees on either side of the gravel road just as a clap of thunder broke from the night sky. A second horn blast loomed closer; its very volume seemed to bend the trees towards the ground. Drops of rain began to bead up on Bessie's windshield as the instrument panel lights flickered on and off.

Invisible icy fingers of fear massaged Jesse's scalp as he watched a gaunt, nearly skeletal figure lumber out from the darkness towards the downed man. The pack of hell hounds parted as the figure stepped into the strobing headlights. Dressed in a tattered frock and wide-brimmed hat, the ghoulish spectre looked like someone from that '70s movie version of *The Scarlet Letter*, the one he'd watched in English class with the actress who played Hester Prynne with the weirdly blue eyes.

Drones and their sentinels, Jesse thought, recalling Agostino's description of the hive legion. Several bony growths had penetrated through the felt hat, holding it fixed against the taut membrane of mummified skin that wrapped tightly around its skull.

The truck's engine began to stall out as the lights and radio faltered.

"Lurker!" screamed Rust.

"GO!" yelled Rick.

"I'm trying! It won't start!" Jesse screamed. He frantically jostled the key back and forth in the ignition to no avail.

Jesse froze. His eyes were locked on the approaching lurker. Its sagging and torn flesh revealed segments of bare bone beneath as it ambled towards the felled man, lumbering forth on atrophied limbs like an arthritic marionette.

The ghoul knelt down, straddling Farmer John's chest as it writhed back and forth over him. The motion turned into a convulsive fit as a gush of fluid and sludge spewed from its mouth, drenching the downed man's head and shoulders. As the ghoul rose, Farmer John stirred to life, crawling to his feet, where he stood dazedly.

The lurker ambled towards the forest with Farmer John on his heels as the awaiting hell hounds trailed obediently behind.

"Okay. I'm really starting to hate this fucking town." Rick reached into the glove box and pulled out the Hand of Doom. He flicked the switch and the machine whirred to life. "It's hot," he said, tossing the device through the back window of the cab into Rust's hands.

"Get fucked, creep!" shouted Rust.

He leaned over the roof of the cab, aimed the weapon in the direction of the lurker, and pulled the trigger. A concussive wave of distorted sonic energy surged forth from the parabolic dish and broke upon the revenant.

The lurker was pummeled by the sheer force of the acoustic wave, flickering in and out of existence as it smashed against a thick oak tree. The force of the blast was so strong that one of the tree's low-hanging branches had pierced through the lurker's skull, which poked out through its eye socket like a kabob skewer being stuffed through a grape tomato.

The lurker flailed at the limb that split through its skull, causing it to wriggle free. It landed face down on the ground and rolled into the barrow ditch where it lay motionless.

Bessie's instrument panel shot back to life.

The headlights revealed an open road ahead; the pack of hell hounds had vanished along with Farmer John.

"Did you see that shit?" asked Rust, brandishing the Hand of Doom high over his head. He shook the discharged dislocator and handed it back to Rick. "This shit's cashed, man. It's one and done."

"Punch it," Rick said, pumping his fist on the dash.

"We can't just leave the old man."

"Dude, he's long gone by now. Besides, we can't follow him into the woods with those fucking things running around. We stick to the plan."

Just as the words left Rick's mouth, Mazes ran past his window towards the forest.

The Lynn brothers turned their attention to the drummer, who had picked up the felled lurker and was carrying its desiccated body over his shoulder towards the truck.

"What the fuck are you doin', dude?" asked Rust. "You got your armor on too tight or somethin'?"

Mazes climbed in and hoisted the lurker down into the truck bed.

"I've sworn an oath to protect the realms from the undead." He scanned the woods warily and spoke through a rare frown. "There are certain rituals I must undertake to prevent this abomination from coming back to wreak its unholy havoc yet again."

"Are we seriously gonna allow this? That thing has got to be a health hazard."

Mazes smiled and shrugged his massive shoulders. "My apologies, Master Rust. However, this decree has been formalized by our covenant."

Rick nodded without turning his head.

"He's right." He folded his arms across his chest and muttered under his breath. "It's the only fucking thing he requested be put in his contract. Something about 'turning the undead.'"

"Whatever. Let's just go," Jesse said. "We don't have time to argue."

Free from the sonic influence of the lurker, Bessie started right up when Jesse tried the key. He slammed on the gas just as the engine turned over, causing Rust and Mazes to tumble backwards over their gear and onto the floor of the truck bedz. He watched in the rear view mirror for any sign of movement as the gravel drive beyond the radius of the taillights disappeared into the night.

3

Agostino had rented out an old farmhouse on the northern edge of town off Route 12. By the looks of the structure, it was a relic of the original townsite settlement that existed long before Macomb Springs was incorporated. *The perfect rural getaway for the ethnomusicologist-turned-guidance counselor-turned demonologist. Or whatever the hell he really was.*

Despite Agostino's enigmatic persona, he was the only person in town that seemed to know what the hell was going on, but more than that, Jesse had grown to trust him. He believed the others were coming around as well.

When they arrived, Agostino was already out front, directing the work of establishing a perimeter of spotlights, audio gear, and a tangle of speaker cables and extension cords that surrounded the house. Jesse immediately recognized the muscled retail clerk with the heavy scar and thick bowl cut from RadioShack who assisted him.

"Two distinct blasts, two minutes and sixteen seconds apart." Agostino clapped his hands. "Did you hear them?"

"Yeah, we heard," Jesse said.

Rust tossed Agostino the Hand of Doom.

"Thanks for mentionin' that we only had one round with this piece of junk." Rust gave him a cocky, headshot-ready grin. "You're lucky I'm a good shot."

"So the prototype *does* work? That's wonderful." Agostino examined the device with a raised eyebrow. "With all that has been going on lately I never had a chance to properly test it."

The remaining members of Hell Patrol and their manager exchanged a cold look.

"Quick, follow Henry into the lab." Agostino waved the group towards a white metal shed at the back of the farmhouse. "Get everything inside the sonic barrier."

"This way," Henry said. "And try not to break anything."

The group unloaded the gear and followed Henry out back per Agostino's instructions. He led the group into what appeared to be a recently erected metal shed. The pristine white powder coating stood in stark contrast to the adjacent farmhouse, whose rough exterior had not seen fresh paint since before Jesse's parents were born.

As Henry opened the front double doors of the shed, an overwhelming stench of decay lingered in the air.

"Fuck me, they caught one," said Rust.

Jesse's eyes were drawn to movement coming from the back of the shed. In the dimly lit interior, he could make out a large transparent tank covered in chains and pad locks. Inside, a captive hell hound was pacing back and forth, seemingly oblivious to the arrival of the group. A small speaker monitor was mounted on the inside of the tank.

Despite the hell hound's movement, no sound came from the tank. A smaller wire cage, draped in an opaque black cloth, abutted against the tank that held the captive sonopod.

A series of workstations lined the walls of the shed. The source of the stench seemed to be emanating from another hell hound carcass that was laid out on a nearby workbench. Its abdominal cavity had been pulled apart, exposing its innards. Heaping piles of greasy soft tissue and organs lay strewn about on either side of the exposed specimen.

Distracted by the horrific scene, Jesse barely noticed the pale, hairless man with blue-grey skin who hovered over the body of the dissected hell hound. The man appeared to be attempting to connect the creature's organs to an array of electronic equipment, the likes of which Jesse had never seen.

"Everyone, this is Rune—a close family friend and colleague," Agostino said. "Rune was a prominent biomedical researcher in his homeland and has worked with our family for several —"

"For a long time," Henry interrupted.

"Rune does not speak much, but as you can see he is happy to make your acquaintance," Agostino said as he turned to face the strange man.

Rune turned from his work to offer a polite bow. Jesse was reminded of the Crypt Keeper puppet from the *Tales from the Crypt* TV series as he absorbed the man's strange features; the same blue-grey skin color permeated his eyes and mouth.

"And I believe you have already met my older brother, Henry," Agostino said. "Henry's expertise is in evolutionary biology and engineering. He does his best to keep our research grounded with a healthy dose of scientific objectivity."

"That was the path my father had laid before me. But as far as you all are concerned, I'm head of security for this op." Henry saluted the group. "I guess you could say that Vinny here's the brains, and I'm the brawn."

"And lemme guess," Rick pointed at the man with the blue-grey pallor, "he's the good-looking one."

"We've met," Jesse said as he eyed Henry. He began to see the familial resemblance beneath Agostino's bearded countenance as the revelation took hold in his mind. "You never mentioned he was your brother."

"My apologies. A preoccupation with recent events has kept my manners at bay."

Rick pivoted in his chair as he surveyed the interior of the prefab laboratory. "You guidance counselors really take your work home with you."

The comment seemed to widen Rune's smile.

"Guidance counselor is my job, but I have another calling."

"Oh, yeah? What's that?" asked Rick. "Demon Hunter?"

"Let's just say that the urgency of recent events have forced our Forgotten Order from the shadows."

"Hold on." Rick looked around the room as though suddenly aware of his surroundings. "You guys really are some kind of Fortean witch doctors?"

"Nothing gets past you," Jesse said.

"Perhaps we can discuss further once this is all over," Agostino deflected, growing more uncomfortable with the line of questioning. "For now, I think it is best if we continue our collaboration with as much discretion as possible, given the current situation."

"You should consider yourselves lucky," Henry said. "We normally don't expose our operations to civilians."

"I feel anything but lucky," Rick quipped.

"Geez." Rust pulled his shirt up over his nose. "It smells like rotten eggs in here." He pointed to the dissected corpse strewn across the metal slab. "What the hell are you doin' with that thing?"

Henry jumped in before Agostino could respond. "Rune and I have been studying their anatomy in order to figure out the resonating frequency of the sonopods' living tissue." He hung his head in defeat as he continued. "These little bastards are all we've been able to get our hands on."

Jesse elbowed Mazes. "In that case, I think we have something you might want to take a look at." He looked up at his companion, and cocked his head towards the truck.

Mazes's perennial smile faded. "So long as we properly dispose of the remains afterwards."

Jesse nodded.

Mazes slumped his broad shoulders, dragging his feet as he made his way out of the shed.

Agostino pointed towards the array of audio equipment at one of the nearby workstations. "Unfortunately, as Henry mentioned, the technology to gain a precise measurement of such a bio-frequency does not yet exist, so we have had to improvise."

Rick wheeled over to an adjacent workstation with a state-of-the-art stereo system. "Nice gear. Do you guys serenade them before you study their anatomy?"

Agostino returned a blank look.

"I bet this one does," Rick said, giving a knowing nod towards Rune as he continued. "What's your pleasure, my bald brother? Maybe a little Minnie Riperton? Some Donny Hathaway or Teddy

Pendergrass to get the juices flowing?" He covered the side of his face with one hand as he rolled his eyes towards Henry. "I'm gonna go out on a limb and guess that your colleague's taste in music isn't quite as discriminating."

Rune doubled over in the midst of a silent fit of laughter.

"I pegged him as a Bread fan from the moment I saw him."

"Actually, I prefer avant-garde industrial music," Henry replied, stone-faced.

"Fuck me."

Henry shrugged. "It's good workout music."

Knowing someone's musical tastes revealed more about that person than could be gleaned in hours of conversation. Jesse filed away Henry's revelation into the back of his mind, feeling slightly more grounded about his present company in the process. Dealing with Agostino's eccentricities was one thing, but it really added up when you brought his meathead brother and the Crypt Keeper into the mix.

Agostino pulled aside the black cloth that lay draped over the cage next to the living hell hound. Inside, a red-eyed, white haired rabbit was strapped down in the center of the cage. An array of wires and electrodes covered its entire body.

He pointed to one of the active monitor screens on the work-bench where the rabbit's biometrics were displayed in real time. "All organic beings produce an array of biochemical endorphins, especially when frightened. You may have commonly heard of this described as the fight-or-flight response."

"I think I'm having one right now," said Rick.

"When compared to humans, the relatively low biochemical output of the rabbit does not appear to register with the sentinel."

As if on cue, the hell hound rested on its haunches.

"Rune, you're up," said Henry. He rummaged through one of the metal storage cabinets, and produced a large, elegantly framed painting.

Rune strapped on a rubber skullcap outfitted with a net of electrodes that ran to the workstation displaying the rabbit's biometrics. A second set of biometrics flashed on the adjacent monitor as Rune donned the skullcap and approached the hell hound tank.

Henry held the portrait, depicting a regal-looking woman dressed in flowing medieval garb. She was standing in what appeared to be a stone courtyard with a rural village in the background. Her face was frozen in a scowl.

Rune recoiled from the painting, physically trembling as Henry held it up to his face.

"Who's mommy's little monster?" Henry asked, turning to face the bewildered group of newcomers. "He's terrified of his mother. Works like a charm."

"Was your mom like a queen or somethin'?" asked Rust.

Agostino lowered his voice as he stood next to Rust. "She was a prominent member of the Scandinavian nobility during the Middle—"

"During the mid '70s," Henry cut in. "She locked Rune in the cellar for a couple years, and forced him to drink colloidal silver—hence the permanent smurf impression. She thought he was a vampire because of the alopecia."

"A very superstitious lot back then," Agostino looked to the ground, shaking his head.

A flurry of activity appeared on the second monitor. The hell hound suddenly reacted to Rune's presence, snarling and snapping at the blue-grey spectre who lingered near the tank.

Agostino stepped towards the cage. "Once this sonopod sentinel—or *hell hound*, as you prefer—detects the biochemical output from our friend's induced hyperarousal, it will begin to emit a sonic beacon, marking Rune's location for the drones to harvest." As Agostino spoke, the bulbous resonating organ appeared to swell beneath the creature's jaw. The hell hound appeared to call out, compressing the air-filled sac as it swelled and released again and again like a pair of fireplace bellows.

"Don't worry. His friends might have the ability to teleport through matter, but this one isn't going anywhere," Henry spoke, pointing to the cage. "These hell hounds don't have the same arsenal of sonic weaponry as the rest of the legion infantry. They're bred for recon."

The hell hound attempted to claw out of its cage as Rune drew nearer, backing away from the portrait. Agostino waved Henry off of Rune, who appeared relieved to remove the skullcap.

"The degree to which these sonopods are able to manipulate matter appears to be relative to their function within the hive legion—an ordered hierarchy of duties similar to the division of labor that one might observe among a colony of ants or bees."

"And as it turns out, they aren't metal fans," Henry said, pressing play on a modular cassette deck attached to the state-of-the-art audio receiver.

A looped sample of the opening chord of "Black Sabbath" *by Black Sabbath, from their eponymous debut album, released on Vertigo records in 1970*, blared over the receiver's monitor speakers. As the sample played, the hell hound recoiled from the small speaker monitor mounted inside the soundproof tank.

Like the lurker they had recently witnessed on the drive to Agostino's farmhouse, the creature briefly phased in and out of being, flickering like an image shot from a stuttering film projector.

Henry pressed stop on the cassette deck.

"Who knew demons would be so fuckin' square?" laughed Rust.

"This can never get out," Rick said. "All we need is for *Hit Parader* to catch wind of this and the industry will be in the toilet."

Agostino draped the cloth over the rabbit's cage as he spoke. "Through the course of our experimentation, we have attempted to reverse engineer the stratified social order of the sonopods within their legionary hierarchy," Agostino explained. "It's possible that the sentinels' lack of matter manipulation points to their own evolutionary origins, as Henry suggested—possibly bred for their purpose through millennia of artificial selection."

Rune audibly cleared his throat.

"Yes—very well." Agostino bowed to the pale man. "I'll defer to Henry on this matter."

"Thank you, Vinny," Henry started. "We're operating on the theory that the lesser demons—hell hounds, and potentially other ranks within the sonopod legion—were themselves harvested from other worlds during previous visitations. Other than the horns, the lack of homologous anatomical structures provide no evidence of a shared, common ancestor, particularly one geared towards life in a subterranean habitat."

Rune closed his eyes and bowed to Agostino.

"Is that why they set up base camp in the old mine?" asked Jesse.

"They appear to prefer karst formations within the earth's mantle—underground caves devoid of light, and therefore also lacking subatomic interference from the vibration of photons. These *thin places* also happen to be conducive environments for developing rifts in the spacetime continuum," Agostino replied.

"Wouldn't it be easier if they just beamed down to the surface where all the Twinkies are instead of bein' stuck underground?" asked Rust.

"Humans haven't always lived on the surface," Henry said. He led the group to a large map cabinet stacked with rows of shallow drawers. "If I was a betting man—and I am—I'd put my money on the cave system beneath the mine sharing physical characteristics with the sonopods' indigenous habitat. Not to mention that caves are natural acoustic resonators—a perfect environment for organisms highly adapted to sound."

Henry pulled out one of the rollout drawers and rifled through a stack of simplistic illustrations of human hands, crude animal drawings, and one image of a great horned beast surrounded by a pack of barb-tailed minions. "Caves were the Ritz-Carlton of early human hunter-gatherers."

Jesse examined the illustration depicting the great horned beast and its surrounding minions.

"So somewhere around the dawn of time, these subterranean fear junkies got hooked on caveman brain, and now it's time for another fix," Rick said.

"Pretty much."

"These samples of parietal art, namely cave paintings and petroglyphs, confirm this chronology," Agostino said.

"They were probably keeping tabs on the planet from the beginning, waiting until something appetizing came out of the evolutionary oven," Henry said.

All eyes shifted towards the shed entrance as Mazes returned with the lurker's corpse. Rune excitedly directed him to an empty slab next to the dissected hell hound carcass.

"Collect them all. Available at participatin' restaurants now," said Rust.

"We came across this one on the way over here," said Jesse. "A pack of hell hounds had just cornered this old farmer when this thing came along and somehow took control of his body."

Mazes slung the corpse down over his shoulders and laid it out on the stainless-steel slab.

"Harvesters." Henry marveled at the lurker's corpse.

"Incredible," Agostino added. "We've been hypothesizing that these harvester drones have significant roles within the legion hierarchy, but now... to finally get to examine one in the flesh —"

"Not much left on this one," Rick interrupted.

Rune shone a penlight into the gaping hole in the lurker's skull carved out by the oak branch. The atrophied remnants of flesh and sinew creaked in protest as he turned the lurker's mummified head to reveal the back of the skull. He then selected a pair of pliers from a set of mortuary implements that had been neatly laid out next to the stainless-steel slab and fished inside the base of the lurker's skull.

The taciturn technician's eyes grew wide as he picked up a wand-shaped device from a nearby workstation. The cable that stemmed from the base of the implement was plugged into an oscilloscope and signal generator, similar to the setup from Mrs. Ford's classroom.

Rune pressed the device to the lurker's fractured skull as the signal generator emitted a series of distorted tones.

The lurker's jaw quivered.

As the volume of the signal increased, a viscous yellow discharge began to pour from the lurker's ear canals.

Rune's smile grew wide as he pulled out a wet mass of organic tissue that had become dislodged from the lurker's skull and placed it into an Erlenmeyer flask.

The contents of the flask began to move, slowly, like a starfish crawling across the ocean floor. Long, hair-like filaments hung off the end of each slimy lobe. A large lesion perforated the center of the tangle of mucus and flesh, nearly splitting it in half.

"This little guy has been through the ringer. Takes a lickin' and keeps on tickin'," Henry chimed. "Looks engineered to me. What do you think, Vinny?"

Jesse noted the excited look shared by Agostino and his brother Henry as they examined the organic deposit under the light. Rune selected a long metal probe and poked and prodded at the organism, causing it to squirm against the sides of the flask.

"Symbiotic parasitic automatons!" the brothers called out in unison.

Agostino reached into his wallet and pulled out a twenty-dollar bill which he grudgingly gave to his older brother.

"Anyone care to explain?" asked Rick.

Agostino smiled as Henry transferred the bill to his wallet.

"Henry had posited a theory that the worker caste of the hive legion might be comprised of symbiotic parasitic automatons—"

"Mindless slaves, hand selected from the sonopods' interplanetary menu. When infected with this clever little beauty here, they are somehow able to control the host behavior," Henry finished.

"Thus the task of transporting the human battery cell to the nexus is fulfilled by the host itself," Agostino said.

"Sort of like forcing someone to dig their own grave before murdering them," added Rick.

Agostino nodded. "In a manner of speaking, yes. And in exchange, the parasite is rewarded with sustenance as it moves between hosts."

"And, by the looks of it, the symbiosis could span hundreds of years or more," Henry said.

"Until somebody shoots you with a sound gun and you get shish-kabobbed," said Rust. "And you're welcome by the way."

"I would guess that only a small number of harvester drones such as this are created from elite sentient hosts during the sonopods' feeding cycle," Agostino said, motioning to the lurker's corpse on the slab. "The harvesters likely serve as the dispensing mechanism of the parasitic organism, which is then able to quickly replicate through some type of spontaneous parthenogenesis when they encounter a bio-energy source, such as humans."

"High price for immortality if you have to spend it being controlled by this runny little snot ball," said Rick.

Agostino lightly touched the tattered frock that hung off the edge of the table. "Judging by the garments, it would appear this specimen is a remnant from the sonopods' last feeding on Earth—nearly three centuries ago."

"Looks like he's about to serve us up some Quaker Oats," Rick said.

"Agreed," Henry said, craning his neck over the slab to inspect the lurker's corpse. "I'm thinking late-seventeenth century colonial Massachusetts. North Shore region perhaps? Maybe Salem or Wenham?"

"Might have been someone important—magistrate or vestry-man by the looks of all that brass."

Rune nodded in agreement with the brothers' assessment.

"So what's going to happen to Farmer John after he got *Night of the Creeped?*" asked Rick.

Henry returned his attention to the parasite specimen, tapping his index finger on the glass. "So this little beauty here takes control of the host's nervous system, delivers it to the nexus. And then… "

"And then what?" asked Jesse. He suddenly felt a knot growing in the pit of his stomach.

"Eventually acts as a catalyst to some sort of bioenergy transference that converts the biochemical essence of the host into a palatable form of energy that will sustain the sonopods' passage into our world for a mass feeding," finished Agostino.

"Jesus Christ, where's Ripley when you need her?" asked Rust.

"What I wouldn't give," sighed Henry. "Which brings us to the upper echelon of the hive legion … the monarchy."

Agostino nodded. "The sonopod hierarchy presumes the existence of an ultimate authority—a leader being who alone possesses the ability to open the door between worlds."

Jesse began to synthesize the information. "The horn blasts."

Agostino uncovered a large leather-bound tome from a nearby workstation. The words *Ars Goetia* were scrawled across the cover in an ornate script. "As I mentioned before, the infestation that presently occupies Macomb Springs has plagued our world before." He opened the book to a marked page that depicted an image of a unicorn-headed, humanoid beast who wore an ornate crown and carried a trumpet in one of its elongated, clawed hands.

Jesse felt the blood drain from his face as he pored over the image.

"That's the thing from our album cover," Rust blurted out.

"This one is known in the *Lesser Key of Solomon* as Amduscias," replied Agostino.

"We've taken to calling it the Rift Lord," chimed Henry. "Sounds cooler, right?"

"Amduscias is considered by early occult demonologists to be a Great Duke of Hell, commanding several legions to do his infernal bidding. This particular demon is directly associated with music and sound, and is believed to have the ability to summon thunder and bend the trees to his will with his voice."

"Well, at least they got that right," scoffed Rick.

Henry nodded. "Like the old man always said, '*Hell was a warning.*'"

Agostino carefully closed the book and patted its cover. "Despite the lack of scientific objectivity, there is much to be gleaned from these early descriptions."

"*Demons* are just a human construct," Henry agreed. "We co-opted these early sightings and wrote them down in our big, black books."

"That's great and all," Rick said, "but in the meantime, what do we do about the fact that these *constructs* are about to make a buffet out of our town? And you're sure this dislocating frequency is gonna work on the Rift Lord?"

Rune mimed what could have been confused as laughter at Rick's inquiry.

Agostino gestured to the Hand of Doom. "Because of the success of the prototype against the varied orders of the sonopod legion, both sentinels and drones, we can infer that there exists a common resonating frequency among them, despite the potential for disparate evolutionary origins."

"They may have gotten on at different stops, but they all took the same bus to get here," Henry said. As Henry paced back and forth his perfectly symmetrical bowl cut resumed its alignment on top of his skull with each turn. "Imagine that bus—the nexus—is made of some type of living plasma that has gotten mixed up with the different hive castes as some kind of integrated epigenetic extension of itself, combining with individual sonopod DNA as they pass through the bowels of time and space."

"And the Rift Lord is the source of this subatomic masking," Agostino said. "It is the source of the nexus. We destroy the nexus, we have a chance at destroying the Rift Lord."

Rune nodded in stoic agreement.

Jesse's mind was clouded by thoughts of Mal being sequestered with the sonopod legion. "Look. I appreciate all that you guys are trying to do, but I'll just take my chances with the prototype. Seemed to work pretty good so far."

"You don't want to take a knife to a gunfight," Henry said.

The brothers shared another of their weird, non-verbal communications before Agostino turned to meet Jesse's eyes.

"In anticipation of the current infestation, we set about weaponizing the sonopods' dislocating frequency as soon as we had adequate data," Agostino said. "Which we do. Not a complete or exhaustive dataset, but it is enough to work with."

"What are you trying to say?" asked Jesse.

"In addition to the prototype, there is also a production version," Henry said.

Agostino led the group to an equipment closet positioned against the back wall of the prefab laboratory. "The production version projects a highly concentrated dislocating radius, narrow enough to allow for safe passage in and out of the partitioning membrane without destabilizing the nexus between worlds."

"Assuming the power supply I rigged together is adequate," Henry said. "Not my finest hour, but it's the best I could do on short notice."

"What's wrong with the power supply?" asked Jesse.

"The amount of power required to attenuate the sonopods' resonating frequency in even a ten-foot radius cannot be sustained by presently available technology for more than approximately twenty minutes."

"So that's all the time we have to go in, find Mal, and get back in time to close the nexus for good?" asked Jesse.

"Yes," the brothers answered in unison.

"All right." Jesse looked over his companions. "We're ready. Other than the backline gear, what do we need to get this show on the road?"

Agostino stopped in front of the equipment closet and turned to Jesse. "Unfortunately, only one of you will be able to cross over."

Jesse stepped forward. "How?"

"With this."

Agostino opened the door to the closet, revealing a nylon flight suit, outfitted with all manner of speakers, wires, and battery packs. Jesse's eyes went to the breastplate at the center of the suit: Alex's boombox. Only it was rebuilt, modified with heavy-duty external wiring, extra speakers, and a large LED power display.

"I hope you don't mind Henry taking liberties with the original design. I recently discovered this derelict machine when taking the last batch of observational readings at the mine."

Mazes knelt down on one knee and averted his eyes. "Behold, a wonder of the realms."

"We call it The Ripper," Henry said. He rocked back and forth on his heels, arms crossed, marveling at his creation. "Vinny thought it would be fitting, since you guys are into Priest."

A heavy-duty power cable ran from a large port in the back of the suit. The plug on the end of the cable looked like one of those big industrial ones that came with a dryer or an air conditioner compressor. A modified motorcycle helmet hung next to the suit inside the equipment closet.

"Holy shit," said Rick. "We gotta get these guys to run sound for us."

"To that end," Agostino gestured towards the gear that had been staged near the shed entrance. "We will need to upgrade your equipment to be able to broadcast the dislocation frequency." Agostino pressed his hand on Jesse's shoulder. "I believe you have a basic understanding of electronics, yes?"

Jesse nodded, dumbfounded as he held The Ripper in his gaze. "Yeah, whatever you need."

"This is a rescue op, boys," Henry addressed the group as they formed a half-circle around The Ripper. He pulled down a screen on the wall that detailed a sketch of the old mine. "We believe the sonopod nexus lies somewhere within the natural cave system beneath the Spring Creek Mine. Despite reports from the historical tunnel collapse, it is our hope that a portion of this system will still be accessible by descending the vertical mineshaft."

Agostino placed the augmented motorcycle helmet over Jesse's head and began a series of adjustments.

"Your objective is simple. Get in and get out without becoming demon food," Henry said. "Once you rescue the hostage, and secure any other viable townsfolk, Vinny and the band will use the backline to override the resonant frequency of the portal, destroying the connection to our world, sending the Rift Lord and its legions straight back to hell."

Jesse snapped open the helmet visor. "What happens if I find her and she's got one of those things stuck inside of her head while I'm wearing the suit?"

"Hopefully nothing more than a brief, albeit painful, expulsion of the foreign body," Agostino said.

"Hopefully?"

"Collateral damage," Henry said. "It's a chance you'll have to take."

"The good news is, as we have just observed with the harvester specimen, it should be possible to return the survivors back to normal with an induced sonic therapy," Agostino said.

"No problem—right, guys?" said Rust. "All we have to do is wander down into the pit of hell and fight off a legion of demons. Mazes practically lives for this stuff—piece of cake."

"Just think of the street cred this will buy us," Rick said, more to himself than anyone nearby.

Henry counted on his hand. "First we'll need to lure the Rift Lord out from the nexus long enough to prepare the mine and setup the gear."

"How do we do that?" asked Jesse.

"We will need a distraction," Agostino replied. "The portal is growing strong enough that Amduscias can move out of close range from the nexus, but only for short amounts of time."

"So who gets to be the bait?" asked Rick.

"Rune and I will lure it out with these." Henry held up the bulbous, hollow resonating organ from the dissected hell hound's chest cavity, attached to a series of electrical cables. Rune's handiwork. "If we fire up enough of these repurposed scout emitters to generate a substantial sonic marker, the harvester drones will come running." Henry tossed the emitter organ on the stainless-steel slab.

"If enough harvesters show up, the Rift Lord will not be far behind," Agostino added. "The legion advance guard are largely dependent upon Amduscias for transport to and from the nexus."

"Gentlemen, I've heard enough," Rick said, eying his watch. He cracked his knuckles and pushed his glasses back over his nose. "I'm the manager of this outfit, and now you're on my schedule. And it's almost show time."

4

After a solid hour of tinkering, Jesse and the Forgotten Order had successfully optimized the Hell Patrol backline. The gear was quickly loaded up as the entourage made their final preparations to set out for the mine.

"Once we are on the road, Henry and Rune will activate the sonic beacons and continue on due north." Agostino gestured towards the woods beyond the gravel drive. "The rest of us will head south, in the opposite direction, to set about destroying the nexus."

"Hey—so you guys never mentioned what happens if the Rift Lord doesn't show," said Jesse. "What the hell do we do if he doesn't take the bait?"

Agostino and Henry exchanged one of their telepathic conversations, shaking their heads in unison as if to say, *Not an issue.*

"Amduscias is desperate for energy—it will show, and once it does, we will not have long," said Agostino.

Henry nodded. "Once the ploy is discovered, the Rift Lord will likely head back to base to recharge."

Rick called to the others from Bessie's passenger door. "Whenever you guys are done kissing goodbye, we have a show to play."

Agostino exchanged a few private words with Henry before they set the plan into motion. Despite being younger, Vincent appeared to be the more mature of the Agostino siblings. Other than a slight hint of rivalry that surrounded the theoretical foundation of their increasingly bizarre familial research interests, a clear fondness existed between the brothers.

Jesse helped Rick into the cab as Mazes and Rust made a spot for Agostino in the back. "So what's the deal with these guys? Forgotten Order—what's that all about?"

"I get the feeling they don't wanna talk too much about the family business."

"I'm starting to feel like they've been planning this for a while," Rick said. "The backline, you going down into the mine in that suit...it's kinda fucked up."

"Fucked up has become the status quo," Jesse started. He watched as Rune climbed into Agostino's Bronco and flashed a shark-toothed grin at the Lynn brothers. "I get it. Trust me. But they're the only ones who seem to know what's going on around here, and we don't exactly have any other options."

"We could leave," Rick said. He let the words soak into Jesse's ears before continuing. "We could jump in the truck with the gear, get the fuck out of Dodge, and forget this little science experiment ever happened."

Rick waited for Jesse's stony gaze to falter. It didn't.

"Nah, just fucking with you." Rick laughed off the silence. "You're all fucked up over Elvira, and saving this shithole town—I get it. I'm with you, man. That was just a test."

5

Rune led the caravan in Agostino's Bronco with Henry riding shotgun.

Jesse and the others followed in Bessie down the gravel drive that led from the farmhouse. The late fall Mourning Moon was nearing its zenith by the time they were on the road, shot into the night sky like a silver pin ball.

Henry's voice broke over the two-way radio that Agostino had provided. "Night Crawler here, do you read me?"

Rick answered back. "I can't properly respond unless you use my handle."

After a few seconds of radio silence, Jesse heard Henry sigh through the speaker. "Please, Rick. Don't make me say it."

"Come on, man, quit screwing around," Jesse pleaded.

Rick held his palm out, fingers splayed, towards his brother. "International radio protocol dictates that you communicate to my handle."

After another brief pause, Henry responded, his voice heavy with reluctance. "Night Crawler here, do you read me, Big Prick?"

Jesse could hear the smile in his brother's voice as he answered back. "Big Prick here, copy. I read you loud and clear, Night Crawler."

"We are ready to arm the beacon," Henry replied.

"10-4, Roger that."

At the end of the gravel drive, Rune turned the Bronco to the north and pulled off onto the side of the road. Henry jumped out and powered up the array of hell hound emitter organs that had been hooked up to the loudspeakers on Agostino's Bronco. A chorus of low-frequency bursts resounded into the night. "Beacon armed," Henry's voice broke over the radio. "Stand by to engage the emitter sequence."

"Copy," Rick said.

Jesse wished that Mal had been with him to witness what might be the last twenty-four hours of his short life. More had occurred during that small and seemingly trivial amount of time than Jesse could fathom. He reasoned it might take the rest of his life, if that was still in the cards, to sort through it all.

As though sensing their intentions, the still night air had begun to build to a steady headwind as they set off down the winding gravel road to the south. To the mine. To Mal. The swelling wind pelted dust and debris from the surrounding forest against the truck.

Rick closed the back glass and gave a thumbs up to the others who were piled in the truck bed. Rust adjusted the pair of safety glasses and sound-dampening headphones that the group had been outfitted with from Agostino's lab. He yelled something to Mazes and Agostino, then returned the gesture to Rick.

"Stand by, we are beginning the seq—" Henry's voice cut out over the speaker.

"Night Crawler, we're getting some interference. I couldn't make out that last part. Please repeat. Are we all clear for take off?" Rick asked into the handheld radio. "Over."

The wind had whipped up a thick cloud of dust over the gravel road, limiting visibility beyond the headlights of the truck. Rick called again over the two-way radio, but there was still no answer.

Jesse put the truck in park and opened his door to get a better vantage on the Bronco.

"Dude, stay in the fucking truck," said Rick.

"Chill out, I'm just trying to see what's going on." Through a break in the dust Jesse could see the red glare of the Bronco's brake lights flickering on and off. "Something's wrong. They're not moving." A slow-moving shadow appeared within the radius of Bessie's headlights, causing Jesse to freeze in his tracks.

"Lurkers!" Rick called out.

Jesse jumped back into the driver's seat. The truck rattled and fell silent as the headlights strobed in the surrounding dust cloud. Agostino darted past Rick's window towards the Bronco, arming the Hand of Doom as he vanished into the wall of dust and flying debris.

A muffled cry resounded from the darkness, followed by what sounded like the blast of a bullhorn feeding back. Once the sound abated, the interior lights of the truck lit up and Jesse was able to start the engine.

"All clear," Henry's voice resounded over the radio. "The sequence is armed and ready. We're off. Now it's up to the rest of you. Good luck. Night Crawler over and out."

Agostino bounded catlike over the side of the truck bed and knocked on the cab window. "We are clear to depart for the mine."

Jesse put the truck into gear. The low-frequency sonic blast bludgeoned his ears a split-second before he was showered in an explosion of glass. He looked up from the rattling glass shards that danced upon the dashboard towards the towering shadow that stepped into the headlights.

The wind stopped.

A monstrous shape emerged from the woods, nearly the height of the trees, and loomed over the vehicles. The Bronco's rear tires kicked up a spray of gravel as Rune and Henry made for the north. The beacon, now fully armed, was emitting bursts of low-frequency calls. The sound trailed behind the vehicle as it sped off into the night.

A field of dark, snaking tendrils orbited the unearthly being, obscuring its form as it stood motionless in the headlights. From beneath the veil of dissipating darkness, Jesse could make out the band of translucent flesh across the creature's abdomen, hinting at the inner workings of the beast. The snaking tendrils seemed to emanate from the physical anomaly.

It was riddled with the appearance of bony protrusions that grew out from the ash-grey flesh that covered the bulk of its body. Up close, Jesse could see that the crown adorning the creature's head was in fact growing out of its skull like horns (or whatever gleaming, metallic biomaterial served as horns for these demons from another plane of existence).

Above the wreath of horns, an accordion-chambered organ erupted out from the center of the creature's elongated snout, giving it a vaguely unicorn-like appearance. The spear-like growth retreated into its bellows as the creature drew breath, causing the limbs of the surrounding trees to bend down towards the ground. A deafening blast erupted from the chambered organ that sprang from the top of the Rift Lord's skull.

Amduscias. The Great Duke of Hell.

Bessie lurched forward into the night as Jesse slammed on the gas. As they headed down the long and straight section line road towards the south, the others looked on in stunned silence as the Rift Lord pursued the Bronco into the night.

"I think it's working," Rick said as he watched through the side mirror. He called out over the two-way radio. "Night Crawler, be advised, you've got one hungry Rift Lord on your six."

Jesse white-knuckled the steering wheel until they were in sight of the service road that ran through the Old Townsite industrial center.

Almost there. Almost to you.

CHAPTER NINE

INTO THE RIFT

1

Rick tapped Jesse on the shoulder. "Slow down. There's something up ahead."

A halo of white light surrounded the ridge directly above the concrete incline that led down to the Hell Hole.

"They made it!" Rick yelled.

As they drove towards the light, Jesse began to make out the individual headlights that lit up the surrounding woods. Twenty-some-odd cars had created a makeshift parking lot just off the old service road in front of the mine.

Jesse parked Bessie on the side of the service road, allowing the others to climb out of the truck bed.

Rick shoved both middle fingers into his mouth and uttered a loud, shrill whistle. A handful of roadies emerged from behind the circle of lights and began pulling out the gear and schlepping it down the incline to the mine entrance.

"Reporting for duty, your Prickness," shouted Robb-O, Rick's old roadie buddy who had sold Hell Patrol the discounted backline.

"Here to do our part, dudes," said one of the black-clad crew who raised horns at the road-weary Hell Patrol.

"Rick the Prick delivers once again," Rick answered back.

Jesse felt a twinge of nervousness at the shit-eating grin his brother was broadcasting.

"Now that's a crowd," said Rust. "How did the hell did you get so many people to show up?"

"I may have told them there was a DIY protest show coming on the heels of the church record burning."

"They all showed up to see us?" asked Rust.

Rick continued beaming at Jesse.

Jesse calmly turned off the ignition, shook the glass shards from his hair and jacket, and looked his brother dead in the eyes. "What did you do?"

"I did my goddamned job. You and Professor Venom worry about the demons. Let me worry about putting on a show."

"Seriously," Jesse folded his arms. "Why are there so many people here?"

Rick lowered his voice as he peered over his glasses. "They might have been told you were opening for Prisoners of Flesh."

"What the fuck?" asked Jesse.

"If you must know, I also alluded to the possibility that there would be free beer. Don't worry—it won't come out of our end. The Forgotten Order is picking up the tab." Rick looked out of the side of his face. "I billed it as the best *underground* show of the year. At least that much will be true."

"What happens when a legion of demons pours over this place?"

"They know what they signed up for—metal or death." Rick screamed out the words "*metal or death*," a sentiment echoed by each of the roadies as they carted out gear from the caravan of vehicles. "See?"

Agostino appeared outside Jesse's window. "I am afraid we do not have much time…"

"This is fucked up, dude," Jesse said, glaring at his brother.

"Put it in a letter," Rick replied. "If we survive the night, you have my permission to be pissed."

2

A command center was quickly established in the central control room. The road crew—a mix of musicians, roadies, stage hands, and other fixtures of the regional underground music scene—made quick work of setting up the backline. They even managed to provide lights and power by tapping into the mine's dormant power grid with an industrial-grade generator. A mile of electric conduit snaked through the central tunnel between the control room and the impromptu stage being set up near the entrance.

Under Rick's direction, a beer station was quickly set up in the Hell Hole, just outside the mine entrance. By the time the gear was set up, there were nearly forty people on site.

Away from the prying eyes of the bustling entrance, in the dark recesses at the end of the central tunnel, the expedition to the nexus between worlds had established a base camp inside the derelict winch house near the opening of the vertical mineshaft.

Agostino helped Jesse into The Ripper.

"The suit is fully charged. And I should warn you, it is going to get very hot once it is powered on. The interior is lined with a thermal protectant and cooling fans, but the amount of power running through the battery array is still dangerous."

"I'll be okay. As cool as this thing is, I don't plan on wearing it home."

"That is agreeable, because at full power, the battery packs will only be able to sustain the dislocating barrier for about twenty minutes." He pointed to the four green bars that represented the power supply on the boombox breastplate's LED readout. "Each bar represents approximately five minutes. Keep an eye on the gauge."

Jesse nodded. "Got it. Back in twenty or I'm demon food."

"When you are ready, we will lower you down in the bosun's chair. The partitioning membrane surrounding the nexus should not be far off once you reach the bottom."

"How will I know when I'm near the nexus?"

"You will know." Agostino demonstrated the toggle switch on the power console. "When you are ready, all you have to do is press this switch to activate the suit by placing it into FULL from the default STANDBY position."

"Kinda like turning on a tube amp."

"Precisely." Agostino moved his fingers over the boombox affixed to the suit's midsection. "Once the suit is powered on, press play on the cassette deck, and the rest will take care of itself."

Agostino decoupled the suit's power supply and toggled the suit's power switch into STANDBY. Immediately, the suit lit up. The LED lights from the boombox and surrounding network of auxiliary speakers allowed Jesse to see a few feet into the abyss as he leaned over the lip of the vertical shaft. The cold darkness plummeted down beneath, causing a twinge of dizziness as he tried to fathom the depths of the descent.

"Just make sure that the tape keeps playing when the sonopods are near. The weaponized sound field created by the suit should repel the sonopod resonant frequency within a radius of ten to fifteen feet."

"I'm ready," said Jesse.

"I have produced a mixtape just for this occasion." Agostino opened the cassette deck to demonstrate. The door to the player opened, but no tape could be seen. He tried the second recording deck. Empty. He felt his pockets and appeared dismayed. "No... this cannot be."

"What's the matter?" asked Jesse.

"Henry was supposed to load the tape back at the lab."

"You've got to be fucking kidding me." Jesse suddenly felt strangled by The Ripper's claustrophobic confines. "Will anything work? There's an army of metalheads out there."

"Anything on cassette will suffice. The suit itself converts regular sound waves into the dislocating frequency, but it is preferable that the source is one of extreme volume and aggressive tonalities."

Rust jogged up to the winch house with Mazes in tow. "Hey Jess, I think I found us a guitar player."

"That's great, but we're kind of dead in the water until we get a tape for The Ripper. Can one of you guys check with Rick and see if he can score something?"

"I've got you covered." The squeaky voice cut through the hum of activity coming from the mine entrance. Jesse turned to see a skinny teen with a backwards ball cap, biting into his lip with a pair of oversized front teeth. A guitar was strapped over his shoulder.

"Alex!" Jesse shouted, unable to believe his eyes.

Alex reached into his battle vest pocket and held up a Maxell cassette tape. Jesse instantly recognized the title flanked by a pair of inverted pentagrams: PAINKILLER. "Heard you guys needed a guitar player."

Jesse hugged Alex despite The Ripper's awkward girth. "I thought they made you burn all your tapes?"

"Just the cases," Alex smiled. "That collection was my life's work, man. I wasn't going to toss it into the fire for some fucking Jesus freaks."

Kara appeared next to Alex.

"Alex filled me in on the way over," she said. "If there's a chance in hell we can bring her back, I want in. Got room for one more?"

Alex looked Jesse over in the suit and smiled a wide-toothed grin as he placed the tape into the boombox's cassette deck. "Go find Mal."

3

The sound of a guitar being tuned up resounded off the tunnel walls and down into the vertical shaft where Jesse's descent was being staged.

"Sounds like the band is almost ready," said Rick. He was on standby near the winch house, overlooking the descent, fiddling with the two-way radio in his lap.

Jesse pulled on the cable from his perch on the bosun's chair—a dusty old harness with a plank seat they had found in the winch house.

"The young mage has signaled his readiness," called Mazes from the winch controls.

The winch arm creaked and groaned as Mazes and Agostino manually lowered Jesse down in the bosun's chair. Even with Mazes's brute strength, the rusted steel cable had to be forcibly separated from the drum with each turn of the crank, causing the descent down into the vertical shaft to be slow going and methodical.

Jesse tried to steady his breathing inside the claustrophobic suit. The light from The Ripper's LED power meter illuminated the rough stone shaft as he inched deeper and deeper into the abyss. Once he was out of earshot, he heard Rick chime in on the two-way radio built into the noise-cancelling headphones that were mounted inside the helmet.

"How's it going, man? You holding up?"

"So far, so good," Jesse said. "Agostino was right about the suit. Haven't even fully powered it on yet and I'm burning up."

"Just hang in there. A little bit farther and the professor says you should be nearing the bottom. When you touch down you should be seeing some kind of spacetime disturbance. Follow it to the source, and you'll be at the nexus."

Just your average day in the life.

After a few minutes, the cable went slack as the bosun's chair touched down at the bottom of vertical shaft.

"Okay, I think I'm here," Jesse spoke into the headset, relieved to be once again on solid ground.

"Good work, little bro. I'm going to pass the mic—Professor Venom over here is getting all twisted."

"Jesse, it is Vincent—I mean, Agostino."

"I read you."

"You should be coming up on the partitioning membrane's outward extent at any moment. Follow its signature and you will likely end up somewhere within the natural cave system beneath the mine—at least the portion of it that remains undisturbed by the collapse. Look for an open cavern or chamber—somewhere large enough for the hive to amass."

Jesse surveyed the bottom of the shaft in the scant illumination cast by The Ripper's LED lights. He immediately noticed the large tunnel that shot off from the base of the shaft. As his eyes adjusted, he began to notice movement within the inky blackness. The very air seemed to writhe on top of itself like a nest of snakes.

"Standby. I think I see something."

Agostino's voice resounded from inside the helmet. "When you turn on the suit, remember to monitor the power gauge. And whatever you do, give yourself enough time to make it back up the ascent." The radio turned to static as Agostino's voice faded.

Jesse had never felt more alone in his life. He took a breath and powered on the suit. The Ripper's power supply began to hum, sending out jarring vibrations that pulsed through his entire body.

Mal's voice filled his ears as he conjured her image in his mind's eye. "Do you ever just feel like you're stuck between worlds?" she had once asked.

He closed the visor on the modified motorcycle helmet; a faint greenish hue flashed across his vision, indicating the low-light filter had been engaged. *Night vision. Looks like the Brothers Grimm thought of everything.*

As he stepped into the abyss of shifting darkness, a brief tingling sensation swept over his body. Once the sensation subsided, he found himself inside a partially collapsed antechamber that announced the formation of a vast, open space beneath the earth.

Just as he rounded a pile of fallen stone that lay in his path, an unseen weight landed on his shoulders, causing him to reel forward. His balance was off-kilter in the cumbersome suit; the force of collision toppled him over onto the ground.

As he tried to regain his footing, he came face to face with the snarling hell hound that clawed at the helmet visor. The bulbous resonator organ in its chest swelled to bursting as the creature let out a bellowing howl. The sound was muffled by the noise-canceling headphones, but Jesse knew that the summoning call had already dealt its damage.

He reached for the cassette player just as a second hell hound wrapped its jaws around his arm. He tried in vain to wrestle the demonic minion loose as the hound's vice-like grip tore through the outer layer of the reinforced suit. Jesse rolled to the side to avoid being pinned down, and with his free hand he smashed down on the cassette player.

The soundburst pulsated outward through his chest, spinning him around like a top as he fought to regain his footing. The descending hell hounds recoiled from the noise, allowing Jesse to get his bearings in the heavy suit.

The antechamber was awash in the rhythmic drum intro of the first track—"Painkiller" by Judas Priest, *from the album* Painkiller *released on Columbia Records in September 1990 after a six-month delay resulting from the much-heralded subliminal message trial.*

The explosion of sound had attracted the rest of the pack, who stood their ground at the opposite end of the antechamber. One of the larger alphas emerged from the pack and charged towards the intruder, clashing head-on into The Ripper's invisible sound barrier.

As the alpha approached the field of weaponized sound put forth by the suit's array of blasting speakers, the creature's flesh bubbled and fizzed. It recoiled from the onslaught, appearing to howl in pain, though Jesse couldn't hear its cry over Rob Halford's piercing vocals.

Jesse took the initiative and grabbed the staggering alpha, pulling the hell hound into him. The creature writhed in pain, but Jesse held firm, wrapping both arms around its neck and holding it against the boombox chest plate that protruded from his torso. The alpha struggled frantically to be released from Jesse's grip before exploding like a balloon filled with two hundred pounds of organic sludge.

The rest of the pack turned to flee at the sight of their leader's abrupt demise.

Jesse wiped away the sludge from his helmet visor and checked the suit's power gauge. One of the four green bars representing the suit's power supply had already turned red. *Still enough time. Almost there. Almost to you.* He pressed stop on the cassette player to conserve energy.

With no sign of the pack, Jesse proceeded through the antechamber, following on the heels of the retreating hell hounds. He thought of Agostino's description of the hive hierarchy and reasoned that they might be heading to the core of the nexus to protect their master. Jesse lingered at the mouth of the large natural opening, awestruck by the enormity of the vast cavern that lay ahead.

The transition into the natural cave system awakened some reptilian memory within Jesse's evolutionary subconscious. Henry had mentioned that these alien demons—these *sonopods*—preferred human prey because of their tendency to live in caves back in prehistoric times. It was hard to deny the ancestral connection he felt to this landscape as he gazed upon the void within the earth.

In the center of the vast open space, a great column of weeping stone connected the floor to the ceiling of the spacious chamber. Jesse had been to a handful of state parks throughout the South— Alabaster Caverns, Carlsbad Caverns, and Meramec Caverns (where they filmed *Tom Sawyer*, according to one overenthusiastic

tour guide)—but none of those underground marvels had prepared him for what he was about to see.

An enormous chrysalis had been formed around the circumference of the stone pillar, the exterior of which was comprised of
a tessellation of translucent, hollow capsules, each roughly the
size and shape of a standing, adult human.

The bottom-most layers of capsules within the conical structure
were filled with a viscous liquid that appeared greyish-white in
the low-light filter of the visor. Jesse conjured the memory of the
royal jelly from the beehive that Mazes had found in the woods
near the Hell Hole before their first practice. And again he felt
the familiar sense that there was something unsettling about
witnessing nature order itself in such complexity, especially when
it involved kidnapping your girlfriend and extracting her life
force in order to feed a legion of demonic aliens.

Undissolved scraps of clothing and dense skeletal matter hung
suspended in the liquid matrix of the lower capsules, each one an
individual cell in the great psychic battery that would be used to
power the sonopods' passage to Earth. Jesse reasoned that the less
fortunate among the population—vagrants and transients passing
through the quiet streets of Macomb Springs—were likely some
of the first occupants...now empty husks devoid of life that stared
up through their hollow orbits at the domed ceiling.

He recalled Agostino's hypothesis, "... *a catalyst to some sort of
bioenergy transference that converts the biochemical essence of the
host into a palatable form of energy that will sustain the sonopods'
passage into our world for a mass feeding.*"

Above the fluid-filled chambers, row upon row of clear capsules
were stacked several stories high, many of which were occupied
by human captives. Farther still, spanning from the midsection
of the chrysalis to the top-most extent of the structure were
even more rows of capsules that remained fully empty. In all,
the structure was reminiscent of an ear of corn that someone had

eaten from the top down, bursting with ripe, untouched kernels at its base.

Fashioned from the same organic concretion that formed the support structure of the chrysalis, a narrow spiral walkway had been formed around its exterior, trailing upwards, running from the cavern floor to the very top of the immense structure.

In the distance, barely visible in the scant light provided by the helmet's night vision, similar structures were being developed around lesser columns throughout the cavern.

Jesse scanned the rows of capsules that appeared to contain recently captured townsfolk. He recognized some of the faces even through the low-light filter of the visor. A majority of the captives appeared yet to be processed by the infernal machine—recent additions, he reasoned, taken from the night of the Community Cleansing.

His eyes stopped as they fell upon Mr. Summers, his hand outstretched towards his son, Kenny, who lay unconscious in one of the adjacent pods.

Jesse muttered in disbelief into the comm mic inside the helmet. "Half the goddamned town is down here."

A static-filled, garbled response echoed in his ear as Agostino's voice broke through the interference, "...band is ready. Once Amduscias appears...to the surface."

"Right on cue," Jesse whispered into the mic.

A swirling vortex opened up near the chrysalis. The portal came to life, pulsating and expanding to accommodate the dark shapes that began to take form inside of it.

The nexus.

Amduscias materialized, passing through the open nexus along with a throng of recently infected hosts plucked from the Macomb Springs populace. A handful of the lurking, skeletal harvester drones and their hell hound sentinels passed through the nexus last, ushering the new arrivals towards the towering chrysalis.

The townsfolk were marched up the inclined walkway in a slow, almost ceremonial procession; plodding along without protest, interring themselves into the next available cells in an obedient offering to their new master.

Against the dark backdrop of the cavern, Jesse could see a faint umbilicus of energy being drawn from the great demon into the heart of the nexus. Amduscias flickered into being and rose to its full towering height. Jesse watched in horror as a second shimmering umbilicus erupted from the Rift Lord's chambered resonating organ and attached itself to the battery of captive human hosts. As it did, the shimmering vortex of the nexus seemed to grow.

He scanned the structure, desperate for any sign of Mal within the chambered tower. The efficiency of the sonopods' operation was repulsive, yet wondrous at the same time.

His heart stopped as he saw the body of a young woman lying slumped against one of the translucent walls of one of the center-most capsules. A tangled mop of dyed black hair pressed against both sides of her face. Her darkened eyelids fluttered momentarily as the procession of host automatons stumbled past.

Jesse whispered to himself, forgetting about the helmet mic. "I'm here, Mal. I found you—and you're still alive."

Without hesitation, Jesse pressed play on the cassette player. The second track, "Hell Patrol," raged forth from The Ripper as he charged into the gathering of hell hounds and harvester drones at the base of the chrysalis.

Like wildfire, comes roaring, mad whirlwind, burning the road…

Jesse screamed involuntarily as The Ripper tore through the ranks of the Stygian horde like a sonic juggernaut. A ten-foot radius of weaponized sound carved through the otherworldly legion with each beat of the drum and screech of distorted guitar.

The harvester drones ceased in their corralling of the townsfolk to focus on the interloper threatening the desecration of their ritual.

As the drones fell into the radius of The Ripper, their ears burst in small explosions of viscous mucus. Many of the more ancient lurkers burst altogether as they tried in vain to stop the intruder.

Black thunder, white lightning, speed demons cry—the Hell Patrol...

Jesse fought his way to the spiral walkway and began to climb. He pushed his way through his fellow townsfolk—now empty-minded zombies destined to become adrenaline smoothies—and trudged up the incline, feeling every ounce of the heavy suit as his legs carried him forward. The captive human hosts fell to the ground, clutching their ears, as the governing parasites were forced out of symbiosis by The Ripper's sonic onslaught.

Night riders, death dealers, storm bringers, tear up the ground...

As he traversed up and around the chrysalis, he could see a second contingent of lurkers amassing below on the walkway. Even in the greenish hue of the helmet's night-vision visor, the harvester drones were easy to identify from their host counter-parts. Jesse could tell them apart from their antiquated dress, and the deteriorating condition of the human bodies being driven by the sonopod parasites.

He had seen more than one harvester among the horde that did not appear to be wholly human.

Finally, he reached Mal's capsule. As he pushed through the cell's thick, translucent membrane, The Ripper's sonic field reso-nated through the confined chamber. Mal collapsed, convulsing on her back while clutching both sides of her head.

"I got you," Jesse said. "This might hurt a little." He held her up as the nodular parasite was expelled in a wash of fluid from both ear canals.

After her fit subsided, he pressed STOP on the cassette deck, pulled her out on the walkway, and lifted the visor.

"Everything is going to be okay," Jesse spoke, more to himself as Mal fluttered on the edge of consciousness. "Now we just need to get the hell out of here."

As Mal lost consciousness, Jesse surveyed the path ahead. *Only way out is the way through.* Before he could hoist Mal over his shoulder, he was stopped in his tracks by the advancing column of harvester drones that lumbered towards his position on the walkway.

At the head of the column strode a familiar figure, more ambulatory than its ancient, skeletal counterparts.

He closed the helmet visor to engage the night vision to be sure his eyes did not deceive him. But there, on the walkway, closing in, was the unmistakable frown cast by Principal Anderson. The standard-issue pantsuit was torn and frayed, and the wreath of tightly set curls was in disarray, but it was her—or at least what used to be her.

Jesse pressed PLAY on the cassette deck.

Fist flying, eyes blazing, they're glory bound—the Hell Patrol...

Without hesitation, he strode towards his former adversary and braced for impact. The lurker—formerly known as Principal Anderson—recoiled from the wall of sound emitting from the suit, its face twisted with rage. He met the automaton head-on until it was inside The Ripper's sonic radius.

The enslaved principal fell to the walkway and clawed frantically at her ears. A gush of fluid streamed out of her nostrils and ear canals. Jesse looked on as one of the parasites that squirmed out from Anderson's left ear began to bubble up within its mucus sac like a fried egg until it exploded on the walkway next to its host.

Believing the lurker threat to be neutralized, Jesse turned to retrieve Mal. Instead, he found himself alone on the walkway.

His eyes darted towards movement on the path below. Mal's body was being pulled behind a demonic harvester the likes of which Jesse had yet to observe in the wild. Unlike the lurkers that he and the others had witnessed up to this point, those who had taken on human hosts, Jesse was gazing upon the corporeal form of a non-human being.

The creature had rough, spiny skin, including several progressively larger horns that ran up the length of its spine to the tip of its skull. In its wake, a barbed, prehensile tail thrashed angrily behind it as the lurker carried Mal toward the bottom of the chrysalis.

She had summoned the strength to kick and flail against her captor, slowing the demon enough for Jesse to catch up.

Using the higher ground to his advantage, he leapt forward and wrapped his arms around the head of the demon, dropping his feet out from under him. The full weight of the sound suit caused the demonic lurker to topple backwards.

Mal rolled safely to the cavern floor, looking up in disbelief as Jesse grappled with the thing torn from nightmares.

The demon squirmed as The Ripper began to liberate the flesh from its body. As it turned to look upon its assailant, the hourglass-shaped pupils shifted inside the pair of narrow, reptilian eyes. A look of pain transformed into a mask of rage as the harvester faced down its prey. Jesse responded by shoving his arm into the gaping maw of the creature, reaching deeper still until the speakers that lined his arm fully penetrated its gullet.

Brutalize you, neutralize you, gonna go for your throat as you choke, then they'll vaporize you...

The harvester drone convulsed as the sound waves shook through the core of its being, causing it to reel back and forth with each note of the slashing guitars that burst through its innards. Small geysers of internal fluids erupted from its orifices as the song raged forth.

Terrorize you, pulverize you, gonna cut to the bone as you groan, and they'll paratamize you...

With his other arm, Jesse pulled the flailing drone towards his chest. Pressed against the speakers of the modified boombox, the flesh of the sonopod began to boil. The drone tried desperately to hold itself together as it was torn apart from the inside out.

Chrome masters, steel warriors, soul stealers, ripping out hearts, they're devil dogs—the Hell Patrol...

As the outro chorus raged through the speakers, Halford's ear-splitting falsetto flourish gutted through the sonopod, resulting in a brief implosion that resonated through the creature's insides in a rebound structure of sonic destruction.

The demon foot soldier's rough outer flesh split down the middle at the spine and fell to the ground like a freshly skinned game pelt. Jesse instinctively stepped back as its soft insides oozed across the walkway in a pile of steaming-hot sludge.

Jesse pressed STOP on the cassette player and opened the visor of the helmet. He could hear the scuffling of sonopods within the stillness of the cavern and the horrified gasps of the surviving townsfolk, now free of the controlling parasites.

He reached out into the darkness and gently pulled Mal towards him as he whispered. "Time to go. We're gonna be late for the show."

At the recognition of Jesse's voice, Mal smiled and fell into his arms.

"Stay put, help is on the way!" Jesse called to the darkness, hoping that the other captives could hear.

The solitary, flashing green bar on the power console brought back the urgency at hand.

He threw Mal's arm over his shoulder and pulled down the visor on the helmet. Together they waded through the wake of carnage left by The Ripper, slipping and sliding on the demonic viscera that lined the floor of the cavern as they proceeded towards the antechamber.

A deep bellow emanated through the cavern, causing the ground to quake under Amduscias's wrath. A large stalactite fell from the domed ceiling as the chamber began to cave in on itself. The remaining legions answered the summoning call and rallied around their leader, who remained ensconced in the rippling vortex of the nexus.

Jesse managed to avoid large sections of the crumbling cavern as he navigated Mal through the antechamber. A flood of angry, dark tendrils chased after them as they approached the bosun's chair.

"Get ready to pull us up!" Jesse shouted into the mic.

The snorts of hell hounds mixed with the deep, resonant blasts of the Rift Lord grew closer.

"We might have some company."

As Jesse helped Mal into the bosun's chair he noted the minuscule sliver of green left on the last power bar. As soon as he laid her down on the plank seat, she drifted off. He cinched her tightly into the harness and pulled hard on the winch cable.

With no response from the two-way radio, Jesse pulled off the helmet and called up to the others. "Pull us up, now!"

As Jesse's words echoed up from the bottom of the deep, vertical shaft, he hoped some remnant of his call would find its way to the surface.

Jesse heard the arrival of the pack before he could see them in the dim luminescence of The Ripper's LED lights. He took one last look at Mal before donning his helmet.

"We almost made it," he said as he brushed the hair from her eyes.

Jesse Lynn, former bass player and founding member of Hell Patrol, strapped on the helmet and marched towards the amassing horde as he hit the play button on The Ripper's cassette deck once more.

4

A squeal of feedback resounded from the two-way radio as Agostino pressed down on the talk button.

"What's going on?" asked Rick.

Agostino shook his head. "Probably just interference from the nexus. As long as the suit has enough power, Jesse should be fine."

Rick wheeled over to Agostino and grabbed him by the wrist. "The fuck—*should* be fine?"

"As long as he follows my instructions, there is a factored probability—albeit a small one—that he will return unharmed."

Rick furrowed his brow and met Agostino's eyes. "If anything happens to my brother down there on this wild goose chase you've sent him on, I'll roll these twenty-six-inch wheels up inside your asshole."

Agostino visibly gulped and nodded.

Rust and Alex jogged up to the winch house.

"We're all set up. What's the word?" asked Rust.

The winch arm began to pivot and creak as weight was applied to the bosun's chair from below. Agostino ran to the winch mechanism where Mazes was already turning the hand crank. Together the two began to pull up the chair from the bottom of the mineshaft.

Rick wheeled up to the winch platform and called out below. "Jesse, you okay? Talk to me little bro."

The groaning of the rusty winch cable and the din of the amassing audience near the stage were his only answer.

Alex gasped as the bosun's chair emerged from the darkness of the deep, vertical shaft. Mazes and Agostino hoisted the limp, sludge-covered body from the chair and laid it on the ground near the opening of the shaft.

"Mal!" Alex shrieked.

A plume of dust and stale air erupted up through the vertical shaft as they pulled Mal to safety. Her eyes fluttered open as she struggled to speak.

"Jesse…"

"Save your strength—try not to speak," said Mazes. The tall youth knelt down to Mal and picked her up gently, cradling her in his arms. "Jesse's fortitude is very high. He will survive this trial," Mazes said as he carried Mal out towards the entrance.

"What the hell was that?" asked Rick, wiping the dust from his glasses.

"Something must have caused the remaining portion of the natural cave complex to cave in on itself," Agostino replied.

Rick turned to Agostino. "He's still down there."

"We don't have time to send the chair down again. Jesse will have to fend for himself until we close the nexus between worlds."

"I can't just fucking leave my brother down there with a bunch of fucking demons," said Rick.

"If Hell Patrol does not start the override sequence soon, we will not be able to destroy the connection between our world and theirs." He laid a hand on Rick's shoulder. "They will devour the town and everyone in it."

Rick looked down in silence.

"Who's gonna fill in for Jesse on bass?" asked Alex.

All eyes fell upon Agostino.

"Do you know any covers?" asked Rust.

"I would suggest 'Black Sabbath,' by Black Sabbath, from the album, *Black Sabbath*. This song features an exemplary execution of the tritone. The modified backline will do most of the work in broadcasting the resonant frequency override."

"Wait a minute," Alex squeaked. "Do you even know how to play it?"

Agostino took off his tweed blazer and neatly folded it up before handing it to Alex as he headed towards the stage.

Rust punched Alex on the shoulder. "Relax man. That dude has a degree in Black Sabbath."

5

Rick surveyed the eager faces of the audience as he adjusted the noise-canceling headphones that Professor Venom had talked him and the others into wearing. He took a deep breath as Rust lowered the mic stand.

"Thank you for coming out tonight for another Rick the Prick production. It's good to be back, Macomb Springs!"

Chants of "*Rick the Prick*" rose from the crowd.

Rick shushed the audience as he continued. "What you are about to witness is sure to be known as the most insane underground show of the year."

The audience burst into applause.

In his heyday as a local promoter, Rick had managed to put together some momentous bills. Before he was prematurely retired from his calling, Rick the Prick had rubbed shoulders with some of the greatest bands in the world.

In the summer of '86, he and his pal Robb-O had managed to talk their way into humping gear with Metallica's road crew for a couple of dates on the American leg of their Damage Inc. Tour. *Master of Puppets* was changing the world—even more so when Cliff didn't make it back from Europe a few weeks later. It was grueling and often thankless work—and Rick couldn't get enough of it.

Within a year's time, he had managed to infiltrate the coveted underground network of regional promoters and talent bookers—the *Sleaze Brigade* as they were commonly known. He had quickly garnered a name for himself when he nabbed Voivod on their Tornado Tour with Kreator as direct support. *Killing Technology* had just come out, and the band was hot shit. That's when he knew what he wanted to do with the rest of his miserable life.

All that was left of that life now was the highlight reel.

It wasn't until his little brother and his shitty cover band came along that he ever even considered he might have a second chance at life, let alone the music biz. A spark had been rekindled, and he was coveting the flame. If by some miracle they managed to survive the night, the stars would be the limit for Hell Patrol.

He would see to it. For Jesse. He owed him at least that much. Particularly if they managed to save the town. *You can't buy that kind of PR*, he thought again to himself.

"Without further ado, please welcome to the stage Macomb Spring's own sons of metal—Hell Patrol!" He pivoted his chair towards the stage exit and muttered under his breath. "Also, we regret to inform you that Prisoners of Flesh had to cancel tonight's show—but fear not! You are about to see a show you will never forget."

Rick tried to ignore the audible question mark that hung above the audience as he was helped off the stage. The awkwardness was soon dissipated by a deep and sustained horn blast, echoing up from the depths of the mine shaft. A second blast repeated, much closer to the surface, shaking the walls of the central corridor.

"Play, goddammit! Play the fucking song!" Rick yelled as he wheeled off stage.

Rust pulled the mic off the stand before the audience had time to process the latter portion of Rick's announcement, or the thunderous call from the deep.

Mazes counted off on the hi-hat as the explosive first chord of "Black Sabbath" by Black Sabbath rang out through the mine.

The ring of the opening chord resonated from the amps that were facing down the corridor. A sustained wall of sound gathered strength as it reverberated off the stone walls before flooding into the depths of the mine.

Rick looked beyond the lit stage towards the winch house. Dark tendrils of shadow flickered into being, rising up from the depths of the vertical shaft. They stretched across the walls of the sparsely lit central tunnel like inky fingers, reaching out towards the stage.

A towering shape materialized from the confluence of shadows. The metallic gleam of Amduscias's crown preceded its snarling, equine visage as it emerged from the darkness. The contracting resonating organ stood fully erect atop its brow. The demon passed through the central tunnel as several of its legion charged forth from its veil, making for the stage and the oblivious audience that surrounded it.

"Now would be a good time," Rick called to the stage.

Agostino stomped on the foot switch that enabled the frequency dislocator. A thunderous roar emitted from the amplifiers, so powerful it physically pushed back the front row of the crowd, sending many off their feet to the ground.

The Great Duke of Hell pushed through the sonic assault as it descended upon the fragmented audience. Within the glow of the utility lights, Rick could see the veil of shadow that transported the Rift Lord beginning to falter. The shimmering tendrils of living darkness were being pulled away by the explosive sound wave, trailing off towards the open vertical shaft.

The cheers of the crowd echoed through the central corridor as the audience began to rally towards the stage. Rick watched the ironic display of flashing horns, pumping fists, and banging heads as the legion descended on the crowd.

"These idiots think it's fucking special effects," Rick whispered to himself, shaking his head in disgust.

The demon swelled up to let out another deep, bellowing call that shook the central corridor, causing pieces of stone to fall from the ceiling.

The concussive effect of the blast caused most of the remaining audience members left standing to short circuit and tumble to the ground.

Agostino was motioning to the others on the stage to keep playing.

Amduscias reached into the crowd and plucked a fallen audience member from the ground. The man, a portly bearded fellow, flailed and screamed as he was brought high in the air before the Rift Lord flung him against the tunnel wall like an insect.

Nearly a dozen of Amduscias's demonic legion ambled towards

the stage, exploding into wet clouds of organic mist as they neared the amplifiers' weaponized sonic field.

As Hell Patrol reached the instrumental break of "Black Sabbath," Amduscias had visibly slowed. The demon lord struggled with each step as it tried desperately to dig into the stone. Snaky black tendrils spewed from its translucent abdomen in all directions. Its presence grew more unstable with each ring of the massive tritone chords that shook the interior of the mine, causing the great beast to briefly phase in and out of existence.

The Rift Lord gathered its strength and lunged forward, swiping at the band. Alex and Agostino both managed to dive out of the way as Rust leapt from the stage, mic in hand. Mazes, who was stationary behind the drum kit, was less lucky.

Rick looked on helplessly as Amduscias held the large brute in its elongated grip and attempted to crush the life out of the paladin.

Despite being under attack, Hell Patrol sustained the sonic assault on the sonopod nexus as the guitar and bass continued to blare through the line of modified amplifiers. Rust was screaming his heart out into the mic off to the side of the stage.

Rick watched as a late arrival emerged from the dissipating vortex of shadow that surrounded the demon lord. A large humanoid shape, larger than most men, lumbered forth. It stepped clumsily into the light, revealing a disfigured demonic form carved straight out of one of Agostino's arcane history books—barbed tail, horns, and all. It entered the fray, pitting itself between the band, now minus its drummer, and Amduscias.

The demonic legionnaire clawed frantically at its torso as it struggled to reach deep into its own chest cavity. A barrage of sound that rivaled the volume of the band caused the creature's outer layer of flesh to explode, revealing what appeared to be a bulky, grey skeleton with a boombox-shaped ribcage in its place. In place of the muscles and tendons were a series of wires and cables attached to an array of speakers. Where its skull should

have been, about a head or two shorter, sat a tricked-out motorcycle helmet.

"Jesse!" Rick cried out. "He fucking did it!"

Jesse charged towards the Rift Lord as it attempted to crush
Mazes, launching himself into the center of the hulking monstrosity. The impact of the heavy suit and its field of sound was
enough to knock Mazes loose from the demon's clutches as it
staggered backwards, losing its foothold against the pull of the
collapsing nexus, sending it careening backwards towards the
vertical mineshaft.

Jesse and Mazes were caught in the pull of the imploding shadow
gate and tumbled into the shaft after the Rift Lord.

Rick navigated through the tangle of fallen showgoers, spinning
his wheels as fast as he could towards the winch house.

Jesse held onto the edge with one hand while he scrambled
to grab onto Mazes with the other. The hefty paladin fought
desperately for a handhold on the sheer rock face as he slipped
farther and farther down into the abyss.

Just a few feet below, Amduscias grated its claws against the sides
of the shaft to brace itself against the pull of the collapsing nexus.

Rick sped towards the winch pulley crank, toppling out of his
chair in the process. He managed to crawl the remaining distance,
pulling himself up to the release mechanism. Once the line was
released, the bosun's chair went into a free fall towards the bottom
of the shaft. The pull of the collapsing vortex brought the steel
cable within reach of Jesse and Mazes.

"Grab the line!" Rick screamed. His voice became lost in the
cacophony of overdriven guitar and bass that flooded the central
tunnel.

Mazes wrapped the line around his waist as an anchor and
grabbed Jesse. Together, they kicked off the edge of the rock wall,
swinging freely just a few feet above the struggling Rift Lord. Rick
leveraged his full weight to turn the hand crank as he pulled up

on the lever with both arms; the movement secured the line and pulled it taught.

Mazes and Jesse were thrown against the walls of the shaft as the pull of the vortex increased. Amduscias floundered as a portion of the rock face gave way beneath its claws.

At Rick's back, the earsplitting groan of the mine cart added to the sonic fray as it was pulled along the ancient track. Free from its rusty shackles, the cart lifted from its tracks as it was sucked down into the mineshaft. It crashed hard into the Rift Lord, sending Amduscias reeling into the abyss of the imploding portal.

As the demon plummeted into the deep, a final low-frequency blast was cut short as the earth shook beneath the mine.

Rick rolled on his back, narrowly avoiding the falling winch arm.

A geyser of dust and debris erupted from the shaft, blanketing the upper level of the mine in a powdery soot. The mine continued to reel from the quake, rendering the light and sound of the stage dark and silent. The faint sonic residue produced by the modified amplifiers resolved down into the depths of the mine as the earth settled.

Silence filled the mine.

Rick belly-crawled over the rough stone ground towards the mouth of the vertical shaft. The impenetrable cloud of dust made it difficult to get his bearings; his glasses were covered in the stuff.

The sound of muffled groaning resounded in the darkness near the mouth of the vertical shaft. He proceeded towards the sound with his heart in his throat. A soft halo of light beckoned from the dark. *The Ripper*, Rick thought to himself as he inched closer to the light.

Agostino appeared next to Rick just in time to assist pulling Jesse up over the lip of the shaft.

Rick pulled the helmet off just as Jesse succumbed to a raucous coughing fit. His brother's hair and face were drenched with perspiration.

"Jesus fucking Christ," Rick said. "You gave me quite a scare, you little shit."

"Brilliant strategy using Amduscias's nexus to transport yourself to the surface," Agostino added.

Jesse's eyes were starting to roll to the back of his head. He struggled for breath, producing only the word, "Mal."

"She's all right," Rick said. "You did it, man. You fucking did it."

Just as the words left Rick's mouth, he heard the loose rocks near the surface of the shaft buckle under the weight of the large, dark shape that appeared, reaching out towards him.

"Master Rick," a disembodied voice called. "Did we fell the beast?" Mazes lunged out from the darkness and collapsed on the ground next to Jesse.

AFTERWORD

Mal burst into the green room brandishing a rolled-up newspaper above her head. She dangled the offering above the coffee table where the Hell Patrol inner sanctum were gathered.

"Is that what I think it is?" asked Jesse. He sat his new Fender Precision bass down against the couch where he and Alex were warming up.

She smiled coyly. "Who wants it?"

Rick snatched the newspaper from her hands and began to tear through the copy. His eyes darted back and forth as he devoured its contents.

"Of course. Barely a mention of the heroic efforts of the road crew who pulled up all the survivors." He tossed the newspaper on the coffee table and crossed his arms. "Or our touring schedule. I knew that hack reporter was going to drop the ball."

Alex jumped up to grab the paper before Rust could swoop in. He began to read aloud as Mal took his seat beside Jesse on the couch. "'As a result of the incident, the Macomb Springs City Council has passed a resolution to demolish any and all vestiges of the derelict mine to avoid future trespassing attempts.'"

"Typical," said Rust, adjusting his studded leather jerkin.

"Glory is its own reward," Mazes smiled.

Alex continued. "'No charges were filed against the suspects, who were deemed instrumental in the rescue of several townsfolk who were detained by the secondary collapse of the Spring Creek Mine. Many of the survivors could not account for their whereabouts on the night in question, and appear to have experienced hallucinations from exposed toxic gases while trapped within the abandoned mine. When asked for comment, the Macomb Springs Police Department claim there is still an open investigation into the matter, but declined to elaborate further.'"

"Instrumental is right," Rust smirked. "I could barely hear my vocals over those hot-rodded amps."

"Hold on, there's more…" Alex traced the script with his index finger. "'The events that transpired on the night of the collapse revolved around the performance of an unauthorized rock concert put on by up-and-coming heavy metal band Hell Patrol, who also include members of Macomb Springs High 1991 graduating class,'" Alex finished, letting the paper drop to the coffee table.

Jesse threw his hands up and hugged Mal. "They mentioned our name!"

Robb-O entered the green room with several rolls of gaffer's tape dangling from his arm like oversized bracelets.

"Sound check in five. You guys ready?" he asked.

"We're ready," answered Rick. "All right, everybody fall in. Circle of fists." He gestured to Mal. "Do your thing, publicist."

Mal produced a bundle of sage from inside her jacket. She lit the dried herbs, and fanned the smoke around the small room.

Hell Patrol, their manager, and their newly appointed publicist/ photographer formed a circle around the coffee table, putting their fists together above the report from the *Macomb Springs Chronicle*.

Rick closed his eyes and recited the band prayer. "With metal hearts, we call upon the metal gods from the altar of the stage." He opened one eye before continuing. "Please watch over our brothers, Hell Patrol, as they embark upon their first headlining gig, complete with a catered green room, and adequate cash guarantee."

"Is it over yet?" belched Rust.

Alex responded with a sharp elbow to the singer's ribs.

Mal gave Rick a supporting nod.

"Brought together by denim and leather, we shine, as one, like a rainbow in the dark. We promise to never say die and to never break the oath as we seek and destroy all that impedes our path to victory along the highway to hell. May our fans bestow fortune upon our efforts. And may a hole in the sky open up and bring raining blood down upon our enemies, and so on, until we close our eyes forever," Rick finished. "In Iommi we trust, hallowed be thy name."

"Hail Satan," said Rust.

A resounding grunt of disapproval issued collectively from the group.

"Hail the demonslayer!" Mazes offered as he pounded Jesse on the back.

"Fucking Hell Patrol," finished Mal.

ABOUT THE AUTHOR

R. D. Tarver is a science fiction and horror author who lives in Norman, OK with his wife and two cats where he works as a geoarchaeologist interested in hominin evolution and Paleo-American hunter-gatherers. In addition to writing fiction and geoarchaeological research, Tarver is also a long-time musician affiliated with the bands Rainbows Are Free and Grim Gospels.

For information on R. D. Tarver's previous and upcoming title releases, please visit www.rdtarver.com.

Made in the USA
Columbia, SC
19 November 2021